The Children of Atwar

The Children of Atwar
Heather Spears

A Tesseract Book
Beach Holme Publishers Limited
Victoria, B.C.

This edition is published by
Beach Holme Publishers Limited
4252 Commerce Circle, Victoria, B.C. V8Z 4M2
This is a Tesseract Book

Production editor: Elspeth Haughton
Cover art by Daniel Goldenberg
Cover design by Barbara Munzar

Canadian Cataloguing in Publication Data

Spears, Heather, 1934—
    The children of Atwar

    Sequel to: Moonfall.
    ISBN 0-88878-335-3

    I. Title.
PS8537.P4C5 1993   C813'.54   C93-091103-2
PR9199.3.S62C5 1993

Contents

for Benjamin

Prologue

A marvellous moon shone through my window;
I went to the roof, carrying a ladder.

Yes, it was a marvellous Moon, stayed in his fall by
the child Atwar, and the world rejoiced. Only Atwar,
being small and crippled, had been able to enter the
ancient car left in Fu-en by the Outdead—that ancient
race who had predicted Moonfall, and invented the
means to prevent it, but who themselves had died out
so long ago. Much knowledge was lost, and the new
race were well-grown—tall, seemly twins, single-bod-
ied, too large to benefit from the inheritance left them so
unwillingly. But at Moonfall, when the Moon's unsta-
ble orbit began to threaten the earth, Atwar's mother
was born—Tasman, one-headed—and the people
looked to her to make the journey. Yet in the end she too
was too large—it was only little Atwar who could, and
who went laughing. All that story is recorded, and not
forgotten, and spoken aloud still in the *Tale of Tasman*[1],
in Book and in the streets. But in the World were left of
that family only the Sorud his fathers, who died, and
Tasman who went away, and his brother Betwar.

This is the story of Betwar and his generation.

One

Do not slacken the bowstring, for I am your four-feathered arrow; do not turn your face away, for I am a man with one heart, not two-headed.

1

Betwar in those years grew to manhood. It was the purpose of the scholars at Fu-en to bond him, so that his children would continue that race; because with the Sorud they had found other cars left by the Outdead, farther under the Sheath, and they were determined to direct them into the Moon. But each car was—like the first—very small.

So Betwar, because of their importunity, allowed himself to be bonded to women from the forest northeast of Fu-en, whose body was very light and small. They ate no root, and later gave birth to separated female twins, unicephalic like himself and his mother Tasman, and his brother Atwar.

They were named Ard, which is the oldest word on the earth and means earth.

Nearly three years after this, male twins were born, also separated. They were named Ur. But because of what happened later, they were commonly called Saska and Ask, which means ashes.

These four children were bound with tight bands from their birth, not only their heads (as is the custom of the eastern people) but also their legs, so they could not freely extend them and grow. Because of their purpose they were called the Children of Atwar, although they were the children of his brother.

Betwar was a silent man with large hands, and very gentle, and when the children were born he felt some inpouring of love, so that his being seemed partly filled up, where before it had been empty. But he was not sure how much he dared to love them in return, because they were the children of purpose, whom he could neither keep nor follow.

Betwar's father, The Sorud had died of a long fever, not old men, but as if burnt away, and it was said that the Twel Sorud's helplessness consumed them, because he could not redirect the spirit of the world from the way it was deflected, and there came to be less and less correspondence between this spirit, and the world.

The Sorud extended greatly that knowledge left by the Outdead, held like a secret language in the near-minds of the ancient machines. But, though it was the Sorud who were charged with the preservation and direction of the cars, they suffered disappointment, and were not helped in any practical thing. And they were forced at the last into agreements they could not bear.

Betwar caused his first children, the infant girls Ard and Tared, directly after their birth to gaze into the faces of the Sorud, before they saw any other—in order that they would remember them. After that, the Sorud died.

2

"My children, it will be a laborious business to teach you in this way, and when there is so much that you must learn by heart already—all the maps and directions, and what you must carry with you from here into the Moon—the great Tales, and the first Tale, and the Tale of Tasman which is modern and in which I lived also, and my brother Atwar.

"It would be easier for me, and for you also, if you were not ever in Book—if we could sit comfortably together on the shore, and I could converse with you, and answer your questions—this we do, as much as we can. Always I have told you, quite reasonably, that the Tale does not correspond where it tells such-and-such, because I remember perfectly well what happened.

"Yet you must learn from me, and unlearn as well, so that you can tell my brother what has become of the world in our generation, because what you learn in Book will not tell him."

Betwar's voice ceased. He remained still, looking down at his hands that lay palms-up on his thighs, as he knelt in his house in Fu-en. It was dusk, and the city was beginning to rouse. Already he could hear the first clatter of the shuttles, uneven and gathering, as the weavers took up their work. The white roof breathed, the lengthened leaf-shadows moved on it gently, and the scent of orange blossom entered through the weave with the orange-rose colour of the diminishing light. He got up, and then, stooping, looked at his sleeping children. He had to hurry now, to tell them properly of all these things. How much they would listen, he did not know; in Book they were so well persuaded! It was difficult, and it did not look as if it would get easier.

"Nothing is right." The words walked across his

mind on their usual path, slow and familiar. Perhaps it would be easier if every speech he prepared for his children were prefaced by these words. It was not that nothing at all corresponded, for of course things were as they were, but there was a warp in them. The world had lost something essential—it was as if people saw it through dust, or water.

The girls Ard and Tared were lying just within the east-facing door, each in her own direction, Tared close to the wall with her dress twisted and her pitiful bound legs exposed; one of her feet was clasped loosely in Ard's hand. Beside them the Ur lay with their arms around each other but their faces turned aside—and the bindings on their legs were loosened, because Ask was artful. Those who bound them had been, however, more successful with the boys than with their sisters— by that time they understood better what they were doing, than when they had first attempted it. And Ask knew, if he loosened the bonds, his father would not interfere—they all knew Betwar's stubborn ways. They remembered how morning after morning, when they were very small, his fingers had gently loosened their headbands. So the children were scarcely narrower-templed than the old western people, they were not "half-heads"—it was a term Atwar had whispered to his brother those years ago, when they came with Tasman and the Sorud into the east. A term which, like "nothing is right," had its persistent footpath across the desolate landscape of his mind. Again he murmured.

"Nothing is right. My children, tell this letter to my brother Atwar, when you find him."

His tears returned then, for there was no resolution or finishing, and in that recurrent storm his body's boundaries became indistinct and his thoughts inarticulate. It invaded him as with a present pain, but afterwards when he was quiet, his grief slept.

"Nothing is right. When we were children, and Atwar went away from the world and the Moon was turned between his hands like a dish of yeast turned in the sunlight, and the air was made sweet and quiet and the Earth set about to heal all her bruises,

"When we were children and the people were made joyous by the end of fear, and laughed and called to one another, and the women refused root, because to increase happiness was their desire,

"When we were children, and wrists clapped against wood and the eastern people stepped to that beat in the streets, and laughed aloud because the Earth was hard and no longer shook like water under them, and their house-cloth hung straight down and no longer tore and fled with the Moon's wind,

"When the Moon's wind returned to the Moon, when we were no more children but alone,

"When Atwar went away from the world and became a child-king, a god in their eyes,

"When the shapers of arrows came down from the north and rejoiced in the city,

"When we were alone,

"When my mother Tasman mad with grief ceased to speak, or to remember me,

"When Sorud my fathers turned away entering the house of their minds and pulling up the door, when over the city gradually, as a white cloth from the weavers' hands gradually, the temper of the times spread and sank down, a silence, a temper, a distemper, a white garment, an argument without answer, when I was alone—"[2]

3

Tared shook herself, pulled her foot free of Ard's grasp and wriggled her moist toes. She sat up, and wiped back a strand of hair so it again lay flat against her head. She looked back at her father whose voice had ceased, whose broad face in the half-darkness was the ordinary, quiet background of her life.

Wide awake she had a cool, measured look, and her eyes were not white and black, but contained distance—the cool, bluish sclera of her Lofot inheritance. And like her perceptibly darker twin, her hair was Western and unruly. She took a fierce pleasure in subduing it, forcing it back so the threads that held it dragged at her scalp. It wanted to shape her as her limbs were shaped, into that perfect purpose for which she was born.

Scared eyes. Bruised eyes. Sockets: the dreams fled back as always into the dayheat—her constants, the paired insults, the array, whatever it was that she could deny only as long as she was wide awake. To Betwar, used to her awakening, she seemed for a few moments blind, so inwardly she looked, till her eyes cleared and she saw him and sat up, and with the known gesture pressing back her hair. The dayheat clung to her with the rumpled cloth of her dress; she was sweat-drenched. But cool night was coming, smudging and darkening the leaf-forms on the roof, the dirty central puddle, pressed where it dipped, of dust and dried leaves, a promise of coolness. Tared pulled her dress away from her chest, and blew into her head-sleeve. She would want to swim, and Betwar was ready to take her to the shore. The sea would be cool.

"Let-us swim. Ard, Saska! Ask!" She shook her sister.

The coast at Fu-en had changed after the Moon was stayed. The sudden retreat of the water before the last, great wave had been followed by a more orderly, gradual drop in the sea level, a gentling of the tides. After the catastrophic changes, these were almost negligible, yet year by year they persisted, and in Great Book the scholars busied themselves with new calculations, and were forever worrying over and altering them. Betwar had seen through the years how the beaches grew, how the canals were eventually abandoned to become beds of salt mud, then saltings and meadow. Now people lived under the bridges; the position of many of the old canals could made out only by a dip in the haphazard pile of house-roofs, the occasional bridge or broken row of saplings that had sprung up around broken, ancient trees, and the old waterways were dry and hidden beneath new houses with their bright unblemished cloth-walls.

Betwar and his children had chosen to live in such a house, north-east of the high city and near the sea. The diaspora people from the west still preferred to live under ground, and it was a relief to go down into the canal in dayheat to sleep. His house was built close to an ancient stone bridge, that partially supported it. Eastward past the bridge, the clustered dwellings dwindled and spread towards the shore.

The bed of their canal had been dry and cracked, with only tough salt-grass growing. On its walls, striations of years of drouth and high water could be seen, and there were two separate lines of round, imbedded pebbles, many-coloured, that here withindoors became the toys of his children. Yet when Betwar had levelled the floor he had found a metal track—the trace of the ancient system of cars, like those he had ridden in the west when he and Atwar were children, but had not encountered east of Lenh. He had left it exposed: it too, traversing the room and shiny with their touching, was an odd feature of the house, and a kind of toy.

Other western people had settled in that northern-most part of the city with its dry canals. But those who had bonded with Fu-en twins, and all those who had joined the Walking City from the central desert and the north, lived over-ground now and bound their children's heads, and slept in slings as though they had never known the other ways.

Betwar was closest in friendship to the Nev, who had run with him and Atwar out of the marsh country towards Pechor. Among all those children only the Nev, in their maturity, had house-bonded western twins. At the time of the Moving City, in Yar, they had become adults and were short-bonded to old men. But in Fu-en they were laughed at, and left that, and became house-bonded to young women who had walked with their parents out of Pur, whose heads were only slightly shaped after the custom of the plains. Their children were now fourteen.

These Sons of Nev were big, ordinary twins by western standards, and (Sorud Twel having desired it) their heads had been left alone. They were the last of the western children born here who grew up unbound; they were swart and vigorously haired, like their fathers, and they knew and spoke the True Speech informally, that was otherwise used only in ceremony, and spoke it always with the western people, when they were among themselves under-ground. Betwar's children grew up speaking it also. They and the Sanev were much together from their infancy, in and out of each other's houses.

The Sanev were late-weaned, that is, easy in the world. They went to World, not Book, choosing without quarrelling. As they grew they spent more and more time wandering away from the city, and had been on the long walk to the Disk in the pointed desert, long before they were grown, and into the northeast as far as thirty days, over Kamchat and seen that sea, and come back with arrowheads as if they were adults. They were clever makers, and Ask and Saska loved to visit them and watch them, and try to help them. Their house was ever littered with bits of stems and clay. Their mothers Ludh were passive without being gentle; they allowed them anything, and Betwar's children imitated the Sanev in paying little attention to the Ludh—in that house, it was the burly Nev who stroked and petted the children. The Nev once remarked to Betwar (Ard heard it) that their sons had demanded the breast years longer than their mothers liked it, or cared to touch them, simply because the Ludh had not the resolution to laugh at them and deny them.

The great wading sea extended now southeastward as far as the shelf, and the water still ran in over it, in places so shallow that in Lightening the people stood far out to their waists, to harvest the tiny, rootless small-leaf that had begun to wander the surface wherever it pleased, greener and more plentiful year by year. It had a strong, bitter taste that seemed good. The wind came seldom now, and when it blew it was as the tides, low and steady. The scholars said the air grew cooler; if so, Betwar could not discern it. The eightmonth across the end of Lightening was as burning hot as always, it seemed, and the people continued to shun the dayheat, and sleep through it the year round. With such a Moon they were not much troubled by darkness, and their eyes were used to a lesser light; their pupils dilated greatly. "This world's sun," said the scholars, "is so bright we must teach our children not to look at it." It was not unnatural that people preferred the dark.

Out at the shelf-edge lay the Oldwo, the Old City of metal and stone, that in the last days of Moonfall had shown itself only before the great waves. It was red, reddest at sunset, though those who dived there said it was another colour under water—silvery, and speckled with black. They said it liked the light because it reddened then, but Betwar, who had once seen it close, remembered his fathers and knew it did not—the red was like dead snakeskin; air was corroding the old city.

He had taken his sons once to the Oldwo, at the neap tide, for they swam strongly and had begged him. The water had withdrawn utterly from the wading sea and its sands were hard and in places drying in the heat. They had had to skirt the trench and then another— which was not marked. Ask had wanted to swim along it but Betwar could not mark its direction and the open water seemed nearer, and he had carried them on across the sands. Then they had come to the edge of the shelf—ah—it was strange to stand so far offshore, on hard ground! They had hidden in their hair from the great, flat brilliance. They had swum across to the city.

But its beauty was false—it was ruinous and dangerous close by, and he had brought the children back, not before Saska had cut his foot on a spar—that had been a fever-wound, long in healing.

Southward beyond the Oldwo, reaching out from the land behind the high city, was the line of the Sheath, the nearest of a seemingly endless series of great, convoluted promontories now further and further exposed, rising out of the sea. Black, sleek and forbidding, the Sheath marked the limit of the knowable, habitable world. It girded the earth, inland without break traversing the continent at that latitude, as far as Scandinavia and the western sea. Whatever lay within it, ancient Outdead cities and all their secrets, was sealed forever as in agate. The heat lay over it like an invisible, constant fire, burning up the air that could not cloud or dew. Once from the west along its bounds, Tasman and the Sorud and their children had wandered with the Moving City, and into it the Sorud had ventured once, to find nothing but death.

Here at its edge in caves against Fu-en Atwar's car had stood from ancient times. Here was the Great Book of Fu-en, where the scholars watched for Atwar. And here, far out under the first promontory, scholars had worked with the Sorud, and found the four other, even stranger cars.

The Children of Atwar swam with joy. They had been born in water, as was the custom, in pit-pools their mothers prepared in the marshes north of the city. And they had never forgotten how; though their legs were crippled by binding, their arms were strong. The freedom of moving in water was worth the increased tightening afterwards as their bands dried. At the end of houses was a deep trench that never quite emptied, and almost every night when the tide was up they swam there, before Book and after.

Tared had her way, and Betwar carried her to the beach, returning to fetch Ask, who had slept longer and wished first to eat. As always, people came forward to carry the children; when that house roused, there seemed always folk lingering nearby: they materialized from among the jumble of housewalls; it was considered good to touch the Children of Atwar. But Tared claimed her father if she could.

While they swam, Betwar walked off northwards along the beach, as he was used to do.

4

Tared swam deep into the long, full trench, and dove for the deepest water that tasted almost cool at her brow. Then she rested at the brink, propped up on her elbows, her hands buried in the cooling sand, her lower body and bound legs buoyant in the water.

Night had fallen, still early though it was well into Lightening, and with as yet no Moon; there was good time to play between sleep and Book. Ard and the boys still swam, and a little crowd of World-children, farther south in the shallows, ran to and fro and splashed and shouted noisily, while one pair stood still, staring outward towards the blurry mass of the Oldwo, their narrow heads so close they seemed merged over their wider shoulders, their sleek hair plastered to their back, their thighs leaning a little against the beginning ebb that swirled in gentle curls of phosphorous under the first stars. Tared could not make out who they were though the sea held so much light—but they could not be the broad-headed Sanev—them, she saw nowhere, and guessed they must still be in the marsh-forests or on the bluffs. Saska had whispered of some new scheme they had, that probably concerned the tools they were trying to copy, that they had seen in the north. These were narrow, peeled stems, pulled taut with strings of human hair. The northern people used them to throw their arrows, but the Sanev had till now no success with them. They played much across the bluffs, and in the system of waterways that generations of World-children were forever making and breaking past the farms. Tared's eyes turned restlessly, looking for them.

If the Sanev were at home, they came always to the shore at dusk, and lately had insisted on carrying her or Ard, or one of the boys, part of the way to Book, staggering, puffing with pride in their body's strength—

at least, as far as the Square of the Doll, and that was all uphill.

Now Saska called out something to his brother in his piping voice, and half-lifted his torso above the surface—how thick and vigorous his back and shoulders had become! Soon Tared, her sister, their brothers would be adult. Her breasts and Ard's were already tender and swelling. She looked down at her redblack nipples on their small, new mounds, and at her smooth belly under the still slick-wet, dark down. She and Ard were thirteen. Adulthood was approaching slowly, as if fearful of its consequences. Lately, the scholars were measuring their heights more often, looking if possible more thoughtful. Her sister was afraid, she knew. Tared herself did not mind talking of what was to come, their purpose, but she did not like Ard to do so, who showed such unseemly fright.

The scholars appeared and called to the children, and walked sedately down to the water's edge to receive them, and carry them into the city.

Tared allowed the Qam to lift her against them. She knew them as her teachers, young scholars who had risen through the Watch, but also informally, because they had lately house-bonded the Siri—twins who had cared for her when she was small. The Siri were only four years older than the Ard, and they had played with the children, in particular with Ard and Tared, in the way big girl-children sometimes play with smaller ones, condescendingly but kindly. The Siri had been despite appearances World-children then, and Ard had had a taste of play, for they had gone to Book late, when their brothers were five years old and ready to accompany them. Before this they had been much with the Siri and lived a little like the youngest World-children, in what was called "beamed-on" freedom, weaned but tended.

This had been the time of Tared's stone-gathering, and she had taken her collection of pebbles very seriously, hiding them from her brothers' inquisitive fingers under the sleeping mat, digging out a depression there, burying them in loose sand brought home in her pocket. It was because of the Siri she had begun to love stones. For they had two in their house, their mothers', and had shown them to her and Ard once, crouching on the beach, opening their pale, scoured twarhand secretively. One stone was dark brown but almost transparent, and one was yellowish, transparent entirely except for a cloudy area of white that partly extended inward from one surface. They were both very smooth, not symmetrical. The Siri said they were generation-stones, that they would receive when they house-bonded, and give to their daughters. "There were once three," the Twel Siri told them, "But our-mothers' mothers lost it."

"In that house?"

"No, this would be in the old house, where our fathers' fathers still live, over on the west hill."

"Do you not go there, and look for it?" Tared was fascinated.

"It has been well searched for. It is gone. It was black, but light cast through it, they have told us. Our-mothers saw it when they were small."

Perhaps they took it to show other children on the beach, Tared thought then. Perhaps they had been careless. She began to look for it on the high beach, where there were a few small stones. But they were dull and rough. The most beautiful stones were in the canal walls. It was difficult to pry them loose. Water had once rounded them, Betwar said. Water had swirled along and scoured them and laid them here in rows, and after that more sand and mud was laid down. When she pulled one loose, it left a smooth round unshape of itself. Perfect, but it was not possible to push the pebble in again exactly as it had been.

The Siri had liked what she showed them. Ard, less interested, kept and lost pebbles frequently.

"My white stone is lost like the Sirimothers-stone," she would explain. To her it did not seem anything special, that a stone could disappear. But Tared thought of it much. The Siristone was surely in the World, and how could you not know where it was, if your heart wanted very much to find it?

When the Siri became adults, they had been short-bonded to weavers over on the other side of the high city, and the Ard saw them only rarely at ceremonies—then, these young, graceful women would come up and touch their feet and shyly greet them. The Siri stayed with the weavers nearly three years, and learned their craft. When these men died, the Siri were house-bonded to the Qam who taught Book, and thus the children had some news of them; they were, after their new-bonding, always at the Square in the evenings, if the Qam came. Ard and Tared watched the signs of their bonding curiously—the Qam's absent-mindedness, the Siri's rosy looks, bright and trembling.

Now the Qam held her high against their twarside, and she encircled their Twar's head with her arms and joined her hands comfortably at their throat. They strode up the sand towards the night streets. Even in their step was their love, even just to see the Siri briefly was their pleasure, and Tared watched and considered this, as Ard did, and wondered about it.

The stars were brilliant, and the high city glowed on its hill. It rose ahead of them in a tumbled, radiant pile of walls and roofs of cloth, dusky or roseate from small lamp-flames, with the deep blood-orange of rarer red-dyed walls among the white. Tiny darker and lighter squares patterned the surfaces—new patches stitched into the ashy whites and pinks. There was no discernable order in the mass, but here and there could be traced, for a short way, a smudge of massy trees along an old canal, or the dense lineal black of a street, sunk in a kind of downy darkness and lost again at a turning. In there the weavers crouched over their pits; the noise of the shuttles was thickened by distance to a steady, blurry chirp, then increased to a steady throbbing as they began to climb. The houses were crammed behind and above each other in half-transparent layers and, as a stronger breeze passed inland, all the surfaces began to waver and tremble, trees and houses alike. The motion ran ahead of them uphill, across all the jumbled roofs and walls, with another and another following. Then all the houses stood still again, the cloth drooping from the poles, while between the lesser hills rose a smoky, hidden pallor, as if secret fires had been lit there: it was where house-walls were all drawn back for coolness, and the soft light streamed out across the hidden lanes.

A sharp reed played, and people walked towards the sound. When they saw the children they drew back a little, but some came and asked to carry them. Tared refused, but the hands, as always, reached out and touched her feet: the whispers reached out too and touched her—"*Atwar walks*," they murmured.

They mounted to the Square of the Doll, at the height of the city. This was no special night, and there was no special ritual, only the *Circling*[3]: as always they were carried once around the Doll before they were taken to Book. At the Turn under the Doll, only Tared among the children glanced upward; Atwar was familiar—and he had not answered her; she felt the shadow of his darker bulk blocking off the sweep of starry sky as they rounded the Square's north side, where he stood. The trudging feet of the circlers kicked up the warm dust; it reached sweetly into her nostrils. Ard was carried beside her and their brothers behind, with an uneven crowd of people trudging in their wake—some of them, women, hurriedly muttering the *Atwar Walks*[4] after the Turn as they went along. She caught the last lines as the circling ended, and the Qam turned away from the open Square:

> *"In his good time*
> *he will speak in wisdom and heal us.*
> *The two worlds, Earth and Moon,*
> *will be friends, as it is foretold,*
> *not silent, but conversing."*[5]

To the chanting Fu-en women it was perhaps meaningless, for they were not schooled in western speech, though all had learned the oldest songs. But the children understood it well. It was a promise.

And there were the Siri indeed, coming close to the Qam and keeping pace with them, which was not seemly; yet they looked only at the Qam, scarcely acknowledging Tared and only lightly touching her feet. Their neatly shaped heads were tilted upward, their smiles unthought and conjoining. They had a narrow bale of newly bleached cloth between their shoulders and it hung down over their breasts, swinging a little heavy as they trod, its brightness making their dress seem grayish and dull in the starlight.

The children were seldom among strangers except in these ritual encounters and at the ceremonies, and never as equals. They did not learn with other Book children; their little Book across the high city was separate, in a house beside downhill against the Sheath. There the Qam and other lesser scholars, without face-boards and in ordinary clothes, taught them, and they were not allowed to choose what they might learn. This limitation did not trouble them much, as they had never experienced ordinary Book, where children were free to learn what they liked. But the boys envied World-children, who could stay on the shore all night long, light fires, swim and play as they pleased. Ask and Saska would certainly have chosen to go to World not Book, had they been given the chance. But if they complained, they were silenced serenely. That they would "walk as Atwar walks"[6] must be their consolation.

Ordinary nights at Book were usually predictable, but at ceremonies like the *Full Moon* or the *Eating of Atwar*[7] (which was the dark of the Moon) the great scholars carried them, and sometimes the Ng in particular came into their little Book as well, looking austere and grim with the face-boards stiff between their heads. They would question the children, or sit with the other teachers to pass on new rote for the children to learn.

Sometimes, too, the children were carried into the Great Book under the Sheath, as far as the Lake of the Moon, and left at the low barrier to cling to the bars, while other scholars went down the narrow steps and unrolled the cloth maps, and walked about on them, pointing. Sometimes the children were allowed to enter the Lake themselves, handed down to the Lake floor, where they could move about on the maps. In this way they familiarized themselves with every detail of the habitable territory so crudely drawn there on the cloth with sticks of ash—the swards and glades, the water-courses, the great escarpments and their wood-clad dales, all under the gridwork that marked the sectors, and their names: Pliny and the Cape, Chmedes, Hadley, the Marsh of Decay, Linné, the Lake of Dreamers, the distant Lake of Death.

But their crawling about disturbed the maps, rucked up under their dragged legs, and this in turn smudged the lines. So it was better, if less real, to stay above the Lake and look down on it.

When the Moon filled, they could see down into the real Moon, cast by the instrument called the Moon's Arm, across new white cloths that the scholars would spread out respectfully on the Lake floor. Then they could watch as in dreams the Moon's wind pouring through distant foliage, the vapours of the Moon's rains.

Or they could stay a little at the screens, silently, where all night and all day scholars sat at vigil and where, at the changes, *Atwar's Grief*[8] and parts of the great Tale were repeated sonorously.

Then there were the nights, that came unexpectedly and now more often, when they were taken past the door of their own Book—into Medical Book, to be measured.

Coming down the steep streets southward from the Square, Tared and the others could not guess whether this night would be one of the rare ones or as it usually was—confined, repetitive and dull.

The cloths were thrown back so the coolness of night could enter the houses: they looked down into warm, rosy interiors, the homely junk of family life: voices and laughter, looping slings, some with babies peering over the sides, lamps, shadows jumping on cloth, light streaming messily out into the street, people squatting around food, heads turning, passive looks, bigger children running forward to stare up at them and, as if daringly, quickly touch their feet and bandages.

Two

*When He congeals the wind He makes of the
wind water, when He causes the water to boil He
fashions out of it air.*
*Since the ears of heaven and earth and the stars
are all in your hand, whither are they going?
Even to that place whither you said, "Come!"*

1

Greenish, the hairless inner cheek of the Twar Ng
receded from Ask, along the warp of the head that
mirroring the Twel Ng's beside it—inner face and
temple flattened at the line of their face-board, lying as
if moulded each to each. The board, seen head-on,
appeared as a narrow white division, and quivered.
Their eyes watched him unwinking.

The children had often argued among themselves
whether these great scholars the Ng were male or
female. The Sanev said they were male; and insisted
they knew this, but would not tell how. In the rare times
one Ng mind was referred to—for these twins demanded the dual and functioned as true-twins though
they were not—the male pronoun was used, so the
children supposed the Sanev were right.

The Ng faces were steep and their features smooth

and fragile. Now, under each of their high, outer cheekbones lay a seemingly identical square of vertical shadow. But the lamplight was dulled in the brilliant room, and Ask could well see the single mole inside the square on the Twar cheek. With all his might he kept his gaze on it. With all his might.

His hands were in their hands and he was standing, naked, his head pulled back on his neck so he could see them as they wished, for they were so much taller—a third again his height. Their skirt was of the sunbleached cloth and reached their gloved feet. Their hair was slicked to their heads and tightly knotted.

Momentarily, Ask's eyes lost focus; their faces swam into one and he blinked, swallowed, concentrated again on the square to the left. His feet ached, and he leaned back more from the pull of their hands, telling himself to rest in their hold, though he knew they might release him without warning. Their grasp was firm and cool. His bald palms pressed against their stone-scoured ones, and he felt the short, perhaps deliberate stubble of the Twel handhair pricking into his skin, sharp as points of sand-grass, and it hurt.

At least his hands were large, broader even than theirs which were so slender and womanish, with naked veins, and the backs—even the wrists that emerged from the dress—almost hairless.

"You have not grown, Little-one of Atwar. But very soon you will be adult; your torso will lengthen then."

"You would have to break my back to prevent it," said Ask, keeping the emotion out of his voice, so that his words sounded only courteous.

They released him at the same moment the Twar said, "Sit down"—he crumpled, and with quick hands righted himself. The Ng walked in a long stride to the door, which was pulled down, and through which the

23

watery moonlight of the white night streamed brilliantly. The Moon was swimming in a diffused radiance; it flowed over the flank of the Sheath beyond the black, shadowed water at the end of the street, and across the lower roofs near the shore. It entered the weave of this roof also, and there was no need for the lamp tied overhead.

The Ng looked out unhurriedly, while Ask waited to be released and taken to his brother; he did not like these times when they were separated, and although he had ceased to be afraid for himself, he feared for Saska who feared them.

They turned serenely. "When your sisters have become women," the Ng Twar said, "and you have learned all the directions, and your minds are composed, retentive and eager—"

"—and the Moon is nearest and we are not yet too big to enter the cars," answered Ask, who was practical and wanted this over with.

"All these threads are weaving into one cloth. Atwar waits. You will be ready."

They bent swiftly and rebound his legs, too hurried now to be cautious but deft with practice. Ask winced, but he would not cry out. The Ng had come to their little Book with the Medical Book scholars who had fetched him and Saska to measure them—they were gone out now with Saska; they were gentler.

"*It is not pain, it is expectation.* You will walk *as Atwar walks*,"[9] they repeated together, quickly and expressionlessly, as they always did.

"I will swim, then," said Ask, who would have lived in the water had he been allowed.

Only in the water he could forget his jealousy of the children his own age at the Circling, who could perform the *Twelve Turns* and the *Heads over Heels*[10] so deftly. Almost, he was not jealous for himself, but for

Saska, whose heart's longing he seemed to feel at those times as if it were aching in his own breast. Ah, Saska watched them sadly as they wove and wheeled. So we will circle on the Moon. He struggled into his shirt.

"In that air, and in those water-courses, you will swim indeed," the Twar Ng, a little more kindly, and picking him up they carried him out to his brother. Once this twin had begun with the twarhand to stroke him, as if tentatively. It was nothing special, just an ordinary adult stroking on his arm. But it had not seemed ordinary. It was not ordinary for the Ng to stroke anyone.

Medical Book was large and sprawling, and comprised most of the houses on the flat ground south and west of the high city, near the Sheath. The sky glowed over the clearing between buildings, hardly darker than the Moon. The closed houses glowed also, the walls warm from the lit lamps. The sharp smells of the plants kept and used there hung in the air, and the shadows of the sick moved behind overlapping house-cloths, dimly and more dimly.

Saska's forehead was cold-hot with sweat. Ask could tell, from the way he half-lay, that the bands were far too tight.

"My legs are furious, you must loosen the bands," said Saska in a whisper, as soon as they were left alone. "Are they through with us? What have they said?"

"Nothing other than usual. We have not grown." Ask stroked him, and Saska came into his embrace, and whispered, "They are so angry, my poor legs, they are crying out—'It would be better to be severed from you entirely!' Do you believe we shall walk there?"

Ask gazed past him at the oblique blur of brightness lying like a pool on the roof-cloth, and he quoted hurriedly: "*Atwar walks well and seemly\ Atwar walks*

*deep in the forests of the Moon.\ No more does he suffer
pain\ From the snake's blow, he is healed.*"[11]

Saska answered him: "*Fald een u ran*[12] (He fell once,
then he ran)." Then he whimpered: "Ah—this anger
makes me want very much to go!"

"Then it is as they say, it is expectation. I think they
want to hurt us, the Twel Ng anyway, so we will come
to hate the Earth and will not regret it. We are much
smaller than the Ard, there is no more reason for these
bands. I will loose you as much as I can"—his fingers
dug at the knots—"and untie you when we get home.
Our-father does not care, and if Tared complains, I shall
strike her." Ask went on pulling at the knots, and
stroking his brother, comforting him as well as he
could.

Betwar arrived before the attendants, hurrying, and
when he saw them, lying there in each other's arms
with their faces streaked with dirty tears, he picked
them up wordlessly, and took them home.

2

For Ard and Tared, Book that night was ordinary
enough. They were reviewing a list of the eastern
generations, Fu-en deeds and names—for Tared not
difficult, for Ard almost intolerable. Fortunately the
Qam were not strict and the children were allowed to
recite in unison, and when Ard stumbled they did not
care.

The door was as usual pulled shut, and the rosy
leaf-oil lamps shone upward on their broad, childish
faces, on the slightly bewildered look caused by comb-
ing back their unruly hair, even their brow- and
cheek-hair, into the high hair-knot, so that it starred out

from their centre-faces in an expression like permanent surprise. All four had the sign of the Lofot people, that their broad-browed father Betwar had not—black, conjoined eyebrows that grew out and upwards finely into the head-hair. But only Tared's hair was really ungovernable—she who most wished to be eastern like her mothers. The boys had their mothers' shallow eyes and paler, almost bluish skin, but the girls were swart, Ard darkest of all—Betwar's colour. Like Tasman's sons, they had inherited not only Lofot brows but also her strangely bald hands and feet; but this was not much remarked in Fu-en, where it was the custom to scour the palms and foot-soles smooth with stones, assiduously, and to wear footgloves almost always. The children's bound legs were thin, short and useless. They could not stand on them unsupported.

Tared had marked Ard's fright when the Ng entered to look at the children one by one in their direct, jerky way. But the Ng were with Medical Book people, and had gone after them when they carried off Saska and Ask only. Ard's body had relaxed at once, and the Qam nodded to them to resume. For the girls, this would be as other nights.

Ard still sat almost behind her sister, slouched in the low hammock and leaning on the stem of the housebeam behind it; Ard's restless arm touched hers from time to time, and without turning Tared could imagine the pout of boredom on her mouth—"Why should I learn it if you others learn it? *We will stand together before his face.*"[13]

But their brother Ask, in wild moods, had said the cars were judged imperfect, because they had been found under water, and that no one knew if they would all survive the journey, or only one of them, or none, or how many.

"We are four and they teach us equally," he said sometimes. "It means they are not quite sure."

"Why do you say that?" Tared would answer with spirit. *"Has any one instrument of the Outdead ever failed? See what they have prepared for us! it is all perfect, only we cannot understand it.*

"Because the Outdead gave us these gifts as to children, who cannot reason or understand, and prepared them for us so that even with our rude hands we could not harm them, or with them do ourselves any foolish harm, but only good."[14]

"Our-father says the Outdead did it for themselves, and hated us," answered Ask, unperturbed by her rapid recitation. "But what they had prepared, they could not prevent."

"Then, it is perfect, because if they could have changed it into another mood, in order to destroy us, they would have."

But these were private arguments, because here with their teachers the children were subdued and made to learn, and not permitted to quarrel.

Their Book, their plain little night-place, had no screens or toys. It was a place for memorizing; and here they heard and learned the Tales of Fu-en and the new Tales about Moonfall and the Linh which Betwar said were distorted and did not correspond. Night by night as the Moon passed over and the distant shuttles banged, they sat in the low slings within these simple walls, more narrow and constricted even than their one-roomed home.

Sometimes what they learned was big and breathy—huge images rolled about, heroic snake-forms and landscapes barren as the unseeded highlands of the Moon, earthquakes and floods: the very walls ran with mind-blood as they listened, the boys wide-eyed and eager with Ask grinning and Saska trembling, the girls dreamy, caught up as well. But most often they studied hour by dull hour the long and tiresome directions, those of Atwar's car that he had snatched from Tasman, that had been written hastily into his bald palms against his forgetting, and of their own cars. They learned the record of the screens and the Lake, of World-seasons and their gradual changes, and how the Moon-seasons compared, and of the Moon and his Quarters, his ways of winds and vapours and the Cast of his Terminator—all of which was rote, and meant little to them, though they were told Atwar required them to know it.

They repeated the history of the western generations, coming to the Tale and Tasman's hidden childhood, hearing of distant Noss and Hoy and the dangerous Sheath where so many had died; their heat-shrivelled bodies like dried stems dragged about by tides, and dried up on the beaches.[15]

Through it all the scholars had never given the children any language in which to question their purpose: there were no words, and therefore no questions. If they remembered Betwar while they were in Book it was as a heavy, uncomfortable shadow, a murmur in the distance that was also as yet wordless. Saska was fearful of nature and had always been so, the one who was protected by the others, especially Ask, who liked danger for its own sake. As for Ard, though she did not know this, Betwar's look was whole ground of what her sister called her groundless fright. Indeed in Book, Tared would not remember Betwar. And what they were taught so carefully taught them something more—every lesson, directed to Atwar, bound them into him more surely, into his distant purpose soon to be fulfilled.

3

The children had not yet been taken farther into the Great Book whereas the water receded (after the world was stilled) a passage eastward out under the promontory had been reclaimed, that had been till then flooded by the sea. In those years of the Sorud's strength, the water had been commanded, forced back gradually and kept out all the way to the place where the cars were found. Ask and Saska talked about the cars often, and speculated, trying to picture them accurately, because their teachers had told them only of the doors, and the internal directions.

And the ancient scholars Azur with their shaved, dented pates and white-bearded arms and hands—who wandered into their Book from time to time and seemed most willing to answer them—always spoke in their accustomed language, as if it were a Tale or Song.

"Your-fathers' fathers made the scheme of it," they had acknowledged, not distinguishing between Sorud Twel and Twar, though they had known them well and worked with them. "They instructed us, poor Fu-en scholars; in our hands was a great Book we possessed but could not use, till the Sorud came out of the west.

"Thus we built one bay farther in along the passage, and emptied that, and then another and another, and so progressed. Because we continued to find marvellous machines in the blackness of the water, in the arms of the Sheath, and when they were unclothed and washed with air, some were seen to shine and move, and others—ah, it seemed that they should, if our poor hands only understood how to touch and awaken them."

"And after that, you discovered our cars," prompted Ask. "What are they like?"

"Ah, they are like Atwar's, like and yet unlike, less

solid-seeming, like his journey branching out into
thought, cleansed and purified. And repeated four
times, black and silver and otherwise most beautiful,
with the light of the surface of the water moving on
them—the Moon's light, his eye."

Ask and Saska would discuss these revelations in
more ordinary language.

"It is a pity our-father does not like Book," said Ask
that morning, when Betwar had brought them home
and left them, and they waited for their sisters, "Or he
could insist on taking us down the passage and we
could see for ourselves." He turned deliberately to the
ever fascinating subject, for Saska was still in pain and
he wished to divert him.

And Saska was courteous and responded. "I think
he will take us soon," he said, doubtfully.

Saska was not so interested in going into the promontory, yet he would have endured it, to see what the
Azur had described, if he could be held by his father.
Sometimes this twin was seized with hope, an idea, like
a sprung seed, that they could eventually be happy. It
was different from Tared's convictions, that were absolute, but had no happiness in them. "It might be soon,
because he is beginning to talk to himself, I think it is
letters to Atwar, he wants us to learn, it means his mind
is walking there now, as our minds are, with-us."

"Have you waked and heard him? Saying letters—
and our heads are bursting already. It will be difficult
to hear them and learn them all at once, if he decides on
it. I have heard him too, he talks them to himself over
and over—and last night, even as he carried me to the
shore—and when I interrupted him, he said, 'It is
something I want you to tell Atwar'—but he did not tell
me what, and we came to the sand and he put me
down."

Saska stretched carefully within the shivery strength in his arms and torso, strength that was so abruptly cut off under his hips, walled off like a walled bay: his mind's picture of his legs was unfriendly; they were distant and besieged him, and the pain was a little red light, a lamp that seemed to be shaped like a rod. Sometimes he could placed it in the farthest corner of the house, or of Book, so it did not touch him. Sometimes, as on this night, it came near. He said, scaredly, "Remember how angry our-father was, when they gave Ard and Tared the red dresses?"

Ask laughed into his brother's cheek, his teeth grazing the skin.

"Tared would wear them, and persuade Ard also. 'If we are the children of Atwar, should we not dress in his colour?'" He mimicked her precise voice.

"But our-father wept, and recited that part of the Tale and then said, he remembered when it was no Tale, but terrible—Atwar's blood."

"Do you not think it corresponds, then, that the snake recognized Atwar, and its mind knew what it did? (*It struck to fulfil the harsh, ancient promise,\ it chose Atwar, it struck terribly, it crippled him*)?[16] Our-father says, what happened to Atwar was an accident."

Ask laughed again. "Our-father was there. Anyway, it is no accident what they have done to us, even if our-father was unwilling about the red dresses."

"I am glad," said Saska sadly, in his sad, boyish voice, "that he is here with us, and now thinking with us, whatever he will have us learn; because it would not be so easy for us, if only the Ng had charge of us."

"No. But whether our-father will take us to the cars when they do not like it, and show us that submerged place—"

"We will be brought there soon, Ask, I think—" said Saska, after a pause.

"After noise and ceremony, *When he causes the water to boil/ he fashions out of it air*? Then we will climb up as Atwar climbed—laughing."[17]

"Once, I dreamed how we swam across that bay, and entered the cars swimming."

"They say swim but I think they say it as in Tales. For the Ng told me tonight 'You will swim in air.' If you swam into the car—then, if you laughed, your mouth would be full of water and you would choke."

"No—" said Saska slowly, "As I was in the dream, I could laugh. I would have drowned in air."

4

The list was finished at last, and Ard's body drooped deliberately; she began to rub at her outstretched legs, pulling back her dress—they had been sitting still too long. The Qam moved, too, as if to give them clear permission, stretching and then standing up—"We will fetch you water," said their Twar, and they pulled down the door and went out.

Tared immediately rolled out of the sling and dragged herself across to the threshold: from here she could see the beach between the houses, there where it curved round to the Sheath-wall; the high water was very light and calm and two big stars reflected in it. Dawn was as yet only a rim of warmer, lesser brightness at the horizon. She could not see the Sheath where it met the water, but its dark shoulder lay heavy over the buildings to her right; there was the Great Book where they sometimes were taken. Ard joined her, and they knelt in the doorway, gazing along the passage to the beach. Sometimes World-children played down there and their far, happy voices reached the children in Book. Sometimes, recently, the Sanev would be standing there at dawn at the lane's end, and would join them and go with them home.

But the beach was empty. Those houses were mostly storing-places for yeast and medical plants. The Ng lived in there somewhere, and the Azur, and others of the great scholars who preferred to have silent rooms around them. The younger scholars of the Watch lived, if they wished, closest to the Sheath, in the last housering. Of all the scholars, the Watch were most regulated; after Atwar's Grief all had been set aright.

Finally the Qam returned with bowls, and clean, folded cloths soaked in them; they squatted in front of the door to squeeze water into the girls' thirsty mouths, then wiped their eyes and faces. Past them the sky had lightened already, overtaking the stars. "Will our-brothers be returned here?" asked Tared, restless to be taken home.

"No, it is late, we will take-you now."

At sunrise there was no ceremony, yet by Tared's desire, because she would sometimes request to be left at the Doll, the Qam and the other attendants carried them uphill through the city, and left her in the Square, and drew back a little with Ard to wait for her.

The shuttles had ceased as the sun rose, first losing that heartbeat unison which came of its own as the weavers took up their work, and becoming then an interrupted clattering, before it dwindled out altogether. Weary Book-children, in little groups, trailed from their Book over the hill. Tired adult voices called—straying World-children were being called home. The forbidding light of day, the still reddish patches of harsh sunlight with their sharp-edged, hot, bright shadows drove people indoors and the housewalls were pulled up and fastened, giving the tilted streets an empty look that invited sleep.

Tared looked very small at the Doll's foot, sitting where she had been put down. She spoke some words then, Ard knew this much but not the words; it was what her sister did lately and when Ard asked about it she had said only, "I am asking Atwar to stop my dreaming," and then closed her mouth firmly.

She prayed, though she would not have understood her act as so formal as prayer—it semed to her serious, heavy play, a copying of the public words of the ceremonies, that also addressed Atwar—the way children play at ceremony in little sunny word-snows adults laugh over, and yet almost believe what they do.

> *Atwar wipe away my fever,*
> *the dream before me*
> *in the evening wakening.*
> *Wipe it, let me not enter*
> *that fearful house again.*
> *Let it remain in there.*
> *Let me turn from there.*
> *Let me escape in journeying*
> *my face dipped,*
> *in clean water wiped,*
> *into your house and bond.*[18]

When they came to the canal the sun was well risen, level over the water and already colourless, striking them under the foliage of the old trees and through the stems of their straggling saplings. They were handed down into their threshold. Ask and Saska had been long home and had already eaten; they looked up, wiping yeast off their mouths with their sleeves. Tared saw at once that their bindings were loosened, Saska's quite unwound and trailing on the floor, but she saw also that Ask was looking fierce and Saska had been crying, so she did not chide.

"Where is our-father?"

"He carried-us home, and is gone to the beach."

"Will you not swim? The scholars can stay and take-us."

Saska turned his back. "We are sleepy, we told our-father this, and he went," said Ask.

"Will you swim, Ard?" Already the heat was push-ing sleep at Tared. But as always she would withstand it, however tired she was. Ard, eating, said with her fingers in her mouth and stubbornly, "We could have swum with the Sanev, but they did not come."

"They are in the marshes," Saska piped up, friend-lier but not turning.

Ask touched him. "Something secret—is it not, Saska?"

Saska turned back to them then—his little, bald face was so dirty with yeast and tears that it belied his serious look, but his eyes had brightened. "When they have perfected it, they will tell-us, I will not," he said.

Tared grinned with her mouth only. "How ugly you are! The yeast will stick fast to your face and grow on it! come with-us to the beach—if for a short time only, to be washed and cool for sleeping."

Ask still looked angry, and she doubted he would leave Saska, whose bent-over posture she knew well—his legs were paining him. But Ard would come, and they could eat first, because the Qam and the others would linger outside for a little while, and she would have her way. She crawled with her bowl over to the mat she shared with Ard and ate there, fastidiously, seated where she was used to sit against the south wall—the hard earth with its polished pebble-rows. Between wall and mat-edge she had kept the dresses despite her father, folding them into the depression she had scoured when she was small, where she had previ-ously kept her treasures, those small, particular stones.

As she ate with her twarhand, she slid her twelhand by habit down to the dresses and fingered them, then let her hand rest inside the fold; it was cool, as if a large, cool hand enfolded her hand.

Atwar's colour. When the Ng had slid the dresses over their heads, she had trembled. And seen Ard as herself, though Ard was perceptibly stouter and darker. Tared had looked at her with a shiver of pleasure. She recalled this, touching the dresses.

Ard had watched Tared, too—trying to make out what she was thinking. Ard, scared of the dresses—and wanting to pretend not to be, as Tared knew. Though Ard longed to live in privacy, and have secrets like other weaned children, she still watched for Tared's judgement and paid attention to it. Even in order to defy it. But nothing in Ard was hidden from Tared. Tared was effortlessly the secretive one: growing up with the bruised dreams, she had learned how to hide anything.

Ah—they had worn the dresses in only one Circling. Then when they were brought home, their father had shouted, and wept, and had gone away and come back carrying their ordinary shirts. The next night, they went to Book in white again, and Tared had been forced to say to the scholars, "Our-father does not like to see us in that other colour." The scholars had not answered. Even the Ng had never spoken of it directly, though they continued to say to the girls, "You will soon be adults, and wear Atwar's colour," as they had said before. So she would keep the dresses; there would be a time for them. Now her hand had warmed their folds and she withdrew it, and smoothed the mat over them.

When she had eaten, she called the scholars, and she and Ard left the house to their brothers and its rumpled mats and unwiped, yeasty bowls.

The girls, revived, stayed on the shore despite the heat. Ard, who was lying on her belly at the trench, pushed herself out on her elbows and stared down into the water, which was at ebb and quiet below her. The sun's oil ran on the surface, but under the bank was a shadow, and when she bared her teeth, their reflection gleamed back at her. She spoke suddenly.

"Will we not go, then, whiteteethed to the Moon, as Atwar did?"

Tared was still in the water, which was just deep enough to let her touch the bottom with her hands. When she squirmed, Ard's image shattered.

"We are to be adults. They have told us."

"But Atwar's teeth are white." Ard rolled on to her back and undid the heavy knot of her hair, letting it swing over the water in a little shower of sand.

Tared reached out and touched the coil, and loosened it between her fingers. It was straighter, shinier; Tared was jealous of her sister's hair. The ends of the wet strands fanned out on the surface.

"He will have blackened them on the Moon. Because everything is provided for him there—*necessary food, necessary water*.[19] So when he became an adult, he blackened them."

"And cut himself also?" Ard laughed, which she did seldom.

Tared, having no answer to this, grabbed at her hair and yanked it angrily.

"Be ashamed! Would you also speak of our-father Betwar in this way?"

Ard sat up, and twisted back her hair as she stammered, "I spoke of Atwar as children—of that time." Atwar as a new adult, perhaps, tall as the Sons of Nev? But she could not imagine him their father's age—

people did not, they kept him childish always.

"In the dolls, his teeth are white," she protested lamely.

"Ah—cloth teeth! Do you not want to go black-teethed?" But Tared, too, looked uncertain. The dolls were accurate, but what if Atwar was changed? The Sanev were changing, and she and her sister were changing. Atwar was their father's twin, and could not be that doll, that little one. People taught him as children, and ate him as children, but what had he become? What had become of him? Suddenly she thought she might be afraid of Atwar.

6

Betwar walked back northward along the beach, stepping in the calm warm breath of the wash with its leaf-bits and sand-float, his long shadow following inland across already burning sand. He shook his hair farther forward over his face against the general brightness, and saw through that overhang Ard sitting at the trench, where its brim was abrupt and made of hard clay, and then Tared as she scrambled up beside her. Farther northeastward, where the trees grew out of the sand and a wide, natural dike separated the sea from the inland marshes, a little group of belated World-children were trudging back to the city, leaving a smudge of steam behind them where they had quenched a fire. The aftertaste of wood-smoke hung in the air. It was the Linh's taste—which had been ever strong in them and even stronger when they laboured and gave birth, as if it were sweated out of their very skin, and the skin of their newborn—ah, he had leaned with his smoky daughters over the Sorud, those last days his fathers lived—

Now, he sat down in the sand, still at a distance from his daughters, letting his mind run unhindered from the Linh, to the thought of his fathers in those last days before they died.

Sorud Twel's words as they lay sick: "Betwar, do not entirely trust the machines. The scholars are sure now, they believe nothing but good can come of what will come. Already they are making a Tale that has not happened, not any version of it, and I am unable to prevent them."

And Sorud Twar's interruption: "But they have begun to make it happen, in these new little-ones."

"I would have wished," their Twel had gone on, "to have lived into these years with the world still in my hand. They make Tales, and I correct them, but the uncorrected are still sung in the streets."

Another time he had said: "Even where it corresponds with the world (he was speaking of the modern Tale) its interpretation does not, and no good will come of it."

Sorud Twar's words: "I do not like the colour which to them seems most beautiful—to me, as to you, our son, it is the colour of great harm. You know that when I was healed I first saw the people dressed in it—most suddenly! And the Old City they praise—till now I have convinced them to leave the cars in the water that is their protection. Do you be sure of this—until the last instant. There are four. Do you be sure they send the two nearest, which are the most certain."

Betwar had said, "Fadel, we do not even know if Atwar lives."

Twel had said, earnestly, "We must believe that he lives, Betwar, and when your children are delivered into the Moon, that they will find him. But this is a strange and terrible thing. Ought you then to keep them by you as long as you can? Were he standing as we desire on the sward, to receive them into his arms! The Outdead did not journey as children, whatever the scholars say. They were as small as children but old—with adult minds."

Betwar got up and joined his daughters, and carried them home one on each arm, for they were slight and thin still, and he was very strong. Their wet white dresses pressed dark gray against their downy bodies. He could feel Ard on his right arm was the heavier: she rested into him more densely, already half asleep.

So he brought them home, and found his sons still whispering. He lay down with his children, with his hand on Tared's narrow shoulders. This is the way they slept: first Saska, then Ard, then Ask, then Betwar, then Tared at last, white morning heat and health and tiredness winning over her resisting, jittering mind.

7

"Oh my children, why were you born with minds? you should have been made as the Outdead's instruments, perfect and obedient. For we have invented you, and made a patent of you. It was not my will, this choosing and shaping and teaching—had you been four trees, and I could have tended the earth around your stems, and drenched you with water and seen you grow without your knowledge of my remorse, my acquiescence! But you see me, you have become selves, impetuous, affectionate, afraid—and if the very making of you harmed you, how have we not harmed you? Nothing is right."

Unable to sleep, Betwar gazed at his children. He saw that Ask's wet bands were well-loosened, and

Saska's lay on the floor; his bare legs were hidden under the general mess of dress and mat-cloth. He got up and knelt over them, crushing the strips of dry cloth between his fingers.

His lips moved with words but the sound was just a murmur, his voice spoke itself aloud in his mind. And he saw in Saska's exhausted profile, pressed into his brother's sleeve, something of their mothers, a likeness that again and as suddenly brought the Linh before his mind as if they had never died.

The Linh from the forest, their eyes frightened, even then, their feet stepping very lightly on the earth. The placid silence of their faces, their youth (his youth also), the way they locked the stubby fingers of their hands together for comfort across their breasts. They were not true-twins, for they spoke together and argued sometimes in their own dialect, and yet they were "of same mind". And they kept those arrowheads about them and used them as knives, as men do—Atlinh, the tent of her shining hair flung forward, awkwardly holding down her head while Betlinh reached and scraped the straight short hairs of her nape, making a clean edge there, the tiny rasp of the arrow-edge, and Atlinh sniffing. Their low voices—their white garment where they sat, in that other house at the water-edge of the city, at the beginning of the marshes. They stank of wood-smell because they tended fires, though they were adult—the quenched fire on the beach—how suddenly and clearly he remembered them!

He stretched, sitting upright on his knees. It was seldom that he stayed with these unsought images of his house-bonded—his mind preferred to run from them; their wood-smell he had run from, only to find them again them in his son's face. Yet in that bonding there had been joy also, the healing from time to time of his grief and emptiness.

"How afraid they were—it is necessary to tell Atwar this—how afraid I was also. The words of the scholars alone could not have moved me, because I still believed Atwar would return. But our-fathers spoke to me, and convinced me to be bonded as the scholars wished. Twel Sorud said, in great sorrow, 'If Atwar could have come back, he would have come before now.'

"But the Sorud did not live to see what was done to you. 'Your twins will go to him while they are small,' was all our-fathers told me—I was holding you new-born before them—Ard, squirming and squinting; but you, Tared, with your black-blue eyes as if fathomless fixed on our-fathers, first on the Twel, then on the Twar, and back again, as if already you understood. The Ludh took you back to your mothers, and I sent a letter of the generations towards Lofot, but I do not know if it was ever taken there or told.

"Before that, before I was grown—ah, it does not correspond that our-fathers turned from me, in those first years, and closed their minds' door against me; for they comforted me much, and kept me by them as much as I would. Perhaps it was I who turned from them, if I must say what happened without any bending of it. Atwar, I would wish to tell a letter to you that corresponds with everything that happened, because so much that the children have learned is without correspondence or harmony.

"The Sorud would have kept me in Book, but I tired of the screens, watching that moonsward hour by hour, not wanting to entrust it to any others. For a time I desired to be the first to see my brother; I thought he would show himself to me, because he was my brother—

"Atwar, why did you not come? You were never aware that we saw you, so why should you show yourself? Yet surely you returned to that place at least once? I cannot believe it was during Atwar's Grief, as they say (because no one can contradict them), those few hours when everyone ran from the screens!

"What else was there, what was it in the forest, that kept you and keeps you hidden from our eyes?"

Betwar was staring upward and now he lay back, supporting his large, tired head on his arms, and the image he had stared at so long in childhood stood forth clear before him, superimposed on the sunwhite roof-cloth—the Moon's moss-green brilliant grass, the edge of the car where its foot was just visible at the bottom left of the screen, the long wall of the larger house to the right and part of the script that was written on the roof of it, and the forest edge pressing in on the other two sides, thick and frothy. Sometimes the trees had moved as he watched, and seemed to move now, vigorously as in wind, and his heart clenched—then, he had been certain that Atwar would walk heedlessly out of them. The picture blurred—sometimes the screen had been blurred, as if clouds condensed in it. And then the terminator passed; he had watched still. The lights in the building had flickered and winked out and never again shone forth; he had seen that, and had watched still.

He never looked now, though he was in the Great Book from time to time, and sometimes passed close behind the screens. In all these years this same scene stared back at them in all the phases, and the scholars kept their vigil, watching for Atwar. In the Moon's dark they watched, and at the Lake floor, also in the darkness for his light; and sometimes they thought they had seen, on the spread cloths, something shining faintly in the Sea of Vapours, and in the Lake of Death.

It was because of this obsessive, useless watching that the Sorud had begun to rebuke them. Because they watched only, while the Sorud argued that it was more important and seemly to search for knowledge, and learn the purposes of the Outdead, and try to understand what had been surely and impeccably prepared. But the Fu-en scholars were happier watching for Atwar, and Twel Sorud said more than once, bitterly, "This watching for him—this is how they forget him."

By that time the scholars were already teaching the people; they had devised the first of the ceremonies, and were beginning to celebrate him.

And Betwar had been slow to Book, though his fathers were patient. He thought now that he was slow because of his sadness and disappointment. He could not look into any screen and not look for his brother—in turning from the screens, he had turned from his fathers as much as they had turned from him.

"And, Atwar, it does not correspond, if my children will tell you that our-mother Tasman made a finishing, and ceased to remember you. I remember her hands holding my head firmly, as a bowl—her eyes—ah, that was strange—she could not eat from that bowl. It was you, Atwar, she could not eat, what you are, the gist and taste of you—she could not, and she knew it, that was the look of her, staring not searching. She would have leapt after you into death, and could not have been prevented—except that you did not go into death. Nothing is right."

What emptiness those years held for him despite his fathers' constancy! To be house-bonded so young, and never having been short-bonded at all—yet that had been at least a change, an end (he had believed) to emptiness.

Three

Strangers from the Unseen have arrived in the meadow; go forth, for it is a rule that "the newcomer is visited."

1

On a night well into Lightening, when the sun had begun to linger, and dusk was long and spread out glowing on the northern horizon and there was no absolute darkness, only a diminishment of light, Betwar remained on the beach alone. Moonfall was over, and its loud ceremonies, and he was waiting for the Moon that would come before dawn, his white rising to be swiftly lost in the roseate one, his great, cool, faded face swimming upwards, in his sweet, imperceptible asymmetry, waning once again from the perfect circular towards darkness and renewal. He awaited the complete pattern of forests blue among the barren creamy highlands, the seeded and vegetable Moon.

In Siya, when he and Atwar were children, they had seen that seeding. He remembered how they had watched together in the clearing, how he had stood between Tasman's knees (for they were unweaned) and how little Atwar had turned blind Sorud Twar's head towards the Moon's rising with his little, narrow hands.

"Can you see the Moon now, Fadar?" Atwar would ask, and Twar would answer patiently that he could, perhaps, if Atwar described it to him. The moonlight on his uplifted face and open, milky eyes. Mostly he kept them shut. He would say, "There is too much light." Ah, Atwar had described much to Sorud Twar, for he was quick and observant and wanted his Fadar to see, as if he could command it—

Anyway, Sorud Twar had regained his sight in Fu-en, and seen his sons. They had been happy then in Fu-en, but also in Siya, it seemed to him now.

Now Betwar wanted to lose himself in the Moon— his presence, not as in screens or maps or mirrorings but there, where he gazed back at him as he gazed. The Moon's thought was not myriad, as the World's, but single and secret and not known.

If Atwar lived. Betwar was not touched by the swollen, ardent faith of the scholars and the multitude, who ate Atwar night by night in the waning, and in high-flown words and ritual believed they were doing him a favour, even keeping him alive, by celebrating him. If Betwar thought his brother lived, it was with a quieter conviction. The people made elaborate dolls, some larger than houses, and touched them, and said many extravagant things, but to Betwar there was no connection between all this and the little, crippled boy who had gone from them white-teethed and grinning, true brother though his body was separated, with all childhood's unpredictable freaks and faults, till that day close to him, breathing and present and real.

"My children, tell my brother (for nothing is right here) that I remember him as he was and is. My mind knows that his mind is grown, and his body—though the snake crippled it, it is an adult body now. But his teeth were never blackened, he was never cut, and for

47

me he is that children's body and child-mind, and his sudden white grin still informs my thought as if he were with me, it appears—as if it were wiped in across a screen, I see it across my mind. And this mind is also stayed, there where he went from me, nothing has touched me since in my mind or heart to make me different than I was.

"No one knows him like this, not even the Nev who ran with us—even for them he is fading, coloured by those fabulous images and songs; he is not what he was.

"Atwar, listen to my children, when they tell you how perfectly I remember you."

2

Again the children had come to their little Book on the arms of the attendants, who had climbed with them to the Square and circled the Doll, then descended southward towards the Sheath by the straightest of the streets.

Again they sat passively, more or less attending, and repeating the lines of section—the grid directions on the Moon—after the obviously bored teachers—the Qam who thought of other things, who spelled each other off verse by verse and attempted to keep the children's attention by calling on them out of sequence. Ard they troubled more than the others.

With no Moon and no indication that they would be taken into the great Book, they had to be resigned; and their voices answered the Qam's more or less accurately, but without enthusiasm, and dawn seemed long in coming.

The wall-cloth was rippling upwards, and Tared knew that Ard was running her hand against it dreamily as she did at home, and watching the pattern of the watery folds in the moonlight. Shadowy figures came and went outside, first the long pageant of the sick being carried on litters, perhaps to the beach to be washed. Then people passing up from the storehouses, their bodies overburdened with sheaves of plants. Others—the slow sick, bent and hobbling, swift scholars upright as if proud of their health—then no one, only the moonlight against the white cloth, and inside, the murmur of voices. Ripple, ripple went the wall, upward, stopped at the roof-stem gap, running into nothing.

But another shadow, instantly recognizable, had paused at the door, the door-fold moved between its stems, and was pulled down by narrow, black, fastidious hands. The Ng entered.

Tared reached back and flattened her hand against the house-cloth to still it. The Ng, inside now, calmly straightened their body. They looked about jerkily, in order to look directly at each of the children. Then they sat down in the teachers' sling, tucking their gloved feet under them. The Qam who had risen crouched on the earth, but the Ng's heads went on jerking and looking at the children.

"Come near-us," said the Ng Twar, who spoke most, but was, in the eyes of the children, less cruel.

Though the Ng were not old like the Azur or other great twins, they moved with the old's deliberation, as if they had anticipated age and copied it. All their movements were graceful yet as if reasoned out, not only at the rituals but for any ordinary times, and their voices, though dark for women, were as the voices of women.

The children slipped out of their slings and pulled themselves closer, the Qam making way for them, after moving the lamp and placing it carefully at the Ng's knees. After a silence, Ng Twar nodded and spoke.

"You have heard these new songs and rumours about the pieces of visible thought, said to have been seen."

What was it he was saying? The children were silent. It was always difficult to understand the speech of the great scholars, and safer to wait for more of it before answering. Even to say, "No, we have not," would be risking more incomprehensible verbiage. Tared had no idea what the Ng were talking about, and was sure Ard and her brothers were as puzzled as she was.

"Pieces of visible thought," repeated Ng Twel in his similar, perhaps even darker voice, which was slightly slowed and slurred. Ask had once said, "Ng Twel is the male, and has no heartside breast—but Ng Twar has no pouch," and they had giggled. But the Ng dress was loose and the rare times they carried the children, it was heartside or loosely—and the Sanev just grinned knowingly and would not be questioned.

Now the Ng heads jerked in questioning along the line of their audience.

Qam Twar's courteous voice from behind them ventured, "You speak of new rumours, not yet Songs, hardly two days old, and we did not think it proper to tell them of it."

"Nevertheless, song spreads like wind, and was heard at the Doll this evening, and people are gathering."

"When we passed the Doll there was no one," said Tared. This was safe enough. Moonfill had exhausted the people's eagerness for ceremony, and the Square had been deserted when they made their simple round, except for sleepers.

"Children of Atwar! What then have your ears heard?" The Ng heads jerked and stayed. They looked last and longest at Ask, who was not afraid of them, and tended to get away with impertinent answers if he couched them in courteous words.

"No thing about visible thoughts, among the heard thoughts. But I call heard-thoughts, speech."

"We are not talking about speech. Have you seen these thoughts that are reported to pass through the air, or have you heard them described?"

The scholars murmured, Saska squirmed, and the others answered "No," because they had not. Tared wondered that it was not loud speech the Ng referred to, the cry of a strong-voiced throat carrying across the city? Nothing special had they heard in this way, and among adults to shout aloud was unseemly, unless it was for news or warning.

The Ng had settled themselves as if they meant to stay, and gestured that the children should come even closer, crowd closer together before them. The twin heads flickered.

When the Ng sat thus they spoke in unison, or else the twin who spoke did so scarcely moving his lips, while the other let his lips remain a little parted. The children's ears heard which twin spoke, but the illusion was so strong it seemed they had one mouth then, and one voice. The voice, which Ask clenched his twelfist to remember, was the Twar's.

"This may correspond, or it may not. Boy-twins playing in the marshes have spoken to people in the farms, of something that soars like a stone, when no stone is thrown upward, and falls without harm."

The children were wary now, and the Ng noted this, nodding as if to say, You have already told us that you know. Ask thought—it is the Sanev bows. He had not yet seen them in use, yet in the Nev house they were not hidden, they hung sometimes half-made on the doorstem; he and Saska had touched them—narrow stems of blond wood soaked and pulled out of shape like the eaten Moon. The Sanev treated them as secret by never speaking of them, that the Ur in courtesy could not begin. But the Sanev were away more than usual, and at home they had spent their time braiding tight strands of human hair: this they begged off the Ludh, whose hair had grown in gray and tough—the Sanev now had many strands, which they separated and measured and pulled taut between their hands.

Yet the bows were but World-children toys, fashioned after what they had seen in the north, to throw the arrowheads they had brought back with them. The Sanev had never seen bows used. For two months they had practised, breaking the strings often; Saska and Ask had guessed what they were playing, for at home they sat shaping doll-arrows of wood, and were ever repairing and restringing the bows.

The thrown arrows had been seen, then. The bows worked. Ask dared not look at Tared or Ard to confirm it, or at Saska, who squirmed again now—he was always half-speaking of the Sanev secrets, it was surely of the bows.

"What have you seen, Children of Atwar?" Again it was Ask they watched. He looked back carefully, his hand still clenched, searching out the Twar mole to hold apart their faces.

"There is no shame in the north, in the casting of arrows," he said at last, very cautiously. Ah, everyone knew of the snake hunters in the northeast, some of whom were cowardly, and liked to pierce the snake from a safe place. Those bows were said to throw the arrows like stones, and with more force. But there were no snakes in the marshes. It did seem, now, the Ng were making a great thing of this, which in the north, as all knew, was ordinary among both women and men.

But the Ng looked suddenly put out, and paused. The Twel said, as if after some thought, "No, there is no shame there. And what you say would correspond, if by chance northern people should travel to Fu-en. They would perhaps cast arrows here."

Were the Ng deliberately leading him? Ask was uncertain. Saska's voice piped suddenly, "It must be people from the north!" Saska would protect the Sanev, if anything they did was challenged.

Now Ask was thoroughly puzzled. It was but play, and no one interfered much with big World-children, who sometimes managed to borrow their fathers' knives unheeded, and liked to play with danger a little, or pretend to.

"Has an arrow fallen into a farm?" asked the Twar Qam, alert to the idea of accident. Siri their new house-bonded were often in the farms for fibre.

But the Ng mouth-grinned; their black teeth so seldom seen, small and pointed, were surprisingly dull with age, and bits of yellowish bone showed at the roots of them like seeds.

"He is no arrow, but a living creature," said the Ng Twar severely. They used the archaic singular kept for single-headed creatures—snakes, Tasman, Atwar and Betwar and themselves. "In rumour he is like a snake, but small as the fist of little children—and he is many."

Saska shifted again beside Tared, and she felt a thrill of excitement.

"Did they-who-found-it touch this thing?" she asked.

But the Ng seemed to have lost interest, and did not answer. They rose. "You are more ignorant that we were led to believe," the Twel remarked. "Yet you are said to be in the Nev house much. We have sent to find these boy-twins past the farms." His profile stayed briefly, as if burnt against the protruding face-board that now hid his Twar, as they stooped in the door. His outer eye closed for a moment in the unwarped socket and, with his bald chin and narrow, sinewy neck, he looked womanish indeed. "Do not allow this to divert you over much, Children of Atwar. A new thread can be tied into the weave, and becomes unseen. How this pertains to you must be studied. Be sure we will care for it."

3

Betwar walked across the city at dawn to meet his children, going by way of the low ground along the shore, then over to the straightest street, which was the way they would be brought. He saw people hurrying uphill, and stopped some World-children and heard the rumour from them: a snake has been seen in the marshes. It is small. It swims in the air, and falls like a stone.

He met his children under the hill, and took Saska from the Qam, and returned uphill with the others. By this time, as it grew hot, people were turning slowly homeward, still talking among themselves. Saska chattered nervously across at Ask—"It was the Sanev, and I knew something of it, but I did not tell the Ng."

"They did not demand it, either, or you would have," said Ask a little scornfully. When something was afoot, the scholars always paid most attention to Ask.

Betwar listened to what he could hear, and when they reached home, and the scholars had gone, he lay down with his children and they talked. Saska, who had not wanted to come in, lay restlessly in the west-facing door, his eyes roving the canal-brim and the leafy sky.

"It seems to me," said Betwar, "that this thing must have consciousness, if it does not hurt itself falling down. Some people I heard saying, that many were seen, and some said, three—first two, and then another one in the evening."

"The Sanev will come and tell us—it was they who saw it," said Saska positively.

Tared reached across Ard and touched Betwar's arm. "Fadar, the Ng say they are thoughts. Like a piece of True Book thrown down—but they must be snakes, and think thoughts, I think."

Ask laughed. "You are rambling like a scholar, Tared."

He and Ard giggled, and Tared, who did not like to be teased, struck out at them, but Betwar laid his large arms firmly over hers and held her.

"Go to the Sanev, Fa," put in Saska. "Tell them to come and visit-us." The others joined in to urge him.

Betwar to quiet them stepped over Saska and climbed out of the canal, and walked to the Nev house, which lay farther inland in the same canal, past the second bridge where the course divided. But when he pulled down the door he saw only the Ludh asleep, with their shirt slid down off their scarred breasts and their arms over their faces. Frowning, he came back past the houses with the risen sun hard against him. He looked about but the people had all gone inside; day-stillness had fallen over the city.

They slept a little, even Saska against his will, curled in the threshold; direct sun woke him striking over the roof-beam. He heard distant voices calling.

People were calling far and nearer, and soon the whole city was wide awake again, and outdoors, calling and running. Betwar lifted the children outside, and they saw the air overhead filled with the new little creatures, little plump snakes, and all swimming northward. A slippery noise, like the scraping together of white teeth, accompanied them. All over the city children could be heard counting, and losing count, and beginning again and arguing.

"They are coming from across the Sheath!" The message spread swiftly, and all the people stood still, staring.

Betwar could see that they were not balls, but wide, and that they seemed to swim sideways, beating their flat, tapered bodies.

"They are falling into the marshes!" a voice shouted. But when Betwar among the running people reached the farms (he was carrying Ask, who had flung himself at him), the swarm of creatures had risen again out of the trees and fallen down farther north among the bluffs: no people who ran after them could get near them.

When he got back, he found the Sanev inside the house sitting with Saska and the girls. It was indeed the Sanev who had seen the first two of these things, and they had kept it secret; but people in the farms had heard them talking, and so the boys had told it to them, trusting them.

"We would have told it generally, but we have no words for it!" said the Twel Sanev, whom the children called Nevi, his eyes squinting with laughter. "Nevar kept saying, 'I have not seen this—it is a *Nothing*!' and shutting his eyes, because we did not know what we were looking at!"

His twin shook his head and grinned good-naturedly. "We opened and closed and opened our eyes, and it was still there," he stammered.

"Snakes—thoughts—the Namers will name them, and so we will know what they are, and all about them," said Betwar a little dryly.

Indeed the Namers found a name by nightfall—in a True Book from the south, kept in the middle country west of Turuk and brought to Fu-en long ago: their name became, for one, *'usfoor,* and for many, *'usaafeer.* That was corrupted in the common speech to *sufur/ asafir.*

4

The asafir stayed, and settled about the bluffs, and began to come into the marsh forests and the farms. The people threw food at them, and they liked some of it but not the black roots, and would not eat any thing, or stay, if the people came close to them. Also, they ate seeds and leaves no people would eat.

The interview promised the Sanev never materialized. They had hidden in the marshes, and were not found before their discovery was overwhelmed in the general one: within a few hours the occasion was public, and none knew more than others.

So despite Ask's fears for Nevi and Nevar's bows, these seemed not to interest the scholars after all.

The Sanev played on, out past the madder farms where the bluffs rose out of dusty meadow. After the asafir appeared, the twins disturbed them much, and began to aim after them. But they were unable to strike any, either in flight or on the bluffs or among the trees; both arrowheads they lost in the marshes.

Then, they managed to catch one sufur cunningly, in cloths they let fall over it, but it had died immediately in their hand. Scared, they had crouched over it among the bluffs. Even without their minds' daring their eyes, caught in amazement by the colour, had examined it carefully (for they had never seen bright blue). They saw how it could have extended and folded itself, and that it was covered in layered shafts, each shaft having two soft feathery vanes, in kind like the wooden vanes slit into the arrows-shafts northern people fashioned, but of great strength and delicacy—and their colour was partly near-white, like the sky over distant horizons, and partly brilliant, unearthly blue. It was a colour so strange there was no word for it, except the word for distance.

The shafts could barely bend and were very light; one snapped in the Nevi fingers and they could not put it right again, or its harmed vanes. It was hollow.

Nevar had wanted to burn the sufur, but Nevi argued that they should first speak to their fathers. So they had torn the cloth and wrapped the sufur in strips, and hidden it under earth, and gone home. They whispered to their fathers, and the Nev consulted Betwar, and they advised the Sanev to fetch it home. They looked at it together, the Ludh watching from across the house-room expressionlessly.

They saw that it did not swim sideways. The extensions were as arms, that supported and propelled it; so it swam forward. The almost round body extended with a third long, tapering extension and forward like a snake's, with eyes like black seeds, but with a nose like bone and no mouth. The forepart was a head, that fell loosely down when it was not held up, and the hinged arms drooped piteously.

Betwar persuaded them to take it to the Great Book.

So that same evening he walked across the city with the Nev and Sanev, the boys carrying it carefully wrapped in the same strips of cloth.

5

It was a late evening they came out of the city, and approached the Great Book under the Sheath. Twin scholars stood like door-stems each side of the entrance; here they would remain through the Watch: they were young adults, hardly more than children, female twins and male twins—apprentices who would later be allowed to watch for Atwar themselves, and think it a favour bestowed.

While the Sorud lived, the order and rotation of the Watch was not yet devised, or even considered. Folk watched because they would—the Sorud would have pitied these their boredom, Betwar thought. Even afterwards, till Atwar's Grief, such strictness was not thought necessary. He saw now how the Nev halted courteously in their tracks, and their sons beside them—Betwar, out of plain habit and precedence, would have walked on in.

The scholars came forward, and the Sanev carefully unwound their little parcel. The scholars peered into it while Nev explained.

"Our-sons are those who first saw the asafir, and who now have caught one; we persuaded them to bring it into Book."

"He died without our wish," put in Nevar—they pulled back their parcel quickly as the scholar-youths put out an enquiring finger.

"Wait, we will speak to the Watch," one of them said, and they ran off through the entrance, while the female twins moved away a little and stood uncertainly. Betwar saw how the Sanev preened before the young women, standing somewhat taller and prouder, for these were round-bodied and fair, and probably of the same age as they; girls grew into adulthood sooner

than boys did, and the Sanev were nearly past their
ugly half-grown years now, nearly well grown.

Great Book had no door, and much was buried by
sand; what was uncovered of it, and what functioned of
it, lay within the part of the Sheath close to the shore;
here the Sheath was strangely shaped, swirled and
tucked and pulled asunder, as if it had hardened suddenly long ago in the midst of cataclysmic bursts of
boiling steam and implosion. The entrance stretched
apart like a mouth pulled into a grimace, and the
interior was a series of caverns—great wallowing vaults,
many wide open to the heavens. Dirty, trodden sand
half-filled the door, whose edges were the in-folded
Sheath-wall, shiny with passage. They could see lamplight farther in and true, ancient light on the lower edge
of the Moon's Arm—the instrument that could follow
the Moon across the height of the sky, and cast its
moving image on the Lake below.

Presently a large group of scholars emerged; and the
twins who had fetched them, with the young women,
were nodded off to the doorway, where they went
reluctantly enough. Hurrying after the scholars, pulling up their long dress so as not to trip over it and
stepping uncertainly, came the Azur, whom Betwar
always liked to see—because they remembered him,
and the Sorud and the old days.

The scholars took the sufur and looked at it, passing
it from hand to hand. They seemed to have forgotten
the sons of Nev, who attempted to keep close by, and
they turned their backs on Betwar and the Nev, and
muttered among themselves, and were silent. The Azur,
pushing in busily, took and turned and lifted the little
carcass, so that part of it bent back and hung loosely
from their hands, bits of iridescence sparkling like
distant water on it surfaces, that were intricate and

manifold. Betwar observed a hush come over the scholars, their glances slowing and widening, overcome against their wills by the colour of distance so close to their eyes.

Nevar spoke up—"Be careful, of holding him—" and the Azur looked towards them blurredly, then tucked back the hanging form with an awkward, possessive flourish.

The other scholars also bestirred themselves, and gestured the boys back. "Leave-us."

Betwar thought, they are not angry with the Sanev, because of their own amazement and curiosity; but to keep this thing they would pretend to be. Even the benign faces of the Azur were soured and inward, and some of the others, in looking towards the boys, had put on ugly scowls.

The scholars now began to walk in a tight bunch over the sand towards the city, the feeble Azur in their midst, holding the bundle rather high before their faces—the hands of other scholars were placed on it as well, and on the skinny, white-bearded Azur arms—it was almost foolish, almost a procession, Betwar thought. He followed, and the Nev and Sanev came as well, more doubtfully, through the crescent house-ring of the Watch and into the precinct of Medical Book. They saw the group enter one of the rooms among the long wards. These stretched back from the street, tight-packed to utilize the last of the flat ground. The door was left open and Betwar looked in, then sat down in the sand where he could see the interior, and the Nev and the boys sat down as well.

"Will they speak to-us?" asked Nevar restlessly.

"Yes, surely, they will say something, since you have brought them the sufur." Betwar wondered whether they would demand an explanation of the boys, of its death.

Inside around the lamps there was much quiet talk and argument. Women-scholars emerged suddenly, stepped around them without a word, and went off among the wards. They returned with more people. The ample form of the An, old twins who healed burns, went shuffling in, fastening their face-board, not acknowledging Betwar. These women had attended the Ludh after Atwar's Grief. The murmuring went on, and over it could be heard in snatches the Azur voices, higher pitched and excited. The Sanev stretched out on their belly, whispering together. Betwar saw their strong, long legs, crossed so easily at the ankles, their big, healthy feet with the sparse foothair wrapped roughly around them—like other World-children they ran barefoot, and their foothair was worn thin, but it sprouted ever under their arches, robust and black. Betwar envied them their strength for the sake of his sons—so the Ur limbs would have looked, had they been left alone. The thought was painful and his mind ran from it.

Now at an even pace, behind them from their house closer to the beach, the Ng approached, greeted them unhurriedly, and stooped into the ward. The voices quieted except for the Azur's—they heard one Azur say clearly, "Now we are assembled, and all will be made to correspond!" But then the group moved farther down the long room after the Ng, and twins came back and pulled up the door.

They resigned themselves to a long wait; yet soon the Ng reappeared, followed by the An and several more from Medical Book. As these made no move to sit down, Betwar and the others scrambled to their feet. Now, he supposed, they would be included, scolded or dismissed.

The Ng leading, they all proceeded slowly down the wards in the direction of the beach. Salt stink reached them. The tide was at ebb, the exposed sands curving steep against the promontory, the water low but close. The Sheath-wall cast a thick, almost furry darkness ahead of it and the scape was halved utterly—twarside height and blackness, twelside flat, bright water and distance and dawning sky.

Betwar wondered whether they were to be invited into the Ng house, which stood off to their left with a narrow space of swept sand around it. That threshold he had never crossed, or wished to cross. But the Ng did not turn aside; they walked on to the high shore, and stood still.

Betwar halted twarside, tall and awkward; the others also had stopped out of the range of their look. But the Ng turned deliberately towards the young Sanev, fixing them with their direct gaze, halved by the board. The Sanev, World-children and wild, had perhaps never been exposed to this before, that his own children faced so often.

"I always look for the mole," Ask had boasted, soon after they began to go to Book, and little Tared had said in her prim, didactic way, "Do not tell them, or Medical Book will cut it off; then what would you do?"

"Throw it at you!" They had squealed and giggled and rolled about, little squirming noisy ones, children of a terrible purpose who did not yet understand.

Now the Ng spoke only briefly. "Sons of Nev, you chanced to see first the asafir, and were the first to touch a sufur with your hands. How did you invite it to you?"

Nevi stammered. "It was alive, until our hands closed over it. It was not out wish—we did not wish it death."

"Walk with-us." Their nod dismissed the others.

Dawn was breaking, and Betwar turned to follow the dispersing scholars, thinking to trudge behind them as far as the little Book, to meet his children. The Nev lingered, looking after their sons, then hurried to catch up with him.

"Those Ng—they might desire more asafir, for their curiosity," said Nev Twar, and his brother added, "Betwar, we do not want our sons commanded of them."

"I think they have enough pleasure in commanding my children," answered Betwar.

"But our sons are wild and unused—", "—they are but World-children, and cannot read—"

"They are not stupid. And remember, where you are concerned, ordinary folk, the Ng have no more command over you that you allow them. If your sons are afraid of them, you have not taught them well."

Saying this, Betwar felt the shameful, irresistible rush of his old despair, and stood still; but the Nev were used to him, and the Twel threw an arm across his shoulders. They went on, the Nev guiding him, and found his children ready. It was morning.

6

The Ng, said the Sanev when they ran in breathless later, had only wished to make sure there were no more dead asafir. And had asked them something of the asafir ways, and had listened more than spoken. "When they looked at us directly, it was as you said," Nevar told them, still panting, "They become as the Moon— and we could not look away."

"Did you try?" said Ask slyly.

"I am sure we could not. I did not want to."
"That is the trick of it, the not wanting."

That night was the Small Eating. Betwar was never at the Square, but the Nev and the Ludh attended sometimes, and Betwar's children took part as always on their way to Book. This night they were delayed.

The Small Eating was finished, and they were already at the south edge of the Square. But behind them the great scholars had remained under the Doll, discussing among themselves restlessly. The children's bearers, and all the people who had begun to leave, turned back uncertainly and waited.

The speakers were not the Ng, whose voices were unsuited for general, loud pronouncements, but strong-chested Tellers from Sakhalin, called Amadu.

"People of Fu-en! You have been waiting patiently to hear our decisions about these new creatures who have come among us, whose name we have called *asahfeer*. Now one is delivered to us, and we have studied it, and our decisions are these: *'sufur's* behaviour, in choosing to live outside this city, and in moving away from any who come near it, and the fact that he chose death, have proved him a living consciousness, to be reverenced and protected. This is our pronouncement to you: 'The asafir are as the trees.'" After that, the other scholars returned into their Book, and the people dispersed, but the Amadu visited the Sanev in their house, and broke their bows.

After the next Circling, the body of the little creature was given to the Doll: the children watched as lesser scholars climbed up and tied it on the sleeve. It smelled after a day in the sun, but then dried up, its hues faded and no one bothered about it.

Thus the scholars named and determined the asafir,

although—as Betwar remarked to the Nev—"the asafir go on eating just the same."

7

For the Children of Atwar, the coming of the "little-birds" meant a respite. The scholars were so curious as to their meaning, and so eager to incorporate this new phenomenon into their system and ceremonies, that they had little time for anything else. They busied themselves in searching out old phrases in Book that could be seen to be asafir prophecies. At the little Book, the Qam came and went more often than sitting with the children, and were obviously distracted not just by their own bonding.

On that evening the carcass was fastened on the Doll, the children had been carried directly home again, and after that, though continued to be carried each evening to the small Circling, they were not brought into their Book; their attendants hurried off and others were allowed to take them home. Evening by evening passed into night and none returned for them.

Free of Book, they did little but swim, or beg to be carried into the marshes, to follow the Sanev and other World-children. And though Betwar told himself this time should be spent with his children teaching them, he let them go.

But the children had not been among the bluffs when the Sanev caught the sufur (the Sanev had kept this secret from them) and Saska wept when he heard of it.

8

There was much talk and rumour in the city concerning the asafir. The Ludh, and other women who had seldom gone to any but the greatest ceremonies, attended even the small Circling, and stood about afterwards with other folk, and there was indeed as much excitement and exchange, and breeding of Song and Tale there among the ordinary people, as in the Great Book. And there was confusion both on the Square and in Book, and between them.

The Ludh concerned themselves much in these rumours. Folk were saying that the asafir were the thoughts of the hypothetical people south of the Sheath, who lived, as it had been conjectured and was now believed, a kind of mirror-existence to their own.

The children, too, argued about these things.

"But it is not exactly the same," said Ask, "or we would have sent them our thoughts as well."

By now most of the ordinary folk believed in the existence, and the good will, of people in that distant and unreachable South, and new, secular songs had begun to spring up about them, even love-songs. A very old Tale from the plains became suddenly popular; the Ludh knew it: it said the *Suidfolk* were all white, white as Whalsay people from the western isles, and that any white twins (the Semer were an example of them—who turn up still in every generation with reddish or straw-coloured hair, and white eyelashes, and who all look somewhat alike) were akin not to their parents, but to each other and to this southern race, their light seed springing still here and there among the swart and blue-skinned people, just as single-headed Tasman and her progeny had sprung from that lost race, the Outdead.

This is the *Old Ludh Song of the Southern Folk*:

> *Past the Sheath everything is backwards,*
> *Twar is twel and twel is twar,*
> *The Earth is the Moon and black is white*
> *the faces of the southern people are white as the*
> *Moon.*
> *Pink as Whalsey their hair, white their faces,*
> *in their eyes no darkness, they squint at the sun*
> *they laugh when we weep, weeping is their*
> *laughter.*
> *If they are born here, ask them as babies,*
> *whether they remember the place all upside-*
> *down,*
> *ask them to tell us about it.*[20]

Arguing about the existence of the Suidfolk had never, till now, been more than a ritual exercise, for there had never been any proof of it. Now the asafir were confirmation that life, at least speechless life, existed beyond the Sheath, and if these small creatures could manage to journey across it in the increasingly temperate air, what else, who else, would come, and finally be revealed? Atwar, on the Moon, saw perhaps the lights of southern cities when he watched the World, and was gathering that information for them in his good time, that would unite them. Perhaps already he conversed with them! It was the stuff of Songs. The Ludh had learned to sing a new, secular Song but their sons laughed at it, and said it was unseemly in the mouths of their mothers. But the children heard it often among women, and Ard knew it before Tared, and taught it her, for it was for two voices. This is the secular duet:

White twins, Semerwhite,
in the south you are preparing
your bed, your body
you send us your distant thoughts
our eyes like weavers worn and weary
look up from the loom
have pleasure in far (blue) mountains.

Ah we will lie and play
black and white in that day
beautiful twins we will bear
together we will teach them
to honour Atwar in beauty.[21]

Meanwhile, some of the scholars searched in Book diligently among the old words, and when they found what they believed referred to the asafir, they told this at the Square. Their pronouncements came almost nightly just after the Circling, and people, even restless World-children, began to loiter there into the night, squatting near the Doll, for these tellings were made much of, and repeated, and the blowers of reeds would stay to hear them, and take them up and shape them.

The words from the True Book found in Turuk were:

A gentle rain in a distant Darkening,
And the birds are blue, are blue,
And the earth is a celebration.[22]

As for the prophecies, they came quickly, for they were already known: the first was lifted out of the song from Novaya Zemlya which Tasman received at Siya, and the second found in the Fu-en version of her Tale, but it had first come from True Book. It was the skinny, ardent-for-Atwar but otherwise insignificant twins called T'ai who, urged on by the excited Azur, strode nervously forth to cry them aloud, while the Azur beamed approval. The T'ai and their even shyer sisters the T'ien were bookish scholars, busy at the Lake, ever searching, still young but looking for the face-board already; they lived celibate in the same house. The prophecies, uttered out of context, were as follows:

> *Your thoughts will cross the barren place\ your body cannot pass\ between worlds, and we will be one world.*

And the second one was:

> *There will be conversation between them in those days; they will turn their faces to each other in kindness.*[23]

But the Ng and many scholars in the great Book began to be angry, and to resist these new interpretations more and more resolutely. The Ng and the Amadu would leave the Square in proud procession with their followers, as soon as the Circling was completed. But their demonstration did nothing to disperse the crowd, so they resorted again to staying on, closely grouped under Atwar and looking serious. The Azur and their followers, however, walked openly about the Square, and sang and pronounced with flourishes, and the people listened, often trailing in their wake. The T'ai, who had been most shy and eager for the seclusion of Book, were now open-mouthed and loud. And the T'ien as well were ready to argue, and good at argument, and some people questioned them for the pleasure of being thoroughly defeated. They said, "The T'ai and their sisters are as upside-down as the Suidfolk, their eyes look into their own heads when they talk to us." Betwar heard all this second-hand from the Ludh or the children, but the Nev had also begun to be interested in seeing for themselves; indeed as the nights passed almost the entire city would gather, some for the Circling and the rest afterwards. Carried around, the children were sure to be closely surrounded by the last turn, and then they too stayed on, kept by their bearers.

Once, out of curiosity, Betwar went to meet his belated children. He came up from the beach in the long twilight, and stood at the northeastern edge of the Square, and could not see them for loitering people. There was no harmony in the crowd—here he heard loud arguments, there broken bursts of song around seated reed-blowers. Children darted between the adults, repeating phrases into each other's mouths, and conflicting voices shouted in song from far and near.

It was on this night that the Ng and their followers stood forth. The voices of the Amadu issuing twinned from that broad breast and throat-pit stopped the general clamour almost at once. People stood up, if they had been sitting down or squatting, and all strained forward towards the Doll. Betwar was tall enough to see, past and between the many heads, a space at Atwar's feet and the Ng standing there with the Amadu and other scholars; then he saw the Amadu scramble up on Atwar's right foot. From this eminence they reached down to help other twins up beside them, reeds were handed up, and now there was a little throng standing awkwardly above the crowds, with the Amadu closest to the bulging cliff of Atwar's ankle, and hidden by its bulk from the main part of the Square, because Atwar faced north. The heads of the Ng with their pristine face-board could be seen nodding below, tilting upward. The Amadu bent to them, then raised their heads and shouted in unison, commandingly, then paused and bent again; they had to pause before each shout, because Ng below were telling them what to say.

So that night it was pronounced that *between worlds* and *one world* and *conversation between them* had always meant, and would continue to mean, the conversation between the Earth and the Moon. These new interpretations and Songs were harmful to Atwar, and those who circulated them—they meant the old Azur's crowd in particular (because they were loudest in the telling) they called heretics.

It was not well to sing heretical Songs. They did not correspond to Atwar's purposes, and to sing them grieved him.

Before anyone could respond or question, the Amadu burst into song themselves, in a Song against Heresy. Betwar thought, they must have prepared this secretly in Book, for he had never heard anything like it. The word "heresy" was understandable enough for all its newness; like the most far-fetched of scholarly speech it was a *snow*, a compound of words into an new picture with a new clarity. It meant false trust, and those who were its propagators were said to press forward like a river, and those who followed them were driven in that current, swept on against their will. This is the Song Against Heresy:

> *Heresy stands in our threshold,*
> *false heretics return*
> *from weaving false imaginings.*
> *Swept by heresy like witless children*
> *foolish folk are persuaded from Atwar,*
> *the heretics want to turn every head.*

> *False scholars doubt Atwar*
> *desiring to increase the Asafir (power)*
> *and believe South-folk white*
> *are more bright,*
> *Fu-en wisdom they put to shame*
> *in order to persuade (us) of South-folk wisdom.*[24]

The song was sung three times and thus was in the strongest emphatic mode. When it ended there was silence. People stared; then a confusion of murmuring began as twin spoke into the mouth of twin. People dispersed quickly and quietly—eager, it seemed, to get to their own houses and talk of this in private. Betwar let them pass and found his children being brought towards him; the Azur and the T'ai and some others followed, talking in low voices; the Qam came with closed mouths. In the clearing Square the group at the Doll could be seen; in no hurry, the Amadu had climbed down and the other twins on Atwar's foot handed down their reeds and then slid carefully into his arms. Someone among them laughed.

But the Azur and their followers, and the hearts of so many people, were not so easily changed. The new songs were still sung, though courtesy kept people from repeating the more provocative verses, like those that stated outright how Atwar conversed with the Suidfolk. Ask and Saska could sing the Azur-T'ai song, and did so lustily on the beach, and World-children took it up across the shallow water. This heretical song was:

> *The Sufur stopped and stayed*
> *from the distant South over the Sheath*
> *from our South-folk friends.*

Burning did not scare him.

Unscorched by distance
carrying distance (blue)
worn (from) difficult journey
guided here by joy.

Sufur guided by Atwar's mind
in the pleasure of blue he has returned.
The Moon stopped close by
in Atwar's hand
Sufur in (the mind of) Atwar ended pain.[25]

Betwar, hearing them, said to the Qam who had come for them: "This time the Ng have perhaps received more yeast than their bowl holds."

The Qam spoke mildly for the Ng. "Wise scholars shape the stream —they cannot block it for long. But sometimes if it is blocked for a little, it will turn of itself."

"Or burst," said Betwar. He was himself outside this controversy, and cared too little about the arguments. His own mind was so filled with its own obsession that it was untouched by these strong public feelings. But he sensed the strength of them in the peoples' minds; and it pleased him somewhat, to see the Ng thwarted.

All came to a head at the next filled Moon, when the Azur, who because of their age were accustomed to much leniency, broke into the circle in front of the Doll and pointed upward with a flourish, their Twel shouting, "Is Atwar harmed? Look, you yourselves have placed the new thought at his breast!"

The next night the little carcass was gone from the sleeve of the Doll. But by the night after, another one had appeared, tied farther down and much dried and bedraggled—it was whispered that it had been found dead on the shore, and delivered to the Azur.

Then began the talk of a ritual quarrel, a debate in which the opponents (usually twins) argue the cause they are opposed to. Betwar could never get this rumour confirmed, yet the Ludh told it unswervingly as the truth, and it may have taken place, and healed the rupture somewhat. But the T'ai and the T'ien disappeared from the Square, and the Ludh spoke darkly of their having gone away—they meant, unwillingly; and the Sanev said, some of the people had taken to chiding their children with this and saying, "We will have you sent-away!" Other people said that the T'ai and T'ien were busy (they may have meant, confined) in the Great Book. The word "unwilling" was rarely used except in Tales or for chiding children, but now it was applied to the T'ai and their sisters almost openly, in the mouths of the people.

And without these mindful twins' sober urgency, the coherence of the heresy was gone. Heretical songs, unsung in the ceremonies, became the shiftless property of the streets and the World-children.

The carcass stayed, and the prophesies, except for the Turuk fragment, were not heard again in their new context, in the Square. The resolution, however it came about, was not spoken of directly. But after this the Azur began to act strangely, ranging along the shore and shouting and scaring the World-children. There were still scholars who, with perhaps more sense, continued to ponder the appearance of living creatures from beyond the Sheath; but they let the Azur be, and were careful to voice their speculations in new words, not in those of ancient times.

Thus the coming of the asafir, their presence and what they might mean, engaged and stretched the people's minds and hearts in that Lightening. There was a new brightness in their faces, and when they greeted each other, some still said, as well as "*Atwar walks*", "*The world is healed indeed.*"[26]

Four

*A strange bird am I, who of my own desire,
without snare or catcher, have crept into the
cage.*

1

Ask and Saska lay at the western edge of the marsh-
forest, looking across at the bluffs and watching the
asafir, and talking not very seriously about how it
might be possible to trap them—carefully, without
touching them, so they would not die.

Here, the trees ceased almost abruptly and the land
changed: it rose gradually over a wide area of sandy
ground that supported only meadow-plants and thorn.
But southward the rose and madder farms flourished,
and inland the cloth-grass waved across the whole
stretch of land towards Semer's Way, and there were
yeast farms closer to the city. The bluffs cut across the
sky to the northwest, white and abrupt. They were not
as high as the Sheath, and wind-eroded into odd little
shapes and holes, and accessible, grass-topped like
shaggy heads, but they were ever dry and grim, and
seemed to keep their heat even in Darkening. There was
one low pit farther in where pure clay was dug for

ceremonies, and gravid women, it was said, visited them sometimes to eat the chalk. But otherwise none but World-children ever went into them, and that infrequently. The Sanev had been there sometimes, but were more often in the marshes—lately, they had played much in the meadows with the bows. And now the bluffs were the domain of the asafir, who were to be left alone.

The day's end was approaching, and the asafir were beginning to return, flocking from inland and out of the marshes, and making their now familiar welcoming noises—gurgles and quick chatterings. Several could swerve and swim as one thought, strongly, and they played, dipping and flashing blue and white against the western sky.

Soon they would disappear, for they slept at night, up among the first bluffs where the forest straggled against the clay-white overhang. It was in the early evenings, and again at dawn that they were nearby, entering the marshes and the edges of the farms, eating and allowing themselves to be seen. And all day now they foraged and returned, but singly, though when they met they seemed to chatter sociably to each other.

"If we could make them a little house," said Ask. "For they like small places, and will enter them willingly—as they do in the bluffs, the Sanev have said."

"Let us get the Sanev to help us then, and make a little house sufur would like, and would go into."

"One that would open inside, into a larger house," said Ask.

"With space for him to swim in—but we must be very careful and never touch him." Saska lowered his voice, as if the asafir might hear them.

"Nevar would tell, he told about the dead one."

"But we cannot make anything useful all by ourselves."

The boys lay over a pile of broken stems that were thick with moss. It was nearing sundown in the long day, and the red light lay in gloomy circles on the tangled forest branches and the brown, clear water among the roots. The Sanev and other big twins had brought them, and were now over beside a pool farther in, where no one cultivated. They were strapping fallen stems together for a raft. This had been a farm, despite its wild look.

The last of the asafir, as if refreshed by the approaching coolness, wheeled unerringly among the stems. They had sharp little hands under their bodies; with these they could clutch the twigs, and look sideways at things, and open and fold their bodies neatly, sometimes with an extra shake and ruffle, as if they were saying, "Just so!" They gurgled pleasantly.

Now, as one, they set off for the bluffs, their colours flashing as they took an extra turn against the sky.

"When they are one-minded, how will only one come to us?" said Saska.

"They swim indeed one-minded, but they fill their own mouths, each one," said Ask.

"And Nevi and Nevar caught one only."

"Perhaps we could make something," went on Ask, "and leave it in the bluffs with its door open—"

"Who will leave it? and who will close the door?"

"The Sanev."

"The sufureen would choose death before they allowed the sons of Nev to come near them again," said Saska.

"Then our-father could carry-us. And later, after two have gone in, we will pull up the door. If the sufureen do not throw themselves out first," he added doubtfully.

"If we persuaded them here in the marsh we could

swim to them, with no ripples and no sound," said Saska, again whispering.

"But they have fingers like little knives, that would tear the cloth."

"They will choose death, I think," said Saska. "Look!"

The boys watched a belated sufur drop straight down into a shallow puddle near them, then shake off the water crossly, and look at them snake-sideways out of one little eye. It opened its tiny hard nose-mouth and gurgled, and with a flick of brilliant blue swerved away, dodging the stems artfully, rising after the others into the open light.

"Sufur-sufur," whispered Saska. "If I could learn his speech, he would not choose death, but would fall into my shirt willingly, and I would take him where we are going."

His brother looked into his eyes then and saw his frightened purpose. Suddenly it stretched in his mind, giving their whole project a new meaning, serious and almost beautiful.

After that, Saska pleaded with the Sanev to take him past the marshes every night, and there he practised the noise of the asafir for hours, using no reed or stem, only his voice—he perfected it, and the birds, swooping from the bluffs in their own play, began to answer him.

Ask, for his part, got the Sanev to teach him the knots they made with their hand-hair—like the Nev, in a half-concession to the eastern custom, they scoured only the twarhand, and kept the twel hand-hair long, binding it back around their wrists. They did not cut it unless they wanted some of it to use as a tool. Ask wanted to learn the ways they could bind cloth to reed-frames intricately. Nevi, teaching him in their house, squinted and asked what he intended to make. And Ask said, "I want to be accurate," and concentrated with his head down—so Nevar put his mouth at his brother's ear and whispered, "Don't chide him—he wants to learn this for the Moon," which, though they knew it not, did correspond after all.

So they carried Saska into the bluffs and marshes and fetched him, and carried Ask between the houses.

2

They continued to carry the girls also, and sometimes touched them. Ard was more interested in this game than Tared. And when, in the fourth month of Lightening, the Nev raised the partition and the Sanev were confined for the cut and teeth-blackening, Ard yearned and dreamed. Now that they were adults—and so warm already—they would surely be short-bonded to some older women immediately.

The Ludh in their uncouth way had spoken of it more than once. "Big, their body becomes. We spoke to the Shui about new cloth. Then, they will have to look about them—"; "—Or be looked for, sister! Remember what those-ones said to-us at the Doll?"

The Nev would not allow this. "Do you begin to meddle—and their voices yet as high as girls?" But the Ludh would laugh, and Ard thought she had seen, then, the Twar Ludh's eyes flick at her lively and settle back into her placid face with a kind of knowing satisfaction.

But when the sons of Nev emerged, they seemed much the same. They treated Ask and Saska as they had before, except when Betwar or other adults were present; then, they pretended to be aloof, and spoke to them condescendingly as adults do with children, and when Ask sat by them to eat (they were visiting Betwar's house with the Nev) they began teasingly to stroke him, and he threw his bowl at them, so yeast spilled down their faces, and they ended rolling about on the earth and giggling.

But they were shy with the girls, and whenever Ard contrived to sit by them, the Sanev discreetly moved. When they looked in now, it was to take one of the boys with them, or both—they were so strong, they could manage to carry Ard and Saska together the short distance across to their house. Ard would watch them stagger off along the canal, laughing and gasping, with her brothers' tiny loose-bound legs sticking out from each side of their sturdy torso.

Ard thought much about their short-bonding. She began to look at women in the street, and at the Circling, carefully and jealously.

One early morning, the Nev had come to visit—the whole family, bringing her brothers home just before sleep; and they had talked long, and finally stayed to sleep there. And Ard managed to lie down by the sons of Nev—she did this by crawling over to refasten the east-facing door, and crawling only part way back.

The twins' long body moved closer into the shaded door-wall to make a place for her, and she lay down beside them stiffly.

Soon she could feel their twelarm's touch against her side, and Nevi's breath on her cheek. Behind her Betwar was asleep; and the dark bulk of his back, with an old mat flung over it, shielded her from the Nev and the Ludh. Her brothers were asleep already—she knew because Saska whimpered then, when he breathed, and Ask always waited for this, and then fell asleep immediately. Tared lay near them—where she herself should have lain—she was surely awake still; Ard felt her attention but scorned it. Had not Tared often enough played at milk-touching with the Sanev too?

The sons of Nev had used to tell the girls that this play was ordinary among weaned children, and common with the ones who went to World, though Tared told Ard privately, "They would like it to be. They do it with us when they can, because they are otherwise watched, even in World, and we cannot run from them." Sometimes lately Tared had pretended to be angry with the Sanev, and made as if to move out of reach, but it was only part of the play—she had never really protested, or prevented them.

Now the Sanev stirred, and the twarhand moved down inside Ard's loose sleeve stealthily, and touched one of her little rounded breasts. The fingers brushed over it, and then pushed back the downy hair, and a finger and thumb took hold of the nipple and held it softly. They shifted their body cautiously, and Nevi's hand (it was strange that, though she was sure she did not like him best, she liked him best) reached up under her dress and brushed across her other breast, then touched it carefully, moving over the whole, swollen surface as if trying to memorize it. She bit her mouth not to move.

They had never touched her breasts like this before—only to compare their flat small-girl-chests with their own, and remark that her nipples were blacker than theirs and Tared's bigger. These were the forbidden places. But the sons of Nev had never heeded adult rules with her or Tared. Then, they had touched her and Tared between the legs also—twice (in the forest) untying their bands as well.

They touched her there now: it was Nevar's hand, and she opened her thighs as well as she could, though it was painful with the bindings. His finger moved into the line. His warm palm cupped the pout of her sex and his finger slid farther between, into wetness (this was new) and a new, tight pulling in and trembling.

Ard lay like a stem. She did not dare to move, even to stroke them in acknowledgment. She could tell how Nevi held his breath, and Nevar was breathing high and careful in their chest—almost not breathing—so their body was taut, almost arched, at her side. Now Nevi's twelhand replaced his brother's, his finger sliding into the wetness, pushing inward here and there; then it moved out again, and slid forward again along another, inner line, and after that his fingers pressed the flesh together, and rubbed it. Then he slid one finger in between and pressed the soft lips together over it, hard, which was delicious.

Their hand pulled away suddenly, and they rolled noisily over on their stomach, dragging the cloths across them, and took some minutes settling. Ard saw, past her father, Tared's wild head lift up and stare at her and grimace and fling down.

Ard held herself tight and wet for hours in the dayheat, as the sun rose higher in the sky and the shade of the canal wall narrowed, till she was lying in the leaf-diffused light as in a thick, hot pool. Slowly light spread over the Sanev as well. She put her finger under her dress where theirs had been. Saska went on whimpering.

She must have slept, because now it was dark, and people were getting up and rolling the mats together, the Ludh stepping over her heavily. The Sanev had already gone home.

3

At last Betwar began to teach his children in earnest—
and realized they had learned most of what he wanted
to impart already. In the years of their growing up he
had told them most of the small things, and the large
one—which was his whole attitude to the world and its
new rituals and the Tales—they had been learning
continuously from his look, his outbursts, his avoidances
and obstinacy. Had he questioned them outright about
the world, as against the Fu-en interpretation of it, they
would have been able to answer him with surprising
accuracy—even Tared, who fiercely compartmentalized
her beliefs.

The children were not allowed to contradict their
teachers, though they knew, if they defended the Tales
at home, what Betwar's response would be. And the
scholars' speech made a kind of elaborate Tale of everything they said. Betwar too had told them fanciful
western Tales, when they were small and after their
mothers died: these were his and Atwar's common
inheritance—the stories Tasman had told them in Siya,
and the Bogdan-a's, whatever he could remember, but
he had also said, in his fathers' words, "It is a Tale, it
does not correspond." He told them also Tasman's
accurate story, that she had been making of the generations, about her own Lofot childhood and first
bonding.[27] He believed it was lost except in his mouth
and (he must trust) Atwar's, for her intention to write it,
as far as he knew, had come to nothing. He was not
certain of this, for he did not know what had happened
to her.

Betwar felt himself to be a poor Teller, and had
retained very little word for word except the simplest
repetitive songs; he regretted that he had not listened
better, and had compassion now on his children for all

they must learn in Book.

They knew the first Tale of Tasman as it was sung in the streets, in their own western language. It was a jumble of verses, moving often disconnected, and forward and backward in time; often, one verse contradicted the next. Yet they were expected to accept it.

The Outdead hated their forefathers, it said.

> *The Outdead fathered us against their will*
> *false, they stared at that summons*
> *they saw, conjoined as is seemly*
> *Janus and all their children*
> *they hated and hurt us because we lived*
> *tall and seemly, they wanted to tear us*
> *from life but they could not.*
> *In one generation, twins only.*
> *They died as we first began*
> *women (replaced by) twin women, twin men*
> *(replaced) men.*[28]

Yet the next verse taught the opposite:

> *No, they did not hate us.*
> *For us (they left) all they had shaped, useful and*
> *beautiful,*
> *against Moonfall.*
> *They remembered us.*
> *Dying, their hearts repented,*
> *they ensured us salvation in trust.*
> *Even Tasman was their seed, (to appear) in*
> *ripeness of time.*[29]

Such distant muddle Betwar could not unravel for them, much less for himself. His father Sorud Twel had condemned prophesy—and this seemed a kind of backward prophesy, that sought to colour the past in order to exonerate the present. His father had sought diligently into the past, as befitted his calling. But his mind was careful, not fantastical. He did not weave Tales.

In the house, Betwar told his children, "There have been generations of scholars in Book, whose whole lives were spent arguing to and fro about these Tales, and the only good to be said about them is, it prevented them from being equally foolish in the world.

"There are such scholars in there now," he added after a pause.

"Are scholars less wise than ignorant World-children then, who grow up without their letters?" Tared had asked him.

"Many are, and would have been wiser without their letters, indeed!"

"The Sanev can count to a thousand," put in Saska.

"Yes, you see for yourselves they are quick enough," said Betwar. "There are foolish scholars and foolish folk, and wise of both sorts as well. Our-mother Tasman told me our-fathers the Sorud quarrelled much, when they were children, whether they should go to Book or World, and once Fadar broke Fadel's arm. But they grew and lived well—they managed much World, for all the Book in them."

Of nearer history, as the Tale told it, Betwar was not so tolerant. He remembered the Semer well, the big fair freckled body with its two straw-coloured heads—mute Semer Twar whom nobody thought about, and Semer Twel who had become a gentle older brother to him and Atwar long ago, crossing the plains.

> *Only the Semer escaped the Two Floods,*
> *they made a raft of human hair,*
> *rode the flood into the east,*
> *swam inland in the water-courses.*[30]

"There was no raft! it was a hand-braided rug, and Tasman's. He came walking, with it wrapped around him. We were far from floods, and there was no water-course where we first saw him."

"He took it from the Say." For Ard, the Say had a certain fascination. The Tale said they had fed Tasman false root secretly, so that she would conceive in short-bond. And she had. The Say were jealous and did it for mischief, said the Tale.

> Look how the Say in Tasman's room
> gave her false Root; so she would conceive
> for they were not her friends,
> to make mischief in jealousy, knowing Sorud
> loved her,
> ah then they (the Sorud) would want to
> abandon her,
> for to make the short-bonded pregnant is
> forbidden.[31]

But Betwar looked at his darker daughter steadily. "You have all been taught to hate the Say, and the Linh your mothers as well. Do you not hate what you know nothing of. As for the Say, they were what they were. That story belongs to Fu-en, we never heard it, our fathers and our mother never told it against them, or thought it."

Then Betwar had walked out, because he had named the Linh, and was unready to speak of them. He stood against the bridge, his fingers scratching at its ancient brim of weathered stone. Gradually his breathing quieted. What did it help, to be so angry? that old story against the Say—who knows what had happened? And it did not correspond, that western people were more gentle than the Fu-en. It was the temper of the time that had made them invent this. Tasman's Lofot mothers had loved any bloody Tale of sexual deceit and jealousy; some she had told to him and Atwar: he had not heard worse here, not even from the Ludh.

His children, in particular his sons, loved like all children the verses about the snake, but they knew better than to sing them in his presence. There were no snakes in the eastern hills, or snake-hunters among the Fu-en people—for Fu-en, the snake was all snakes, a wise, ancient being who had lived since the time of the Outdead, simply in order to cripple Atwar.

> There the Snake found them, waiting with intelligence
> its eye opening baleful from its bed of gravel.
> It struck to fulfil the harsh, ancient promise,
> it chose Atwar, it struck terribly, it crippled him.[32]

Betwar had already told them of this encounter, if unwillingly, in short words they could not doubt. As Ask had reminded Saska, Betwar was there. In actuality the occurrence had the coarse brutality of chance and accident; no recurrence of it in his mind had ordered or explained it, for he had never sought to contain it, but fled from it always. None had comforted him, not then or later when they were reunited with their fathers and mother. For he had not been hurt, only Atwar, and it was he and Semer who had to keep Atwar alive and bring him living to the others. He had run beside the Semer through the trees, the Semer carrying Atwar tied to their back. He had lain close to Atwar when they rested, and wiped his mouth. He had not, then or later, expected comfort. Only now, with little sons the same age, did it strike him how very young he had been.

Once, in Yar, after the first scholars from Fu-en had

joined them, he had heard Sorud Twel remark to Tasman, "Little Betwar squeezes his eyes, he does not like to see the eastern garments because of their colour." And Tasman had sighed and said, "I have seen that—he remembers what happened, Semer told me there was much blood." And Betwar had been helped by their words; with such words, he could order his fear and he forgave it, and stopped shutting out the red dresses, and looked at them thereafter with healthy hate.

The Great Fire (called Atwar's Grief) was so recent it was remembered by everyone but children. Betwar could not yet bear to speak of it calmly, for the accepted interpretation was so invasive and unreasonable. The scholars insisted that, in that short time when Book was deserted because all the scholars ran to quench the fire, Moon-hidden Atwar had appeared on the screens. Blaming the Linh and pretending to blame themselves, they had created the greatest of the rituals, and the Watch with its rigid neophytes and changes.

Almost, it seemed, in order not to blame Atwar himself—for they dared not fault him for his silence; therefore, he must have shown himself. It was a sweet persuasion. That Atwar had shown himself, and grieved, because no one watched for him, and it would seem to him that all had forgotten him. The chant was mournful. In the ritual it was for two voices, yet all adult twins who wished could repeat it, and the ceremony was lengthy indeed. The people had been told that to chant it was like squeezing clear water into the mind, and then wiping the mind as if it were a bowl; in such wiped minds, the shame of Atwar's Grief was cleared away.

> *Only a small time*
> *we turned away, yes we turned from him.*

*Fire's fault it was, fire's fault
but we are not faultless watchers.*

*Atwar! running on the sward,
you looked down and spoke, and we did not
answer.
No you could not see our faces.
Only the empty places, and fire on the hill.*[33]

*Fire on the hill...Atwar's grief...*their claim had to
correspond, because no one could contradict it. Atwar
must have appeared, because for a few short hours
none were there to say he had not.

Betwar could have let himself be persuaded, almost,
for he remembered well enough his own compulsive
watching. Ah, he remembered the day he had turned
away; it had felt like a betrayal. Yet others had gladly
watched, and it would be easy now to blame them for
that one omission, when he had come to trust them.

But he remembered his fathers—Twel Sorud would
have regarded this reasoning with contempt, and Twar
Sorud would have laughed at it sadly. Betwar's shame
was private; it could only be contaminated by the
public spectacle of Atwar's Grief, the scholars' great
doings and reasons, their pretence of possessing and
make generally known what was only his to know and
understand.

It was as though they paced and prated ashore, and
he was swimming—or drowning. Ah, he was jealous of
his love; he kept it close in its simplicity. All that
weaving and show—it was empty, funny even. It was
for their own sakes; like the Doll it was dead, and all
their noise could not bring it to life, or their contrap-
tions.

In the house, Tared only had ventured to recite a bit of Book sometimes, a little provocatively, wanting a response yet not wanting to meet it head on. Once she said, "We are to tell Atwar everything about the fire. Because then he will understand, why we were not watching."

Betwar had not replied: as too often he had got up and gone out, but not this time before he heard Ask saying, "Atwar must have seen the fire."

"It was why he showed himself," Saska put in. "He ran into the sward when he saw fire on the hill."

Betwar had stood still beyond the house-cloth to hear them, and listened to his children arguing to and fro—whether Atwar at that distance could have seen the fire and known what it was, or whether in daylight he could see the city, even the Doll, or how big the Doll would have to be to be seen on the Moon, and whether he had a screen like those in Book, and if so, where it worked and where it was directed. He thought, they are still unable to picture themselves as there, yet in picturing a childish Atwar they try to do so. And like everyone else they accept that Atwar appeared in Atwar's Grief.

And if I said what I want, that we know nothing about Atwar, or where he is, or why he does not show himself—or even if he lives—if I said all this, what would it benefit them?

Betwar reentered the house, saying only, to Tared, "I will tell you about the fire, so that you know what happened." But he did not tell her then.

What the children had to learn in Book was unusually difficult, because of the way the Fu-en scholars taught—and indeed thought—in convoluted imagery. Yet against every snowy image, every confusion, they received some kind of response from their father— even if it was only a denial, or a wordless, angry look, or the evasions of his going out or his tears. They knew his posture well, the whole colour of his mind, and they accepted it as they accepted him, in spite of how little power he had, how little they could depend on him to protect them in any real thing now—just as they accepted without question that he could not or would not spare them in the end.

It was most of all the Sorud's uprightness Betwar had brought forward into their lives, which he could not have put into words, but which had been the world's mood in the time of Moonfall. Though Betwar condemned himself for having turned away from his fathers, he was clearly of their temper. He had never been seduced into the new mood. He remained on the edge of things, never denying his fathers (and never directly asked to), never committed in his heart to what he must submit to with his life.

So his children went on balancing these two worlds as well as they could, and had learned more from him, even before he began to teach them, than they learned at the last.

That morning he sat long over them and watched them into sleep. Not yet, he thought, not yet could he bear to tell them of the fire. Of how he had tried to hide the Linh and keep them back at the last. And of the Ludh—if he had patience with these women now, it was because of what they had done then. The children thought the Ludh dull, and seeming not to care, but they were like their name, dense inwardly. They were as rocks are, he thought, that seem changeless and heavy, because they do not change in human time, though they change calmly in their own.

Five

*And if he promises, "I will come in another
moment," all his promises are but cunning to
beguile you.*
*He possesses a flaming breath, by enchantment
and wizardry knotting the water and tying up
the air.*

1

Saska continued to practise in the edges of the farms,
and the asafir began to answer him. But though he
swam and pulled himself deep into the tangled marshes,
and waited patiently with the brown, warm water
covering all but his head, making no sound till they had
forgotten him, none had come within his reach. Like
World-children who love to gather curious things to
possess them, he gathered the dropped feathers of the
asafir. His eyes found them without his will, caught on
twig or moss or floating on the water. The Sanev had
given him some also, and now he had thirteen; Ask had
four, and Ard two—which she pretended were of no
interest to her but which she had not given him.

There were new songs about the asafir. One night,
one was sung completed at the Circling, and the children were taken into Book to learn it. It was strictly

according to the Ng persuasion, describing them in high-sounding words:

> *Ah they are great thoughts.*
> *From a great distance they arrive on our*
> *thresholds.*
> *The distant mountains are standing*
> *in touch of our hands.*
> *In the pleasure of blue our eyes are drowning*
> *before them.*[34]

But it said nothing about any message they might be said to bear. Only the last verse, as a conciliation perhaps to the Azur camp, referred to Atwar, and to the placing of a carcass on his dress. It played on the old meaning of blue.

> *In your sleeve, Atwar, we have hidden*
> *This blue (distant) thought for your pleasure.*
> *Distance is close by*
> *In every eye*
> *Turn to us, returning*
> *The world heals for your pleasure.*[35]

Ask, rocking homeward on the Qam shoulders in the morning, spoke across them to Saska: "Those words—*Great thoughts from a great blue*—it is like a snake-tale!" Privately, he was critical. Atwar, when he hears it, will believe the asafir are big as snakes, he thought.

He said this to Saska when they got home, leaning over to his ear as he sat bent over his feather-hoard.

"If we do not show him—" whispered Saska low.

"Ah—what if sufur will not?"

Saska fingered his feathers, laying a row from smallest to largest as children like to do, and smoothing the vanes. He kept them, as Tared had kept her pebbles, in a depression—a little "proud-pit" he and Ask had dug with earnest, infant hands when they had first lived in that house—it was low in the northern wall: it had later been stopped with a stone, but this he had now prised out for the purpose. He spoke dreamily.

"This of sufur—to invite him, as we intend—what if we found sufficient feathers, and I made a sufur-doll to carry in my head-sleeve, as the Doll of Atwar did? What if curious sufur saw—?"

"It would not be a doll, however many feathers you bound together."

"But a sufur-doll, that would be possible—"

They had been whispering, but Tared caught the last of Saska's words.

"Our-father has never been to the Doll-makers," she said firmly from her mat across the room. There had never been dolls in their house; they had never held small Atwars at the ceremonies as adults do, and let their children do so carefully as children do. The great Doll was theirs; indeed the Azur had once told them, with twinkling eyes, that they were the four little dolls of Atwar. Tared was preparing to sleep, smoothing out the cloths as was her habit; Ard slept already beside her on crumpled cloths and had not bothered to cover herself, or her eyes against the light.

"The asafir are however new, so it would not be an Atwar-doll. And I already have feathers," answered Saska. He whispered to Ask, "Perhaps we could make him ourselves."

Ask saw it would be useful, if Saska were to carry such a doll, if their scheme to catch living sufereen ever succeeded—the scholars would be then well used to the doll, and not look more closely—ah, but it seemed they would not succeed, with the asafir so wary!

That night Saska spoke to the Qam at the Circling, and they spoke to the Ng who agreed. But there were to be four dolls, and Doll-makers would make them.

<h2 style="text-align:center">2</h2>

It was the Sanev who found the colour. They came running into Betwar's house one morning, Nevar saying triumphantly, "See this stone!" and Nevi explaining, "If we scrape it with our-fathers' knife, it will make the colour of the asafir—look."

They all crept close and watched as the Sons of Nev scraped blue dust into Ard's bald hand (for she had quickly thrust it forward). Nevi licked their twelfinger, and stirred the dust in her palm. When he glanced up she caught his look, as he pressed the finger down against her palm, but the others were looking at the colour, which was as richly blue as sky in the bright morning over trees, or the sea running on a sunny day.

"The little birds are blue, are blue," recited Saska, reaching his finger into Ard's palm also, then suddenly holding it up, and wiping it down the throat of his white shirt. They stared. The colour was very rich and clear; even more brilliant than the asafir it stroked their eyes, as distance strokes the eyes of weavers looking up from their looms, delighting and comforting them.

They called the colour not blue, which means distance, but used the western word *safir* after the stone, because of the pleasant sound of it, and because they had found it, in order to name it before the Namers.

The Sanev brought people to the place, which was an outcropping some distance west of the city, off the road called Semer's Way, and more was found. The partly completed dolls were coloured with it, and stitched finished and shown to the children at the Circling under Atwar. But Saska, when one was held before him, seized it and plunged it down into his sleeve, next to his heart. The scholars made to prevent him, but the Ng jerked their heads at them to move back. So he was let to keep it, his dark hand pressing the round little shape against his breast.

The others were not given their dolls then; these were to be stitched into the new clothes that were presently weaving. But Ask smiled over at his brother—now, he thought, Saska would be less anxious and afraid.

The sufur-doll was as little like the asafir as the Doll of Atwar was like Atwar, thought Betwar, when Saska proudly showed him it in the house. It was a soft, stuffed pocket, coloured blue, with two stitched blue flaps that hung down, and two clay eyes, and no nose or hands. Saska sat with it in his lap, and he and Ask worked hard at sticking Saska's collection of feathers into it—which did not improve it much, for they protruded at all angles. They pricked at Saska sharply, too, when he put the doll back into his sleeve. So he pulled them all out again, which ruffled them, and left little holes in the doll.

But often now he would sit with the doll, when he was at home, putting the feathers in and taking them out. It began to have a bedraggled look. He even swam with it, and it lay in the little dent of his breast at Book, soaked like a drinking-cloth: if it was wet from the marshes, he sucked at it covertly, but sea-water was not good. The doll still kept its brave blue colour; otherwise it was becoming unrecognizable.

Safir became the joy of the streets, when the people saw it. The bright mark on Saska's dress neither washed out nor bleached away, and the Sanev began to call him, half-teasingly, Saska-Sufur.

Far beyond the Sheath
ah beautiful people, beautiful twins awaiting
we have seen your thoughts, between our hands
they speak of distance
Our pleasure is in distance, our pleasure is in
sapphire
come towards us living, come towards us
walking,
come towards us in distance, come towards us in
sapphire,
white of skin and red of hair
blue in your garment, distance in your garment,
sapphire in your garment.[36]

3

The Sanev came often again to the house, and wanted Saska to teach them to whistle to the asafir, but their noises would have scared anything off. "You had better teach Ard and Tared," Nevi said to him, finally, "because we are hopeless—and as soon as your voice darkens you will be hopeless, too."

They all went into the marshes and Tared set herself to learn, because Nevi was right—it was possible that her brothers' voices would darken before they stood *before Atwar's face*—and who would then recall for him the sufur's song?

But the sufur fled back through the marshes behind them when Tared squeaked, and they hid among the trees. Ask laughed and went on laughing, and Tared stubbornly went on trying, but with no more success, though Saska put his fingers against her mouth and throat patiently, and made her touch his throat, to teach her the way.

Ard held tight to the Sanev and let them carry her farther, deeper in beyond the farms.

"Tared will strive to squeak, whether her mouth can or no. She is determined to serve Atwar well," said Nevar cheerfully, his dark adult voice trembling in his throat where Ard's cheek pressed. She turned her mouth into the hollow join of their shoulder. Shadow and brightness swam across them. It was the night before Whitenight, the whitest night, the turning of the year, poised on the brim of Darkening at the longest day. Their feet splashed in and out of brown water, sunk into moss and mud, balanced along natural rafts of fallen stems. She clung to them as they released one arm to hold aside twisted branches or duck under them.

"Go farther," she said when they had entered their playing place, with its mess of half-ordered channels and platforms. They had paused at a sward.

"Where no one can find-us." Her sister's mind, if not her body, might still reject a song lesson in favour of following them.

They went on, at last out of reach of the other voices, where only the little asafir spoke, less and less frequently as the bright night advanced. The Sanev put her down on moist grass, and sat beside her.

"Can we look at you?" asked Nevar shyly, "and show-us to you, how we have changed?" Ard nodded and pulled up her green-stained dress, and they looked at her body and touched her little breasts and nipples with their fingers awkwardly.

"Loose me," she whispered, and sat up to help them. Misunderstanding her, they undid her hair, so it sprang out in wild western fashion. They had often teased her and Tared about their rippled hair and it had made Tared angry, for hers was worst: they had called her a dried sunflower. But there were Ludh tales in which the new-bonded loosed each others' hair, before any other play; and the feel of their fingers now shaking it free was strange and pleasant.

"I mean, my bands," she said at last, and when the strips of cloth were all unwound, they pulled her bunched dress over her head, then they waved it free as weavers wave cloths in the hanging, and spread it out to hide her naked knees.

Nevar wanted most to show her how they had been cut. Ard had seen men: it was nothing special—she looked because they asked.

Their penis was thick now, not small and thin and bald like her brothers', or as it had been when she and Tared last played with them. She reached out and touched it in its tangle of wiry hair, and it sprang against her wrist like a branch that had been bent back. It was naked still, purplish and whitely scarred.

She let go, and lay back down. She had only been a little curious. From somewhere a stubborn anger entered her mind, and involuntarily she turned her head away, her body also, the rough ground digging into her side.—Why show me this object? You will be short-bonded, and those-women will teach you, and show you how to stick it inside them, day after day. And tell you how beautiful it is (Tared had heard that women said this) and you will believe them. Ugly little snake!

She sniffed, but carefully their hands turned her, and she saw Nevi's squinting smile. They began to touch her intimately.

4

"My brother, will they find you? I have told them most of what to tell you, and if I could make them into empty vessels I would fill them as the cloth fills with clear water—because I want you to know all of it. How I live, apart from you, how I lived when the Linh came, and what happened to them, not as the scholars say it, or the Song."

Betwar was on the shore, walking northward away from the city. The beach was narrow here and mostly clay and roots, in some shadow with the protracted day; beyond the old pollard and the marsh-edges the peninsula extended in a white sweep to the northeast.

He squinted far off across the split, caked reaches: here began the saltings, but the people had harvested much salt already and they were seldom worked, except by old men for whom hoarding still tasted of wisdom, who remembered the first years of their appearing as the sea receded, and did not forget disaster. Two pair were in sight, tiny, bending over their rafts.

He sat down, then lay back among the roots and rolled over, his face rasping against smooth weathered wood where a treeroot, gray and rounded as the heel of a hand, emerged from the ground and dipped in again. "It will be soon now," he thought. "The children will be delivered from me, surely forever. From me, towards me—because to go to him is to go into my heart."

He stroked the root, moved his cheek against its coolness. Making love to the Linh had never been, finally, anything but the thought of his brother—for Atwar and himself, being separated in body had never harmed them while they grew—and certainly they had pretended to be twinned like other children, drawing sometimes almost as close as brothers who shared the same body would be. This making love to women could not be more complete. There is progression in that woman-bonding, and a climax; the Linh body was a new bowl, and a many-folded cloth, but ever in the yielding he would forget them, the unclear abiding image of his twin suddenly cleared—and he would be again joined, merged in that former symmetry as he slid into sleep. Ur, Or, primordial—real twins were granted this always, and his sons knew it also, he supposed. But they would never be taken one from the other.

"I am going to you, Atwar, if you will not return to me, in the only way I can." His semen had already made that journey, in becoming the children who would go.

Near here, in the old pollard field full of saplings where the trees were less grown, the Linh had given birth in pit-pool to his children. Ard and Tared had spoken their first words in the house that had stood among green stems, and the Ur had cried out—their mothers had seen them also, heard two voices and laughed and surely loved them. Ah—they had not laughed. Even then, already, the place was filled up with the sick Wan, the Azur, the narrow-headed youthful watching twins (who were the Wan's children Feng and called Ng even then)—and the Sorud were no longer there to temper the others, or the voice of their awful purpose.

The Linh sitting against the greenwhite wall-cloth, their hands braided together, watching—"Nothing is left of that house now, that stood against the brush in its messy yard of clay and half-burnt wood. Or of their voices and strange speech, or their ways. If there is a Tale, unless I tell it, it will not be heard in this generation.

"But, Atwar, I want you to know what they did, and what happened to them."

5

It was high time to go to the Ng, he could postpone it no longer. He stood up and began to walk back along the shore, in the traces the little waves had made as they receded: his eyes tasted how each had left the slate-dust in delicate lines, with a clear edge and shading back, as the wave withdrew, hill over hill half-hiding the ones behind them—how here a larger wave had written a big, pushing mountain over them like Nador's peak—remorselessly obliterating whole intricate mountain-scapes, range upon range, in one sweeping curve, that was even more beautiful than what it had erased forever.

The sunlight made long ruddy fingers through the trees, and out over the water. It was between tides and quiet. Betwar looked outward and saw the Oldwo standing in the sea; it seemed as if it were burning out there without flames. The calm white surface of the water was greening in patches beyond the city. People made small by distance walked out four by four, the forward twins dragging the corners of the great nets that the leaf-harvest would cling to, the others lifting the shoreward corners and walking slowly after. The nets bellied; their white reflections touched them, shaken by ripples. He bent his head and walked faster.

The Ng had sent word through the children—it was Tared who had told him—that he would do well to meet them and see what was being raised at the edge of the Square, behind the Doll—the room for the Ard, and the many rooms. She had not said invited; it was not a formal summons. He had done nothing about it.

Daily he had heard his children discuss what they had seen at each Circling—the new pattern of temporary house-stems and the dye-vats, the new looms and presses working. He had been aware of his son's increasing excitement, his daughters' jittery silences. Tared would glance toward him, but she did not repeat the message. And he had not gone.

Two nights ago had been Whitenight, the festival of the longest day. He had not gone, though the noise from the Square was loud and almost seductive—in the voices rising and falling in strength, and calling out and chanting in unison he remembered the windstorms of his childhood—it had followed him in his ears far up the shore. But that morning, to his surprise, the Ng had returned with the exhausted children to the house, themselves carrying Ask on their arm. It was the first time they had ever visited him; he understood well that their policy had ever been not to provoke or try him, to let him avoid them and range on the short rope and rule in his own house as he would.

Under his roof they would not sit properly down though they were gaunt and sweating from the long celebration, and must have hungered. They hastily took the water he offered, squatting.

But they looked at him close, and said (he was not even sure which had spoken): "We invite you to visit-us among the new houses tonight, brother of Atwar, and sit down with-us on the Hill. It is time to speak together wisely, and heal those hurts which have come between our minds and your mind." Then they had gone out. He had felt Tared's eyes. This child will be satisfied by my obedience, he had thought bitterly.

Now as he paced they were waiting for him in those new rooms on the high city, it was the time they had appointed, the first evening of the sun's withdrawal, the beginning of Darkening.

Six

*You have seized me by the ear—whither are you
drawing me? Declare what it is in your heart,
and what your purpose is.
Since the ears of heaven and earth and the stars
are all in your hand, whither are they going?
Even to that place whither you said, "Come!"*

1

"Tared!"

She wakened as if falling—as if she had been trying
to stand alone, and had collapsed suddenly within the
thick of her dreaming, into the bruised eye and the clear
eye—she fell forward into them as they were widening
terribly—then erasing themselves in daylight. Ard was
pulling at her arm and whispering.

"Tared, we-are become adult."

"Ah—ah, they said it would be." Tared felt a burst
of anger. Why was she not first, if they did not begin to
bleed the same day?—she felt quickly, and there was
nothing. Ard saying we-are! when it was Ard only.
Tared did not want to look at the finger her sister held
up with its telling stain.

"Are you not?" Ard pouted, then looked scared,
understanding suddenly. Tared flung away from her.

But Ard rolled closer, whispering into her hair. Her teeth were actually chattering, Tared could hear them, and she was gulping between words.

"Are you not? Look and see, for you must be as well! Everything they said—why is it, if it is not for us both? that new room they are making, why is it not in this house, why will not our-father build it? Tared, where is our-dress? Tared, what women are they, who will attend-us?"

Tared spoke finally, if just to stop her, still angry. "I have kept the dresses, they are here under the mat, I have them. All these things you know, they have told us often enough. We are to be black-teethed, this is what they have waited for—the Ur will have to go white-teethed, it is to be at perigee." She added somewhat cruelly, "As for who will tend-us, it seems it will be the Ng."

Tared spoke steadily, yet she as well as Ard was overwhelmed by all the Ng had been recently teaching them, though not by any exact words. Perhaps because the words were never exact, but swam in and out in images, as if they were pulled about by dream-tides, half-drownings. She was soaked in the images, it was like her dreams, they dragged at her waking life, blurry pictures of the long stages of a darker and darker ceremony.

It was not always possible to look into the mole when they spoke; often she had grown tired and careless, and she knew Ard was far less careful than she. And the simpler directions that all twins received—about the black-teething and fasting, the rote learning, how female twins ate root (though it seemed the Ard would not) and male twins were cut—these were confused now with what was preparing for them only, rituals more secret and more necessary. And the pictures in her mind were stained over with real ones, what they had already seen—the new activities on the edge of the Square—the steaming bolts of cloth pounded in the redding-vats, and then lifted out on straining reeds, and the gush of their dripping, and how they hung to half-dry on new stems that strained with their weight, with the ground under them all lined and criss-crossed in tiny trenches of dark red. And the damp cloths carried over to be fastened into the stems of a strange, new little city on the hilltop, and tightening as they dried—mazes of roofless rooms and narrow, cov-ered halls, and the dyers walking here and there to slap the sheets so they twanged. New walls, new openings and closings of door-curtains one beyond the other, as if they were mouths saying unrecognized and fearful words. And each one deeper in dye, more roseate—it seemed to her the ones at the centre must be the darkest of all.

Ard broke in, almost whining—"The Ng! how will it be the Ng when it has to be women?"

"How can I tell? If they are women after all."

Ard shuddered. "We have to speak to our-father. He was with them, they will have told him."

"Whether they are women? Ask the Sanev—they said they know the Ng are men—ask them if they saw that penis, when next you are with them!"

Her voice was spiteful and Ard was silenced. Fi-nally she replied dully, "The Ng will choose for-us. They choose everything."

"Then it will be the Ng, who choose themselves. We know no women."

"Not the Ludh?" When she heard that, Tared rolled over and looked straight at Ard and they giggled. To be with the Ludh all those days, to be fussed over and taught by them, would be ridiculous. She relented, seeing Ard's grin stuck oddly across her fear as the laughter passed, as if it had forgotten to erase itself. A thought came to her like a picture, of being lifted into a white lap, gently. She wondered at its rightness, and her own ingenuity. Here would be a good choice, if it could be managed. She said to Ard, "What do you think about the Siri?"

The Siri, seen now only at the Circling. If the Qam carried one of them the Siri would always approach and greet them. Once Tared had recognized them across at the vats, bringing bolts to the dyers, almost staggering. Close up, their white dress was stretched, and spotted with madder like a field.

Betwar would speak for them. It would be a comfortable choice.

Indeed Ard snatched at it. "Ah—I would like to have the Siri with-us!" she said, in a burst of breath. Their brothers stirred, and Tared put her hand across her sister's mouth.

"We must make our-fathers agree to it, and interest first the Qam—they are kind. The Siri were always good to-us when we were small. Our-father said once that their faces are like our-mothers, and that is why we loved to play with them. But I do not remember our-mothers, or any thing from that time."

"I remember something," said Ard doubtfully. "I remember the fire."

Tared puffed out her mouth in disdain. "Ask says he does too, and what can he remember of that? Only, that you say it." But she was angry again, that Ard might have kept a memory of that disaster, when she herself had forgotten it. She did not know that the image she remembered was farther back and more constant, and not changed by words.

Ard had moved to look at the sheet under her. "But Tared, what if the Siri refuse, what if they have forgotten-us, what if it is the Ng after all!" She burst into tears, and lay down again and cried into Tared's hair. Tared knew her sister's mind had opened and swallowed it now—the fact that, for all their talk and plans, she must go alone, and be shut up alone, perhaps with the Ng— to listen alone to what they seemed to begin to be saying. Now she was whispering sharply, frantic: "I will lend you my blood, so you can come with me."

"How can you do that?" Tared asked, scornful. But she stroked Ard's shoulder.

Ard propped herself up on one arm. She was staring. Her hair had come partly loose and fell across her dirty, teary face.

"You, make it happen, then! Open yourself with an arrow of our-mothers—it does not hurt so much. We have to be together, Tared, you must accompany-us." Ard wept and gulped again, saying, "I do not want to listen to what they said."

The Siri attended Ard in those days, however, because Betwar went quickly to them to ask them, and they agreed.

2

Hurrying along the streets with the Siri, in search of the Ng, Betwar was much comforted. He had found the young women sitting alone in their house on the south hill, with their looms behind them silent, and they had looked up at him gladly from some small-mending, the sheets spread all across their lap and around them so they seemed to emerge whitely from whiteness in their simple dress. They had stood up immediately, and deftly folded the cloth together, and gone with him. He saw, glancing across them as they walked, that they were pregnant.

On the way, they asked after all his children, and he told them a little, lightly, about Tared's disappointment and impatience. They reassured him courteously: "Her body will surely relent," and "She will surely join her sister."

He told them also of Saska's preoccupation with the asafir and Ask's with knots and threads. Then, before he could control it, his voice broke. "Yet they do think of what is coming, and they are not fearless—"

The Siri's slender twelhand took hold of his arm impetuously. "Betwar, do not fear for them! It must be well."

"Are you not afraid?" he asked. "No—you are not, you and the others—it is as though the people of the city are asleep. The Fu-en are without fear," he said bitterly "—they make even their fear all backwards in circlings and ceremonies. And if anyone questions it, it is called heresy, and it happens some people are not seen among us any more."

The Siri stopped in the street, and their Twel smiled at him gently. "Betwar, this does not correspond. We have all been afraid, more or less. And being afraid makes the scholars more stiff in their necks as well as in their face-boards! Perhaps those who argue most passionately, and who judge the Outdead as perfect against any argument, are most afraid in their heart. But Qam our house-bonded have been deep into Book, far in near the cars, and there is a small, steadfast light. Think of it, they told us, and now we tell you to think of it: it shone through the waters from ancient days, and it shines now, and tells us the ascent of the Children of Atwar will be as his ascending—the cars will prove themselves and all will be as it was prepared."

"We will give them the gift of our trust," added her sister, when she had ceased speaking, "even though we are afraid, because afraid or not it will make no difference, and it is easier so."

Their hand still on his arm, they closed their mouths smiling, and laid their narrow heads close together in the graceful eastern gesture of agreement, cheek against cheek and temple against temple, almost complacent and almost beautiful. He saw how the lids of their inward eyes, turning back along their flattened heads, merged to one line, and how the inner corners of their mouths, stretched in smiles, met in one extended smile. And found them almost beautiful—for he had grown used to them—as they were used to him, he supposed.

3

Tared remained in the house, impatient and angry. Betwar came and went, also silent, and sometimes sat across the room from her, because she would not at first let him touch her or comfort her.

"Tared, I also became an adult without my twin," he said carefully more than once. But she would not answer.

Later, he spoke again, with effort, "Tared—can I tell you anything else, not for Atwar's sake only, but so that you know for yourself, what it was like then in the world?"

She raised her eyes, and looked across at him. Only the moon's light, aslant on the roof, lit the room in the short night, but it was bright enough to see his broad, tender face, the sadness so perfected it was beautiful.

She spoke, also with difficulty. "Ard says, she can remember the fire. Ask says it, too."

"Not Ask. But perhaps Ard can. Yet I think it was only the small, ordinary fires that your-mothers tended, when you played beside them in the yard, and nothing more. Because Ard scorched her hands more than once—she loved fire, and always pulled herself towards it. The Great Fire we kept you from, the city burning—as for the house....

"When this happened—Tared, perhaps it is not the great events, or what seem now great to us, that are most important and most clearly retained, but something we were too young to understand, and that yet appeared to us in our ignorance to be—significant— whether it was not, or was—"

Tared shivered, not yet understanding. She felt as though her head would burst with what she could not speak of, that dream-part of her life which had no words—too primitive, too unfinished, and farther back than any speech that could have explained it. Not her father, but Atwar would resolve this; he would find in her some way. She would again bring it with her before the Doll, and this time she must find the words. Perhaps Atwar required words—But she was eased by what Betwar had said about her sister, and laughed a little. "Ard looked at fire enough then, in the yard—that is what she remembers, and does not know what she remembers."

"It remembers her, perhaps." He paused. "I would tell this to you of your-mothers. No one knows, and I do not know either, how they died. I believe they chose death, for they could have hid; none died other than they. They were found afterwards, at the ashes of that Doll. I am sure the Fu-en people did not kill them, although they were very angry."

"Our-mothers were crazed."

"You have been told this, and all the people knew of what happened to Tasman. Yet for them—Tared, it was that they could not bear to stay in the world and witness your—grooming. For our-mother Tasman, the grief of loss was very sudden—it could be perhaps likened to the snapping of a leg bone; but for the Linh it was like a long sickness, their body had become gradually more and more angered and they knew how it must end."

The Linh had fired the house, and the first Doll, all this was called Atwar's Grief, the high city had burned, all the houses on it. They had died, perhaps at their own hands. If Tared had a question it was to do with their reasons, which no one had explained. Ask demanded reasons of the scholars, but their only answer was no answer, only the song repeated. She thought her father knew. He spoke of the Linh very seldom, but then evenly and without rancour.

"The Ludh were with them at first, in our house, and kept them from their choice, and helped me to hide them, also after they had fired it. We took you little-ones into the marshes. You children, and the Sanev, do not hold the Ludh for any worth. But they are good women." Tared looked doubtful. "No, Tared, there are good people whose heads are quiet, they tend the small outward pieces of the world, the small minutes as they pass; this is also good, not to have heads full of pictures and imaginings."

Tared broke into his thoughts, speaking slowly: "Did our-mothers wish to choose death for us also, since we could not choose?"

"Ah—nor did they get the chance—" Betwar looked away. "They were very angry. Yet, to have so much anger—there is fire under that vat, and if it boils—it must have been, it was, much love!"

More than my own, he thought suddenly and with shame.

"Then, they did love us—but they were angry with Atwar, what he demanded." Betwar heard her voice lighter than usual, less strident—it seemed as if she were tracing these new thoughts softly across a white cloth with her finger, and looking at them.

"Ah, not with Atwar. Atwar himself made no demands. He was little, as little as your brothers. What did he know of them, or of you all unthought of, unborn? Tared, Tared, this is the wrong colour, Atwar is not as he is in the scholar-imaginings, nor is the world. Nothing, of this colour you have learned, corresponds; nothing is right!"

"This is as Saska said—" Tared hesitated, then began again. "This is as Saska said. You speak as he spoke. Once, he was talking strangely—he told us he had in his head a picture of a new city that would come down and fit over our city so neatly that no one would notice it, except there would be no Doll—and no Tale—and he heard a voice say loudly, *It is all wiped out!* He was dreaming, his eyes were open and still turned inward into his dream."

"He never told me this."

"Or the scholars, or any people but us. Ard and Ask cried, but I struck him, and he came outside into his face, and looked at us. I made him say *Atwar walks*, Ard and Ask also, and then everything corresponded again— as it was taught to us—as the world."

Betwar gazed sorrowing at his daughter, who lay with her eyes fixed on the roof-cloth overhead and her mouth tightly closed on the trembling in her words. Her hand lifted in the familiar gesture and pressed back her hair. As she had finished speaking, her voice had stammered and then become again the voice he recognized.

He knew a sweetness in these times and in speaking with her, even so, and he knew he had eased her jealousy, as though he had become her attendant in some parallel ceremony—this secret talk between them stroked her pride and quieted her restlessness.

Tared for her part thought to and fro about Betwar's words, wanting to trust him and take comfort, to forgive her mothers—Atwar—could it be, that Atwar was heedless of what they had done, did not know of it and would not care if he did? Yet he awaited his Children!

Across her mind walked the Tale of her mothers, heard in the dark woman-voices of the Ng:

> *"The Linh were chosen of all the people*
> *And forfeited their joy.*
> *Born of the fire*
> *They refused to relinquish the fire*
> *And left the vivid air scorched with their infamy.*
>
> *"Death ran before their hands*
> *like grass, like trees in wind*
> *they flashed their blades.*
> *At the house of the Children of Atwar*
> *the cloth ran in ribbons, the ribbons ran in fire.*
>
> *"They rose in day, their arrows flashed,*
> *they opened the liver of Atwar*
> *secretly in the City, his red spilled,*
> *they fired him in blood.*
> *Over the City his face burst, his limbs melted.*
>
> *We could not come near him,*
> *We could not extinguish him.*
> *This was the Linh, remember them.*
> *Ash, ash, ash, ash, ash."*[37]

"Fadar, if he did not ask it of us himself, yet we are commanded by our lives, to go to him."

"Yet not by Atwar. He made no demands," Betwar repeated. "Remember this, whatever they have told you. The demands came later and not from him."

"But you, our-father, you would go to him!" Tared, lying closer to him, had pushed herself upright, and now touched his arm. Her eyes were fixed on him, squinting with pride.

"Indeed I would go to him—all of us would have, then! do you remember the tale, the Semer offering? *But it is not given, to give your life for another.*" Betwar recited the lines:

> (He) desired mute Twar be severed from their
> body...
> but he was unable:...it is never, it is never
> you can give your life for your friend.[38]

"Ah—my mother, my fathers, any of us would have gone. And I would now."

"And we would go also," Tared said fervently. "We have chosen it—"

The thought of choice startled her, reminded her of Saska's dream-city, with all the heavy urgency wiped away. She leaned her head against her father's arm. After a time she said gently: "Would you have that I tell these softer things about our-mothers to Atwar?"

It was a gift, for Betwar knew this child was farthest from his influence—she, among them, was the one who had needed most desperately to defend the scholars' words.

"Tell him whatever corresponds. They loved you, they were your-mothers. But they could not keep you from your purpose."

He mused. "Tell him also of Tasman, what I have told you—it was the same thread."

"Yet, your-mother Tasman did not range in the city when Atwar went, to fire it and destroy."

"No, that was not her way; she was quiet, and became more quiet, to an unacceptable degree—tell

Atwar I will find her," he added, suddenly and harshly, as if he needed to have it said aloud before he repented it.

"She is dead, surely. You have taught us, after your fathers, *do not prophesy*."

"So, do you not prophesy death. She is in Lofot now and not old."

Tared stared. "Had you word of this?"

"No." He smiled. "I am just placing a stem across the stem of your prophecy. Ah—this place overcame me, and all these immediate angers. The world believes I finished with her, but there are, it seems, many pains that cannot have a finishing."

He remembered the Fiada song Tasman had sung to them in Pechor, and with this memory came the taste of her milky breasts. Ah Tasman! After the babies Liv died in Dearth he Betwar, though he was long weaned, had persuaded her to let him suck that milk of pain—

Perhaps this is why I must ever choose life, he thought, surprised. He drew Tared closer and stroked her arm. Yet he found himself trembling. Was it so, that he was not finished after all with Tasman? His mother was gone from him years ago—*let her remain as she was*. The sun travelled, and if its light fell on her in this world, that was her concern and not his. Nor Atwar's either—yet what sort of finishing had Atwar achieved, who had gone away careless and laughing in the sudden gift of a new adventure? Suddenly Betwar sensed his brother's nearness, as though Atwar breathed on his cheek. "This is my daughter, see her—" he almost said aloud. All these threads and unfinishments—they followed and pulled, and would not be unknotted. His mother, his brother—soon his children as well. Atwar, is it so with you as with me, nothing finished, not finished but asleep?

It was good to be silent. Tared's somewhat bony arms were crossed on her chest and he held them loosely, gazing past her at the westfacing wall. The high pocket in the northwest corner—it held the Linh arrows, prised out of their burnt, dead hands. It would be good, if Tared could tell Atwar of the Linh in gentleness.

Quiet now, reticent with each other, they remained in that consanguine courtesy that accepts what can be said and not said. It was the last time they were to be together in innocence.

4

"Will you take-us now to see the cars?" said Ask, when the boys were returned that morning. Because, now that Ard was adult, the time was surely short.

It was the third day of Ard's absence, and he and Saska had been with the Sanev in the marshes, but that night had been fetched into the Great Book. On their way, circling the Doll, they had seen the tired dyers at the vats, their fires slowed, their arms deep among the last bolts that were drawing into their weave the handwarm dye. Others hurried, pressed turfs under the vats till the dye jumped. Steam poured straight upward into the half-dark. The dyers were all stained and dripping red. Old bags of madder lay underfoot in the puddles. People worked, watched, came up to the children; many ran forward to touch their feet. Opposite the Doll, as the bearers paused for the words of the Turn, they had to linger in the stink of piss; here were the urine-tubs, the newly-dyed cloth being sloshed about by the young scholars—part of their learning. Twins came up, all reddled and shamefaced and proud, and the boys felt their wet touch though they tried to draw back. "*Atwar walks.*"

In the Great Book they had been shown the last directions, on cloth, so that they had seen as well as heard, and after that, reverently, some of the True-Book that the directions were drawn from, with its ancient and—for them—unreadable script. But they had not been taken further than the Lake.

Ask had spoken then of going to the cars, and the Qam had not actually forbidden it, only said, "Speak with Betwar, and we will speak with the Ng."

But now Betwar's answer was, "I do not like to go from Tared. And it is a long way."

"Fadar," argued Ask, "People are coming and going—we saw them, there is such activity in the city now, and at Book—if you would decide to take-us, there are many who would accompany-us."

"Then I think they will come and take you, if they intend it. It will be their decision." Betwar turned his face away from the importunate, pleading boy. He saw that Saska, busy with his bird-doll in the corner, was deliberately not listening: this son would not press him. "Sleep now, before the heat."

But he considered, and was unable to sleep, and got up and went out secretly as they slept, hurrying to see for himself.

The cars stood out under water, under the Sheath that was here cool and broken and still over-run by the sea. He had walked quickly, with averted eyes, past the screens where the sleepless scholars of the Watch as ever crouched, and along the near side of the Lake of the Moon, glancing down without stopping to see where new cloths had been spread and marked that night by the careful scholars, searching for more than vegetable changes. From the Great Book, the walled bay extended to the east and downhill, at first lit patchily by rents in the roof, where the blinding sunlight of high morning struck down to make even denser the intervals of darkness. There was dust here, but it was damp and clung to his lungs; he remembered that particular earthy taste on his breath from years back. But the bay itself seemed lower, and narrower, than it had seemed when he was small and had hung about half unwilling near his fathers. Farther in, deeper, were recesses and enlarged rooms. The sound of his footsteps, even of his breathing, began to echo differently; now he was under water.

The broken ceiling of the Sheath had been primitively patched and sealed with stones and the dull fill of fired earth. It looked roughly and hastily done. In places he could see how the damp had entered, and seeped down the makeshift walls. And he felt a sudden shame—he remembered the Sorud's frustration, how they had argued against haste, and said "This will not last, this will not keep!"

The scholars' answer had always been, "Long enough for their purposes." Not even saying, "our purposes." Believing it was all the Outdead plan, not the Sorud's and their own. He felt shame for the ignorance and impracticality of the scholars of Fu-en. They were content in it; as if stupidity was a matter of pride, a display of faith. Healers they were, he had to acknowledge; they could heal the body and it was by their own art. But this of the Outdead—no, they had clung to ignorance despite the Sorud, and had defeated the Sorud, and now they imagined they were somehow justified by their blind reverence of Atwar and of the Outdead. The Outdead, who could not fail in any endeavour and whose works, and even whose supposed benevolence and redemptive plans, were not to be questioned.

Here in the patchy darkness and bad air this was brought back to him most powerfully—and with it his sense of his fathers' steady righteousness—the old world that had not forgotten the Outdead and did not trust them. He was alone in remembering his good fathers. What shame it was and folly, this embroidering and interpreting of the long-gone thoughts and hopes of a vanished race—this glad trust in their making! Nothing was right.

5

The main bay was darker now, and he had to stoop somewhat as he walked. In places, water lay in shallow pools on the floor. His ungloved feet grasped at the somewhat slippery path of black, ancient tile—it was trodden clean though the sides of the floor were filthy with mud and debris. Belated twins coming from farther in passed him—they walked wearily, and were speaking hurriedly together, and glancing behind them. He heard one say to the other, "They are harmless,"—then they saw him and passed him, murmuring "*Atwar walks.*"

Recovered instruments stood in some of the alcoves—they were different from the ones higher up, with a less compacted design—not all sleek and enclosed but complex, and fragile—their surfaces were in places flaky and reddish. Yet some were lit.

Other twins came towards him, and he heard other voices, including farther-off but surely in themselves louder, high-pitched ones. The scholars noticed him with surprise. Then their faces reverted to what he was used—their look marred by the discrepancy between their parted mouths that spoke to him calmly and the narrowed corners of their eyes. Yet they greeted him and did not prevent him.

The passage dipped sharply and opened suddenly,

outward and upward into a high, bluish room, swim-
mingly lit from beyond, and noisy with talk and echoes
though there were few people. Bits of loose tile cracked
off the walls lay about—he realized, he would have
expected this last bay to be more finished, more cared
for. Directly in front of him, past a complex of low,
corroded instruments and panels, it was severed by the
last barrier—a somewhat more finished looking fired-
earth wall buttressed by rocks and stems, with an
gridded inset of glass. The high-pitched shouting, which
was indeed very loud, was coming from the instantly
recognizable Azur, who stood facing the barrier, their
white-bearded arms spread across the glass and their
bald heads flung vehemently back. Their face-board
was askew and their dress was torn almost to ribbons,
and hung down tattered and gray to their feet. Their
gnarled toes, along with unshaven wisps of foothair,
stuck comically from the holes in their outworn
footgloves. A few tired scholars stood about, and seemed
to be remonstrating with them. He hurried across.

Ah, their voices were piercing. "Into the south! Into
the south! They will be thrown into the south!" the Azur
were shouting, almost wailing, over and over.

He slid under their twelarm and put himself directly in front of them to make them see him. The smell
of their bodies was rank and sweet, and their breath
stank like bad fruit.

"My father-friends!"

Gradually they calmed, squinting at him out of their
tiny eyes. Up close, their shaped faces swam together,
deeply scored by wrinkles and blue-black, bathed in
the watery light. The once pristine edge of their face-
board was bent and ragged; their long white hair grew
over it and straggled between their faces, and lay damp
in their throat-join, which was as dark and sinewy as
old roots.

The Twel Azur's face was still blurry and amazed, but Betwar saw that the Twar had recognized him, with a fumbling, searching look that—held—hardened into obstinacy. His mouth chewed a little; then he said in a quite ordinary voice, "Into the dye-cauldron, and boiled clean, all of them."

He gestured past Betwar's head and Betwar turned to see through the glass, climbing up the light-shuddering water, the cars as he had remembered them, and not like Atwar's. Ah, they were most strange—reaching upward through the shimmering water—net upon net of thickening filaments and stems—like, if this could be imagined, the dolls of trees.

A hand plucked at his arm; it was twin scholars, looking at him helplessly. So he turned back, and lifted his arms to half-embrace the chattering Azur and take them from the barrier. Slowly, with many a pause, he pushed and supported them back between the people and machines. "Let us sit down and speak together," he urged, guiding them back towards the bay. "Do you remember when we first met, when you spoke with my Fadar at the Disk, and I interpreted for him, and what you said?"

"Blind he was then, and blind you are now," answered the Azur Twel hoarsely, accompanying his words with a faltering forward movement of his hand, as if he were either blind himself or making fun of the condition—then the gesture changed, as if to avert: he seemed to be fending off a blow, the uncut handhair swinging limply across the rags of their dress. But they climbed with Betwar, he half-carrying them, slowly up the bay. He kept stepping on their foothair and the rags of their gloves. They muttered, angrily and fearfully; he could not make out their words.

Finally they were outside the great Book, and they shook him off, and turned towards the sea. He followed them out onto the dark sand, that lay in shade, tide-wet and cool under the flank of the Sheath. It was here they ranged—they had piled sea-worn stems against the Sheath and covered them with an old house-cloth: whenever the shallow tide disarranged their shelter, or crept in over their toes, they shouted at it, and ran about to rescue and rebuild their hovel before it floated away—and the more daring World-children were sometimes as harassing as the tide.

Now, they squatted outside the tumble of sticks and rags, and Betwar squatted with them.

Nothing they said was in itself understandable. Their scholar-talk had dried into the dust of nonsense. Yet he heard them. They pointed over the Sheath, and jabbered about the asafir, and made low, vague threats about the cars falling.

"Atwar is benevolent in the south, there he stands on his head in the Moon. The Moon stands on his head and opens his mouth—it is a cauldron—into the dye-vat! boil that head clean and put it at his breast. We have boiled a better colour, we have boiled sapphire in the blood of birds.

"Ah, malevolent face-board face! they will fall into that face like birds, they will swim into distance, they will swim into sapphire. They will fall into the cauldron of the south, it has a bowl all humped from the humpbacked potters' crooked hands, the shape of the gibbous Moon.

"Sicken, sicken, they make them smaller and smaller, their leg bones are little stripped sticks. Where are the rafts of the heavens? Click, sticks, click together. Will they row clouds, will their staffs stick in rainwater, will air and absence of air give them purchase? Who has killed the small birds in the pulse of their hands? Who has strangled the small bird with a string of hand-hair artfully?

*"The Doll turns his back and prepares to lunge across the
city. All in his path, run to and fro for his sake! Only the south
makes him kind. Turn his one-head on its narrow neck.
Birds! take each one a strand of his hair, and turn him to the
south at the time of his coming!"*[39]

So they raved, one voice taking up the strain when
the other unravelled utterly. Then their Twar spoke
suddenly in an ordinary voice. "You will choose death,
when you have done it," he said matter-of-factly. His
mouth chewed.

Betwar saw them with sadness. The failure of their
heresy had cooked their minds, or it had failed because
of their craziness. Yet perhaps they were no less wise
than any—than the unbonded Ng with their gliding
walk and their obsessive, humourless stare, or any of
the others who senselessly circled the Doll.

"Ah, father-friends," he said to them sadly.

"Ah, *head-of-a-sufur*! Atwar rises, look to the south!"

He left them finally, after directing some World-
children, who had ventured near, to fetch them
something to eat.

Trudging homeward Betwar was curious, despite
himself, to see the changes, and so he crossed the high
city on his way, passing through narrow, deserted
streets upward to the Square. He emerged at its eastern
brim into unshaded light that bleached his vision.
Along to his left, the new pink and red walls crowded
inward from its southern periphery, against the day-
abandoned dyers' mess. In there Ard was hidden with
the Siri; he had himself brought her to some room in
that maze.

He turned away, and crossed the expanse of blaz-
ing, dusty earth to pass the Doll. And made himself
look at it.

It was the Atwar they had built after the Fire, with the space cleared of ashes and debris and levelled and enlarged around it, so that the people of a whole city could congregate at its feet. This great Doll was far taller than the original, four-or-eight times taller than any of the houses.

It was soft, if solid, its cloth stretched from rains and rare scourings and pulled unevenly in the drying, so that a realistic kind of wrinkling and puckering covered the disproportionate, much-mended legs, that were propped standing. The right leg was somewhat forward of the other, which had a contraption with a series of ropes attached to it and hanging down. The Doll's shrunken, short shirt, with the dirty sufur carcass fastened on its sleeve, had once been red, and the Doll was a faded red, entirely. On those parts they could clamber up and reach, people had tied bits of cloth and tresses, and the whites and blacks speckled its shanks and knees like mole-hairs. Looking up, Betwar saw that even its penis (in which the stuffing had sunk) drooped, and had been decorated with a meagre tag of hair. Beyond it the huge stained torso rose to support a head perhaps overly round (for Eastern people had made this thing), a fair likeness in its main planes and masses, but with a disagreeable expression, caused by the pull of the weather over the years and the cloth's sagging—the nostrils were pinched as if in disdain and the angles of the mouth, tucked back on graying white-cloth teeth, scowled—as if this Atwar regarded the people beneath him with increasing contempt, and would have removed himself if he could. The first Doll had been more benign. But small ones made now repeated this one's expression. Betwar walked around the forward foot and saw, propped between its puffed toes in the dust, old twin women comfortably asleep.

Betwar disliked the Doll, its size, look, colour,

nakedness—but it seemed to him pitiful rather than threatening.

They would cover it before the final ceremony. The dyers would be finished in time, and the new cloth would be bright and clean and orange as blood. It was not Atwar. The children had to touch its feet in the Circling, and recite those ritual lines, but Betwar had made its impotence clear to them, surely—whenever they spoke of the Doll, he had told them "It is not my brother."

As for Atwar, he would forgive the Doll, Betwar reasoned. And if Atwar did, he himself could as well. It had no correspondence with his brother, and no power. "My children, you must tell Atwar when you see him that the world is very funny now, but people have forgotten how to laugh at it."

Seven

In that vat where you dispense dye to the heart,
what should I be? What my love and hate?

1

The Ng had spoken seriously with Betwar only once, and as yet with words that were turned in circles, converging but not converged, so that he had returned from them more puzzled than otherwise. It had been a kind of formal visit and he had received their sour tea, squeezed ceremoniously into his mouth. He noticed when they served him that the Ng had an unsmell, as if they stone-scoured their skin all over and not just their feet and hands.

Their house was deep, larger than twins who lived alone could ever have required, and swept and empty except for the slings. The air too had a sweetish unsmell, though it was so close to the shore. The roof-cloth was neatly mended and stretched taut, but it was built so low that Betwar had to stoop standing.

They had gestured him towards a sling close to the door and he had sat down awkwardly; his weight placed him hard on the hard-sand floor. The Ng too had sat down, prim in their tauter sling, from which they could look slightly downward at him. They wore as always white, their face-board a white slash joining their smoothshaped heads.

They had not, then, demanded that he look at them. Yet his eyes had been caught in their look in spite of himself. Their dark voices, one ever pausing and replaced by the other, were in themselves soothing and cool. Their words seemed woven to calm and dull him, to confuse his mind as with jasmine sweetness. They had spoken at first to him, then of him—as if he were only a listener; they had taken the skein of his chary, obstinate life and stained it, coloured it their colour and woven it into their schemes as if he had never opposed them, as if he were all eager and willing and foolish and undone.

"You have served your brother well, since his going away your being in this world is the conjoining braid, the ingathering of his mind with your mind and so with our-minds. Never can you forget him, never can he forget you. You Betwar have no need to partake in the ceremony to honour your brother, when your body honours him awake or asleep. Your whole life honours Atwar.

"Ah, we are less than you and we seem not to account you, yet we do account you and know you are closer to him; you are the only mind who truly knows him. Do you not come to the Doll, who have no need of dolls and replicas. In your heart is the heart of your brother, in your liver is the liver of your brother. In Tasman's womb were these drawn deftly apart, that you might live separately until you must separate in purpose, to rejoin in purpose at last. There is a Tale of you, Betwar brother of Atwar, in which you are his equal, as the shadow of the Moon follows the Moon, as the darkness returns after the light and coolness after great heat. Without Betwar could there be no Atwar, while Betwar lives does Atwar live also, the world beholds Atwar's shadow among the people, among the people Betwar walks in the shadow of Atwar as in a stand of trees and they acknowledge him without speech; they know and acknowledge him. They honour him.

"When we who are ignorant circle the Doll, when we tell our Tales and recite Atwar's Grief, we remember Betwar on the strand, who lifts his tear-blurred face directly towards the Moon. When we watch unceasingly at the screens, we remember Betwar waiting for the Moon to rise over the horizon, his eyes ready to catch the first light. Between Betwar and Atwar there is no need for words or watching. Ah, he is preparing for the journey, ah, he is preparing his children for that journey of distance. The braid will tighten, the braid will hold; across space, between worlds his children will go to him, they will leave their father to return to their father, they will bring in their small bodies the brother of Atwar into his conjoining."[40]

Betwar could not bring himself to speak, for as he heard these words his mind was all confusion and rising anger; shame made him silent till he had left them. Indeed, they had not required him to speak.

"You will return to-us," they had told him when they dismissed him. No, he would never enter that house again, he resolved through tears as he trudged towards the beach. Ah, even these tears were contaminated by their approval—as if the Ng had commanded him to cry, and nodded beneficently after him as adults beam on the small fires lit by their children, who think they are brave and wild when they are all allowed and constrained! He felt unhoused, he hated his body, and forced back the tears so they drew inward at his throat like burning thread.

The Azur were standing at their shack against the Sheath-wall; they looked forlorn in their ragged white, with tidewater up to their ankles. They gestured feebly, perhaps angrily towards him; but he did not turn aside to greet them. He walked quickly northward in the half-dark; ah, even the Moon—his innate knowledge that the Moon would soon be rising—this had become yet another wound—even his mind's privacy and its small comforts the Ng had somehow entered, and made sick, they had emptied a vat of their sweet, bloody dye across his house—ah, how they had sickened him!

And now again they summoned him to them.

2

He ran northward, his feet pounding the dark sand, throwing the water up against his body as he crossed the little inlets and bays of the high tide. This night was as dark, the north softly light, the northeast very light where again the Moon threatened its rising. One day had passed. Ah, whatever he touched was sickened and sickened him. He had been unable to sleep. The boys had not been brought home—Nevi and Nevar had put their heads in and said they would sleep over at the Nev house. Last night he had come in as if to some safe place, hurrying, and sat down ashudder, wrapping his arms around his knees. Tared only was there. The daylight hitting the roof patches sent dull squares of grayish shadow across the mats and walls. They were not red—there was no red in this house—yet even here, the Ng could have touched it with their words, had they liked. Touched anything. Touched Tared. In his mind he seemed to jump up, and gather her up in his arms, and run with her northward. Yet, she would have resisted him. His sons—Ard, already caught inside their rooms! His mind jittered. None of this was new. It was known, even the knowing was known. Ah, he was all known, all seen.

Tared offered him water, speechlessly. She could see the ugly urgency in his face. He let the water fill his mouth, pressing his teeth into the cloth, swallowing painfully.

"Tared—I have thought that we must go away, but there is nowhere to go."

For Tared the worst was that he did not cry. Waiting for his tears she wrung the cloth, and folded it carefully and laid it back in the bowl. She remained near him. The only sound he made was a harsh swallowing. How could one not cry, if it was a necessary art no one had learned it. After a time, she stroked his arms gently, that he kept clutched around his knees.

His running was hopeless; he could as well have run towards them, straight to them. Yet it eased his mind to run in his body so vehemently, as if almost he could run from his thoughts, so that only the most desperate could keep pace with him. These were of escape— should he run as the Linh, directly into the fire? But it was too late; escape belonged to his youth, to refusing to enter that bond, to a time of no children at all. Or to hiding them then, to going after Semer into Lofot. To another path that had branched off so far back that it was lost forever. Perhaps, with a long, sure plan and much care, to the years having been spent differently, not in helplessness but in teaching them and preparing that secret path, that they would choose—but how could they have withstood, when he had not, when it had ever been inevitable?

He was past the saltings, running under the old polder wall that curved out and around the point. So far he had not been for more than two years, and then at high tide there had been no beach; now it was wide enough, and dusty, with the bitter saltgrass springing—the swollen water did not come here any more. At the point he would turn or not turn. His heart knocked at his ribs strongly. He was running, it seemed to him, bearing all his children—his sons on his back, clinging at his neck, his hair hiding them, their little legs knocking about behind him, and Ard and Tared one in each arm with their arms around his body. So many heads his body had, he who had thought he was bereft! They were a big, running body, with two good stout legs to carry them. At the point, the body would be outlined against the dawn sky, tall and seemly. Then it would go around the point and be seen no more.

He reached the turning, which was long and rounded, not abrupt as he had thought, and saw the northern capes come slowly into view, spreading away into the brightness with the waters of Shelik whitely shimmering. He could make out, he thought, the distant Taygon Range at the brim of sight. The extent of the scape shrunk him back into himself; his woven-children vanished. A tiny cool breath passed across his forehead ruffling his brow-hair, and he sensed a heavy brightness leaning on his shoulders from across the eastern sea. He turned; The Moon was rising, easily lifting itself and settling and lifting in the intervals of his gaze; Crisium and the blue forests, Imbrium at the terminator. It rose where the Ng and the world's blood could not reach it, where Atwar in spite of them waited to put them to shame. Ah Atwar my brother, my brother Atwar.

When Betwar reached the Ng door it was pulled up tight and the house was empty. But twins from the Watch came over to him, and told him to follow them uphill. They brought him to one of the new houses—to a room, rather, in the jumble of little rooms that had been set up against the Square; the scholars had to lead him into it. These rooms were in the last stages of furnishing: new cloth was laid down to cover the very earth; and in places was trodden on and already dirty—in other rooms it was there but rolled carefully aside. He saw a few slings hanging haphazard and empty, some with one end folded on the ground. The house-stems were greenish-white with newness. Everything else was dyed, layers of red, red, red gathering around each bunchy glow of lamplight, and the sterner moon-light falling through in cool whites and grays.

Ard was here—he had himself put her down, but so many spaces and passages had since been built that he could not tell where. Nevertheless he found himself listening for her voice: somewhere here she was closed up with the Siri, fasting and learning.

The Ng were seated in a sling of new red cloth, and motioned him close to them. The space was low and cramped—he could have touched the walls with out-stretched hands, and could not have stood upright. No cooling air moved. It was evening but still very hot, and the walls shook constantly—Betwar, as he squatted down, was aware of people passing behind cloth all around him. But the commotion gradually ceased, the walls settled, and it was still.

One lamp stood against the Ng knees, set into the ground and packed with clay so that its light was shaded from Betwar and shone only directly upward, into their faces.

They looked at him directly from either side of the stiff face-board; thus was he exposed to the weight of their composite gaze.

"Come closer to-us, brother of Atwar."

He knelt in front of them and put his hands awk-wardly between his knees. The Ng hands reached out: he saw them placed, narrow and dark and surprisingly heavy, one on each of his thighs.

"Look at-us."

Ah, he was unused to this scrutiny, and had no practice, no children's tactics for avoiding it. As he lifted his head and looked directly at the Ng faces the board blurred, flickered, and winked out utterly, and their heads swam into one. His eyes were locked un-willingly on this new, round, austere visage, that seemed to distend as he gazed, swelling to fill his entire visual field.

His mind chattered—that he was letting them do this out of courtesy, that he would turn away in a moment. Still he stayed, staring. Ah, they were adept; they had done this so often before, and he hated it.

"We have spoken to you before," said the Ng Twel, and his mouth, that ran into his brother's mouth, scarcely moved. "Your desire is your brother Atwar and this is your reason and your life."

Betwar had no reply, and the voice from the ex-tended, slightly parted lips continued. Now he could not tell which of them spoke.

"You have thought long on these things, never diverted as we by small Eatings and Turns around the Doll, ever constant to your Brother, ever alone. In service to Atwar you have striven with your body to be completed in him, yet you cannot be completed in him in this body—but through the bodies of your children, whom you have made in his image and for his sake, to be his sons and his perpetuators on the other world. You have served him perfectly, and you serve him perfectly."

Their outer eyes narrowed and gleamed. He could perceive two eyes only, and the light from the floor caught at the sclera, finding the chinks under the shallow eyelids. Two-one, two-one. Betwar foundered. It felt as if the earth had slid down a fraction. The pressure of their two hands on his thighs had changed—now it was strangely inverted, so it seemed to lift and suspend him. His own hands he could no longer feel—except that they were imperceptibly, inexorably floating apart, or so it felt to him though he could have seen them, if he could have looked down, and he knew they had not moved.

"You have walked in one path, and we have walked in one path, and our path and your path join now like strands of hair in the braiding. Our path was not yours; yet as you, we have increased our necessity, and it has brought us to this place as swiftly as yours. Often you have considered in your mind, brother of Atwar, how two separate paths may correspond, when one is among folk and ceremony and one is among barren stones. Indeed in the World they cannot. But from a distance, away between worlds far from the feet that tread them, in Atwar's twinning sight, they are twinned in harmony.

"Therefore before the Doll our paths will meet on that day, and together we will turn our faces towards him in harmony. Atwar requires from you only what you desire, and you will ever serve him well. The children are perfected, shaped for his bidding, and he bids them come to him, and in them in all things possible you will also journey to him, as is your desire.

"On that day, your hair will be taken from your head like the hair of a woman in childbirth, and the world's earth will be pared from under the nails of your feet. Your children will wear your hair and eat your earth, the cells of your heels and the salt of your tears will be their skin-oil, and you will deliver into them from your keeping every part, to be a sign of that journey, until there is nothing else to deliver to him. And you will be delivered from your desire."

They closed their mouths across their words at last. There was a silence. Then suddenly, in some near room, a sheet was torn to size—it sounded for an instant like a human scream.

3

He remained before them in silence, his gaze stolen by the irresistible beauty of their composite visage. So was even unright made beautiful, when there was no wavering.

Their belief had stolen his words and his argument—he had never asked any of the scholars, even secretly, whether they had real reason to trust the cars, or to believe his brother lived. How could he have asked the scholars, when none were able to speak any more without masking themselves in fearless trust, in images and Tales? And the Siri had told him simply that trust was easier than distrust. Yet they had said that even the most ardent of all who said Atwar lived (who said, "*Atwar walks*") were not really sure.

But the look of the Ng was terrible and perfect; this visage had no deviousness, no guile. They believed. For his own sake, to still his desire they had spoken, not saying "This must be done because Atwar is dead," or, "Because we do not trust the cars." Only to still his desire. How could their minds, how could any mind that was complete, trust and believe so perfectly? Again he thought, so is even unright made beautiful, when there is no wavering, even in the deepest heart.

He yearned for the speech and ways of his fathers, their strict adherence to what was and corresponded,

Sorud Twel's words like keen and ordinary knives.

How the Ng drew him out! like a thread between their fingers, how they wove him! They had been from the beginning utterly certain, from that day the Linh were first brought to him, that he would comply. It was then in his youth he had conceded and pacted his heart in complicity, and entered into the contract.

As Betwar walked homeward, the Moon a daymoon now and lifting long before the sun, and the sea past the lower city in dark abeyance, it came to him quietly that the scholars had planned it even then, whatever the Sorud had understood or intended—for his infant daughters would have been gift enough, had Atwar lived. Had there been certainty, as infants the Ard would have been sent to Atwar unbound, unharmed, without his waiting. Their faces would have been their speech and Tale—he would have known them, and so known everything.

Even after the Fire, even then more reasonably they could have gone—and the boys also, small as they were, for they had to be weaned; they were motherless. If Atwar were there to receive them, why should they wait till they had to be stayed in their growth, and till they learned to think and fear? No, it was then, in innocence, they would have been sent to him.

But against his doubt was the fact of his life, its transparency. Was not every act of his, every function, as they had described? They did not flatter him when they told him, "You serve Atwar perfectly."

The crazed Azur words came back to him: "You will choose death." What lay before him? He had called his children inventions, yet was he not himself, despite his grief, despite his rages and apparent steady obstinacy, their invention as well?

4

Ask liked to pretend he was as Atwar in the Tale, full of eagerness and delight. But as the time of the journey drew near, this was harder and harder to do; and Saska's fears, and the way Saska hid in dreams, angered him.

"It will be a whole day and a whole night, that we are separated in the cars and may not sleep," Saska was murmuring now, as they lay in the house. He had been scratching his scarred foot; now his skinny fingers picked at the doll on his breast.

"That long, we have already managed to stay awake—the day the asafir came," said Ask. "It is not much." Saska was silent, and Ask waited for the whimper that would tell him his brother slept.

But instead Saska went on talking, his voice a gentle sing-song; it sounded as if he were not really listening to himself. "We will fall down, down, down into the Moon," he said dreamily, as if tasting a strangeness that half-teased and half-scared him. "No—up, up, up like a sufur into the sky—till we are over the Moon, and Atwar will push it under us like a basket and we will be dropped in—we will watch it getting bigger, and bigger—"

"We will watch both worlds," Ask broke in, trying to make the words ordinary. "On a screen as Atwar did, the world receding and the Moon coming nearer—we will fall down into it; you know this, the Qam said it will seem so. It is as the Lake of the Moon, only not flat—the trees grow straight up out of it, how could they grow down, or sideways? Water flows along the courses. Atwar walks."

"Our-father does not think he is there."

"Does he not? Sometimes perhaps it seems he is not sure, but he has never said this. Ah, we will find

Atwar." Ask sniffed; he was weary of comforting his brother—and now Tared never would—there she lay close by with her back turned, perhaps not even listening. And her comfort was too harsh; all she did was silence Saska when he frightened himself, and with Ask she was peremptory and refused to argue. Lately, she scarcely ever spoke with them; she was angry and busy in her own thoughts right now because of Ard, he knew.

Saska sighed, the whimpering sigh that he seldom allowed himself awake, and sat up. Again he scratched at his foot. "I will take my scar to Atwar," he said, examining it. The down was growing in. "If it lasts. Atwar will say, I know which brother you are by the scar on your foot." He laid his hand on one of Ask's pallid, hairless legs where the bands had crossed. When Ard had become adult, Betwar had unbound them and burned the bands. For the boys were still much smaller than their sisters.

"Do you feel this?" said Saska, pressing down his thumb into the flesh above Ask's knee, where it left white dents.

"No."

Saska pressed his other thumb into his own knee. "It feels the same—yours or mine," he said, and rubbed the doll along his leg, then along his brother's. "Just the same."

"How can nothing be the same as nothing?" said Ask. "Yet anger, we feel often enough in our legs, and the blood inside them warms our feet. It is a sign we will walk. Our feet live, and are very strong." He extended his toes.

Their feet had been left alone and were large and long. They were striped with down on the upper surfaces, underneath bald and tender. But they were straight and well-formed. Of their sisters' one foot was badly turned, because it had been laid across the top of the other foot when they were bound; that one leg was also shorter. But the boys' legs were the same length and their feet were straight.

"Atwar has a bad limp, even on the Moon, says our-father," he added, finishing his thought.

"Will we walk more straightly than Atwar, then?" asked Saska doubtfully. Past their short, useless legs, their feet looked like oversized footgloves, or as if they had stepped into dark, clinging clay. And their legs were permanently bent at the knees, the knee-joints locked almost rigid. They fitted against each other skin to skin and dent to hollow. They had been bound upward, as well as across.

"As our-father remembers him, we will walk about as well," said Ask. He was less sure about the Ard.

Tared turned on her mat, and said to them, "Lie down, and sleep!" Then, though they were silent, she left them, and pulled herself over to the space by the east-facing door, and lay down beside her father.

5

Her body felt swollen and furious. She would make the blood come, hurt herself with something—not an arrow—her mind shirked away from the thought of the jagged-edged arrows of their mothers, kept in the wall-pocket by the western door—Ard had said, use one of them. And her father's knife was ever bound on his arm.

Something less harmful—a bit of stem, perhaps. Her body winced. She had tried already, the day before, crawling outside secretly and rubbing herself against the sharp rim of the bridge-stone beside the door. It was where they broke cloth and hand-hair, and had been useful in those milder ways. Blood had come; she had to wipe the stone with spit. But the bleeding was superficial and had not continued.

She imagined speaking to the dyers at the Doll, and asking for a bagful out of the vats. But it was not exactly blood orange; its darks were of a colder colour, though its lights were rosy. It was recognizably not right. And Ard's time was nearly over. She would return to them in no more than two days. Her teeth would be black.

Tared thought she could not bear to see that—yet, she missed her sister. Whatever Ard was learning, it was taking her into other places—it was about being an adult, and about Atwar—and the conversation that would surely begin then, that Atwar, for reasons of his own (which were the Outdead's reasons) had not yet initiated. She was left here; her own body was a blood-bag that would not be pierced.

She lay without touching Betwar, her arms at her sides, wide awake now and staring into the dayheat, the radiance. Her mouth moved.

"Atwar, help me.
"Do not continue in silence/ when we are listening./ Do not remain in the forest/ when we are watching."[41]

6

So Tared fretted, and prepared herself to greet her sister, when Ard would be brought home blackteethed and triumphant with the Siri and many attendants. But it turned out that the Siri came back without Ard, for they were summoned to her—because Tared began to bleed that very night. Betwar had to run to fetch them; it was not seemly that she should be brought across the city unless they attended her.

While he was gone she took out the second of the red dresses, and concealed it from him under her white one, pressing it between her thighs. Betwar returned with the Siri, and then they set off back again up the hill, he carrying Tared and she laughing. The Siri also smiled, but wanly—they looked gaunter, as though they had been fasting as well as Ard, and their belly jutted square under their dress.

Betwar stooped and followed them just as he had with Ard, through the low, sheeted halls with their confusion of hangings. A figure crossed ahead of them— a graceful shadow seen momentarily against the cloth at a turning. Then the Siri paused at an inner door. Betwar put Tared down, and she pulled herself impatiently inside.

"Now, Betwar, do not delay in making a room in your house for your adult daughters," said the Siri Twar to him firmly, before he left them. "They would expect it, even for this short time." They had leaned for a moment against the doorstem—they seemed very tired. Betwar saw how their Twel looked away, across her shoulder, and would not meet his eyes. He stammered a little.

"Is it well with Ard?"

She stammered also. "Very well. It is only that the scholars should expect—when you have prepared a room—or perhaps, otherwise, they would make it a pretext to keep them here until—and that is unnecessary."

Their Twel said, glancing across her sister, "Ard wishes to wait for Tared, but tomorrow we will give her something to eat; she is hungry."

Tared pulled herself across the sheeted floor to her adult sister. Ard was lying in a low sling of red cloth, dressed in her red dress, and when she saw Tared she put her hand across her mouth, covering it. Above her hand, her upper face stared, and Tared was not at first certain whether her look was joy or sorrow—the upper face alone is hard to read—yet, there was intensity in it.

The Siri entered, smiling, and helped Tared up, and dumped her unceremoniously across the red sling beside her sister. It shuddered. The girls embraced, and Tared said, "I have brought the other dress. Will you remain with me?"[42] looking into her rounded eyes. She pulled Ard's hands away impatiently, and saw the black teeth gleaming in a scowl of terror.

But after that, Ard smiled a little. And when the Siri assured her she could stay with her sister, and said some words to people outside and sent them away, she lay back more easily, and drew Tared down against her body, that felt warm and strange in some odd way Tared could not account for, but which might have been the unsmell—because Ard was scoured; the Siri had washed her.

The Siri were now more serious and withdrawn than Tared had ever known them. But they were brisk: everything was correctly proscribed and ordered. Once, while Ard slept, Tared woke up and heard them crying bitterly.

So her teeth were also made black and she became like her sister, and the Siri repeated for her the ordinary things, though without laughter or celebration. They told her also much about the last ceremonies at the Doll, which they would partake in along with their brothers, before they were all carried into the Great Book and to the cars.

"But there, you *will not take leave formally,\ even as Atwar did not,\ he made and makes no finishing....*"[43] When the Siri recited this, they were less believable than when they talked of dresses and responses. Atwar's conversation, like Atwar's Grief, was in another realm, part of the Tales and Songs.

But the Siri Twel said to Tared, in her own words, privately, "Take good leave of your father." And Tared remembered that later.

From now on, it seemed that the burden of their journey was being bound physically across their foreheads, just as, they had been told, the clay of their father's footsoles was to be traced on their faces, mixed with his spit and tears. Tared and Ard did not remember how Betwar had made them touch their mothers' charred breasts with their baby hands, or pressed the Linh ash into their mouths. It was to have sufficed. But something remained in that pocket that was to be emptied of grief, some dregs or stain hidden in the lowest seam, that was personal and that like the cells of their father would also cling to them. For Tared this was heaviest, for she was already heavy with her dream. And for them both it was most private—nothing to do with the general yearning for Atwar, the unfinishment that was the ordinary temper of the world.

Betwar heeded the Siri and made a room for his daughters, binding the cloth to the stems with a braided strand of his own hair. He partitioned off the house, replacing the west-facing door and bringing across an oblique cloth-wall that was knotted by hairlines to the bridge. The boys helped him when they were there, and begged scraps of the torn cloth. He saw how deft Ask was become in braiding and knotting. But they were mostly away in the marshes.

Betwar worked as quickly as he could, raising the coolest part of the floor, which slanted up against the south bank of the canal, into a wide sling as the Fu-en people did; but he could not secure it tight enough to hang clear and gave that up. That side of the room had an oddly pleasant, rounded look, however. When they were home, his sons tidied about, and interfered, but this was seldom; they were more interested in their own schemes.

In the mornings when the Sanev brought them home, Betwar lay down with them in his arms, and if they squirmed in discomfort his arms tightened. But later in the day he sometimes left them asleep, and wandered northward on the shore, and no people went near him.

7

"Atwar, what is the colour of your voice now, that I hear still when I hear the raised, light voices of my little sons? Why have you not spoken to me? One light, one certain light was all I required for a sign. We have become your signs, and your signings, there are no others. Now they have woven you across the ordinary face of the world and distorted all its meanings like pulled cloth. We are a bulge, a pushed tide, but you have not pulled at us; we fall back. We invent you over and over, shadow of a shadow, radiant and diminishing.

"Atwar, what is the colour of your mind? What is it uncoloured by this earthy stain? I have not served you, if I cannot understand. Our life is not their words. My correspondence with you was unbleached cloth—and they have stained it, and say they know our heart. If we had one proper heart, and one beating! Once we lay face to face in the body of our mother, and believed we were one body—then, you turned from me. That was the moment the world turned! the beginning was even then. Whatever happens has already happened.

"Atwar, the Ng have seduced me, because—ah, they have descried my heart—and seen that you are more important to me even than my children, more absent, more present, more absent! It would be better to make myself into small ash, and my children to eat that, and nothing to remain of me on this earth! Why must I serve you by living in this body, breathing, seeing, eating? If I knew you were dead I would do it.

"If I knew you lived, and there was no chance of our meeting I would do it. Chance deranges my heart. I say they are crazed to believe in you, who am myself crazed. They know this, and they have persuaded me to give over to you every thing, even the sweetness of my despair."

But Betwar strove, and thought beyond these thoughts, and it seemed to him he came to wrestle with a greater snake than the snake of his childhood, and defeat it, and go on through a fiery defile more narrow and more dangerous than Narod's had ever been. The world's unblood, the untruth that drenched him was scoured away in an unseen earthfall with a kind of pain that scoured his mind's skin almost to breaking. Those who saw him on the strand—and there were some, harvesters—told that he lay fisted together for a long time motionless, then that his body turned on itself once or twice in a jerky way, and was for some time motionless again.

It was on that same night his daughters were returned to him. And he came from the shore quieted; his look was erased, and his step certain.

8

The Ard, their red dresses covered by long, white women's dress, were carried home in procession—the Siri foremost and then the Qam and other teachers bearing them. At the noise, the Nev, the Ludh, and their sons hurried across, and were seated in the now cramped quarters of the divided house when the Ard were brought in. The Siri entered with them.

It was noisy, and the bright voices of the little boys made it a kind of celebration. The Ur chattered, flinging themselves against their adult sisters, pointing out the new room they had helped to make for them, pushing their fingers between their sisters' lips to touch their new-blackened teeth, and demanding to see their adult smiles. Ard and Tared were thinner, and nearly fainting from tiredness. Betwar gave them water, gently, for he saw that their mouths were sore, especially Tared's. He also squeezed water into the mouths of the Siri, at the same time looking into their faces, searching out some communication from them. They saw him this time, both of them, and their look mirrored his—it was clear and empty. He himself gave the girls yeast—Tared was ravenous—out of new bowls, and then the Siri took leave of them.

Their look, it seemed to him, had called him after them, and he climbed after them out of the canal and walked beside them to the next bridge-end. "Have you nothing to say to me?" He asked.

But they stopped unwillingly, and their Twar said low, "You will yourself have heard every necessary thing."

Their faces were sad and calm, but not as he had hoped—nor did they again look into his face to receive his quietness. What calmed them was different; it contained a kind of coolness and distance. He realized he had wanted some touch, something he thought he had felt before, when he had delivered them Tared. More than that—he had expected without reason that their heart would accept him, and would help him at the last. But the Siri glanced downwards and away; their twelhand rested on their belly.

Ah—they were gravid and bonded, and he was nothing to them after all. They had brought his daughters through into womanhood with gentleness, patience and courtesy. Now they did not understand him, and would not look into his face, where perhaps they would have understood his mind. This he must however bear alone. What they had given him was finished. He watched them walk off between the stems of the trees, graceful under the light and shadow, white dress flickering, sleek heads close together.

It was by now high day, and very hot. The Ard, their curiosity fighting their exhaustion, had climbed into their room, talking low and touching the spaces, and the Ludh had entered heavily after them, looking about as if for something lacking. "The Sanev room is higher than this, and more even"—"And it has an outer door," Ask heard them saying, and he nudged his brother and giggled. In the room, Tared would have answered the Ludh sharply, but Ard had already made to lie down, and the Ludh were forced to come out, and climbed over the bunched cloths, then fastened up the new door busily.

The Twar Nev said, "Betwar, we will leave you now, all of us, to sleep," and they began to get up. But Ask was jumpy and wide awake, and shook the drowsy Saska. "They will tell, now," he said to him in a loud whisper—"about the asafir."

"What is that, then, and who will tell it?" asked the

Nev, but the Sons of Nev, who had been sitting close to the door with their knees drawn up under their chins, nodded to Ask wordlessly and went out.

Ask and Saska squirmed and laughed, and Ask said, "You know, Fadar, how excellent our Saska-Sufur is in saying the unwords of the asafir?"

"The squeaking—yes," said Betwar.

"I could not myself," Ask went on, "but he could, and they learned to answer him and then, because they saw we could not swim to them across the air, or walk on the earth either, they began to come near to us."

"And the Sanev helped us," said Saska. "We have made, with the Sanev, a little house—they are fetching it, now.

"Four, we have enticed into it," he went on. "But one escaped."

At this moment the Sanev reappeared, stepping cautiously down into the house, with a little white basket in their hands. Its corners were knotted over stiff reeds, and the stripped twigs of trees, and its roof was a rough grid-weave of woven thread, strengthened with human hair.

It was full of asafir, two brownish and one blue, which flapped and cringed, and stared. Saska leaned close over them, making little crooning, clicking noises.

"I can touch them a little now," he said, "but not here—and only if I speak for a long while first."

He reached a skinny arm back to Ask, who quickly took Betwar's cloth and dipped it, and gave it to his brother. Saska squeezed water into the basket, trying to make it fall into one corner. "There are bowls in their house for water—" explained Ask—"little ones, we made them also, we cut and plugged up pieces of reed."

Saska, still staring in, reached the cloth back into Ask's lap. His hands settled the box more steadily on the floor.

"None died, but one blue sufur swam away," he said softly. "The thread was not knotted close enough."

The Sanev sat back on their heels, and stroked Saska's arm.

"Saska-Sufur," said Nevar, grinning. And Nevi said to Betwar, "We helped a little with the house—but it was mostly Ask who made it, and Saska who whistled till they came."

Ard, then Tared, woke out of deep sleep to the warmth of their voices, and the odd fluttering sounds, and pushed down their door and looked down.

"It is the world's asafir, Tared and Ard," called Saska. "Not dolls. Asafir for Atwar in the Moon."

Eight

*The moon has returned, whose like the sky never
saw even in dreams; he has brought a fire which
no water can extinguish.
I am as full of light as the clear sky, I am circling
around the Moon.*

*What do I possess other than the thing you have
given? What are you searching for in my pocket
and sleeve?
I am ashamed of respect, therefore I circle shame.*

1

There were very few days left after that, till perigee, and
every evening attendants came for the Ard and the Ur
and carried them to the houses beyond the Doll, and
they were prepared. New cloth, as yet undyed, was
stitched into dresses, and for the boys into short tunics
in the western fashion, with pockets for the asafir (dolls,
as the scholars supposed) and pockets to bind on their
arms and thighs. Betwar, who helped with bringing
and fetching them, saw that the new buildings were
now hidden behind a wall of cloth higher than their
roofs. Before it, lamps had been set into the earth, and
he saw rafts, and people he had never seen before

dressed in dirty unbleached cloth with head-sleeves like hoods, kneeling in the lamplight over chunks of quarried stone: they worked with sapphire, and ground it to powder for dyes—though, apart from on the round dolls, he had not seen where it was to be used.

The Sanev were ever in the farms, and came late to the house with leaves and mud for the asafir, and Saska whimpered to them to make even more effort find the sufur that had fled.

"How can we recognize him?" asked Nevi. "Except that he is now the most wary!"

"We have placed another basket there, do not fear," said Nevar.

Nevi added, "If your attendants would not hang about you so, Saska-Sufur, we could carry you in to whistle for him."

"You must!" Saska's face was burning. "If it be in the dayheat—"

"There will surely be a night, before the last one—" put in Ask, doubtfully.

Tared said, "When there is much yet to be done, for every night—?"

"A day then," said Nevi, looking about. "It would be unseemly, if we were not to be all together playing in the marshes, even once more."

At that, Saska flung himself upon them, and burst into tears, burying his face in the pit of their throat: "Nevi! Nevar! Nevi! Nevar!"

Betwar, in surprise and confusion, took him gently from them and rocked him. "Little son, you are a stormflood! out of the west! Never have I seen you weep so, be still. Ah—you have it rightly from your father—tell Atwar you are like me in this, we have not forgotten how to weep."

Saska's doll had lain against the wall-cloth, forgotten, though the breast-pockets were stitching for all four dolls, on the new dresses. He brought it over to the basket and put it on the roof. "Little stupid sufur, forgive me for forgetting you. I promise to take you also with me, if you will help me to call your brother. See? They are like you, are they not? But they have been in the south. They can tell you many things." So he murmured over the basket and the doll.

That morning the Sanev came, and woke him, and carried him in the heat into the farms, and the bluffs. Saska called over and over, but no asafir came near. The birds were agitated, gathering themselves farther in, keeping close together, chittering and twittering. They would suddenly throw themselves up above the bluffs in a crowd, swirl, then settle again noisily. They circled in the air in harmony, as if their thought were one thought instead of many. "This they have been doing more and more," said Nevi to Saska.

"They have perhaps told each other you are a danger to them," said Nevar. "They do not like you any more."

"How can we know what they do and do not like?" asked Saska, his eyes filling with tears. "The others chose to enter the basket."

"And our fingers chose to close it with a grid," said Nevi and laughed. "Whatever they think, their thought is different now than it was."

The asafir rose again, a large throng. Saska rubbed his eyes and looked up at them with longing. "But in something—they are thinking as we do," he said. "They are restless, just as we are."

As they returned along the marsh-edge a breath of wind shook the trees, and a few leaves fell on the dark water.

2

The space around the Doll was now cleared, the dye pits filled and the vats carried off, with the rafts and rocks and stems for the drying. Only the darkened patterning left by the dripping sheets remained like a strange moon-grid on half the empty Square, which was now swept of its earth-dust and the dust from the quarriers' stone. Only the depressions for the lamps remained—around the Doll, which had been draped with a new, red cloth, and in a half-circle in front of the high white curtain that hid the ceremonial rooms. The people worked far into the day, and children brought them water. Among them the Ng walked gracefully, making some observations here and there but for the most part silent; when they saw anything amiss, they themselves corrected it. They took a besom from other scholars' hands and swept the earth over again close to the Doll, where the long strings were being untangled and drawn down straight and even, and some lengthened. Between each great, droopy cloth toe the last bits of loose dirt were coaxed away.

Betwar watched wordlessly, standing back between the housewalls north of the Doll in the shadow. There was nothing for him to do here. His children had been carried home, but the Sanev had come for them; they must all be still in the marshes. Waiting for them, he had walked uphill; he could not sleep.

By late morning the Square began to empty. He was about to leave when the Ng beckoned to him and, quiet-faced, he followed them across the Square. He had brought them Saska's doll, for they wished to clean it, and they took it from him calmly, and at the same time put a firm hand on his arm. Together they stepped behind the curtaining.

3

The gibbous Moon hung suspended overhead like a rain-filled roof of light, when the people came from the city and from the far places. There were strangers, staring about them at everything they had never seen, some who were swart and a very few with broad, light heads as if they came from the islands in the west, and people with great sleeves thrown over their heads, and brown, coarse tunics and loose hair. There were narrow-headed inlanders from Turuk and Yar, with shallow eyes. There were stunted twins from the northeast with bows, and northerners from the polar world who looked like giants, their fierce-eyed children wearing the skin of snakes and riding sideways between their shoulders. There were the Fu-en folk emerged from their houses, staring at as they were stared at in turn. The scholars from the Great Book were there, subdued but restless, like a tributary or bay of quiet water at tide-turning, standing close to the curtain, wearing new clothes neither white nor red but roseate, half-coloured, about the tone of the faded Doll but of fine stuff and almost transparent, so their dark bodies showed through them when they moved, impatiently shifting their weight from one foot to the other. They had brought something forward from the new rooms, and placed it on the ground among them—a low vat—and in front of them was the half-circle of unlit lamps embedded in the earth.

Ask and Saska were dressed in their new red tunics, of the same stuff as the great cloth that hung about Atwar, the colour of bright, watered blood. They came into the Square in front of Atwar at the north side, perched among the reed-players high on the arms of their bearers, in the procession that had brought them uphill through the darkened city. No light shone but moonlight—every lamp had been extinguished. They sat upright, looking about and then, expectantly, at the scholars across the mass of people crouched in the Square. Their sisters were held up to their right, past their father. The Ard were dressed in red of the finest weave, and lifted high and rigidly by their strong bearers.

Now there was a gleam, and another, as the scholars began to light the far lamps, and the light lifted like a curved bow to separate them from the nearest people, who drew back. The curtain behind them, stretched tight with almost no fold, closed in the Square and hid all its darkened rooms. In the new light it was a firm, matt whiteness, and over it in lamplight, suddenly visible, hung a myriad of narrow bands dyed the blue colour, that hung straight down to the ground. It seemed as if water of the clearest, most exquisite purity was flowing down, as down the face of a cliff or a stationary wave. The garments of the scholars beyond the lamps filled and emptied of light as they moved, translucent and billowing—they were themselves as tall lamps, bending. The face-boards among them winked.

Ask sniffed, and pulled his arm across his face, and reached out and touched Saska with one brown hand— "The Azur are there—look!" he whispered.

With the lamps lit at last, the scholars stood still, the greatest of them with the lamps at their feet—so that a row of high stems of shadow stood behind them on the striped curtain, and they were a row of rosy stems, all glowing. The Azur's bald pates and filthy gown were easy to make out: they stood stiffly next to the Ng in the midst, behind the vat. Then they moved—they were scratching themselves under one arm. Their shadow, agitated, shook on the cloth behind them. The boys giggled.

At once the sharp-pitched call of the reeds sounded

all around. Everyone stopped whispering, as if a wind had passed over and ceased.

Once more, in slow procession, the Children of Atwar were carried around the Doll. First the Ur, with Betwar following, his eyes fixed on their high, bobbing heads, then the Ard behind him and then the players. Their feet stamped to the knock of wood on bone, and the crowd took it up, wrist against temple, low and steady. Only Betwar refused, determined to step at his own pace, but it was soon too difficult; his feet would not deny the pulse of the throng.

Their Circling was large, out at the perimeter of the Square; and more lamps were being lit and set down even as they progressed, with some stalling and bustling, and people pushing back to give them room. The reeds played the *Twelve Turns*, and then the *Heads over Heels*, and children pressed in front and tried to tumble; people took up the chanting, but there was not enough room and too much noise.

Ask and Saska, Ard and Tared, borne ever forward, looked down into the familiar faces of city folk, and into the upturned staring faces of strangers, breathless children and adults alike with open mouths and bewildered, ardent eyes. Their feet were touched by hundreds of reaching hands, and some people held out small dolls to touch them. Tared saw here and there faces like her dream, broad and heavy, but with unbruised eyes. Her eyes snagged on them and her head turned after them unaware. And Betwar saw, deeper inside the crowd, light hair almost like the Semer's—yet, were the Semer here they would not have such hair any more. They would be old and changed.

They passed more smoothly along the arc of lighted lamps, and the line of scholars at the curtain. The Ng's heads turned to meet them, and jerked after them as they went by. Betwar as he approached looked down, and again willed his feet into a shuffle—it was a small, useless gesture. Better to acquiesce. He looked up, and met their composite gaze. It held triumph. He passed.

They continued, circling back to the Doll. The reeds stopped. The Doll loomed.

4

Now there was a commotion at the far side of the Square, and the lesser scholars came walking with tapers towards them directly across it, forcing a passage between the people, who scrambled back as well as they could. The scholars then lit the lamps at the foot of the Doll, moving in some confusion and talking among themselves; one pair went part way back, motioning angrily at the people, who had again begun to settle in their vacated places, to keep clear. Another pair hurried back after the first. Waving their arms, they strode up and down the narrower and now somewhat crooked pathway. It threaded precariously between the impatient people, from the feet of the Doll, where the lit lamps made a space of clear ground, to the vat at the other end. Betwar saw the Azur step forward across the vat and be pulled back with, it seemed, some irritation, by the Ng. His lips curled.

The fact that the Doll of Atwar faced northeast, and stood well to the north side of the Square, did not help to make these formalities more sensible, symmetrical or inevitable, he noticed with some satisfaction. Perhaps Moonfill and the Eating and other, lesser ceremonies, which took place here at the Doll's feet, achieved a degree of seriousness. Yet this most elaborate and untried one—even without the antics of the Azur, it would be lucky if it were carried through without foolishness and accident. And the Doll overhead—Atwar as ever looked very unpleased, with his back turned on most of the throng, and on the Ng and their fancy curtain, lamps and buildings.

The Ng now glided forward across the Square, followed closely by the Azur—and moving rather more swiftly than they would have liked, Betwar suspected, for fear of having their gown trod upon—and all eyes were turned towards the Doll. There was more confused, low talk and some repositioning among the scholars, and stopping of the Azur from doing anything prematurely; but they were finally ready, and stood importantly, holding various of the descending strings. Then the stern Ng and the volatile Azur, who grasped bright red, obviously new strings, pulled at them with a nearly simultaneous flourish, and from the great shoulders overhead the mass of bunched, red stuff that had covered them was released and fell airily downwards—while the noise and movements of the crowd stopped like a held breath. As it fell the stuff had caught against the sufur carcass and the Ng pulled again: it slid loose, but caught again farther down, on the Doll's penis. And even when it had otherwise fallen completely, it hung from that paler member like a door around a face peering, with the Azur prancing about uselessly below and the Ng, flustered, jerking at the cloth and unable to free it.

Betwar and some others laughed, but the people behind the Doll could not interpret the sound and immediately began to shout—and suddenly all the people were shouting in unison—"*Atwar walks! Atwar walks!*" over and over.

And the Doll took a step.

5

It was later, towards morning. Betwar and his children knelt before the vat at the end of the Square. The vat was wide and low, and filled with clay, and around it lay knives, and clean watercloths folded inside their bowls. Betwar's shirt had been pulled down to his waist, and the Ng were cutting off his hair.

They stood behind him, and he felt the sleek touch of their dress, and occasionally the touch of their body through it, against his bare skin, and the rasp of the knife. Scholars took the hair from them strand by strand, and gave it to his children, braiding it into theirs, which had been unknotted and hung sorrowfully down about their lowered heads. He saw in the lamplight that it did not blend—his was coarser even than Tared's, and there was gray in it. He sensed rather than heard the presence of the waiting crowd at his back. None spoke aloud, but he heard whispers and coughs, and more than one baby-voice crying.

The knife scraped, and the short scalp-hair fell over his arms and shoulders, and some into the whitish clay, where it lay in a drift. The Ng now reached across his shoulders, their knives rasping on his chest, the points curling close around his nipples. He could feel their body against him, their little, hardened penis—he was sure of it—pressed into the small of his back, that he winced from, shuddering. They stood up and squeezed water over him and again he shuddered.

"Hair of my head, *what do I possess other than the thing you have given?*"[44] intoned the Ng, together, straightening upright. Betwar repeated it dully after them.

"What do I possess other than the thing you have given?"

They scraped and scoured him with the flat of their knives, which his body found almost intolerable, and flung hair and cells and dirt into the vat. The edges of his eyes also, they invaded with their narrow fingers, and the corners of his mouth, tipping back his bald head with one hand and with the other coaxing. They walked around in front of him to the vat, and wiped their fingers over it. *"What do I possess, what do I possess, other than the thing you have given?"*

Then they scraped the dry skin off the soles of his feet, and the earth from under his nails and between his toes and fingers. In the end he was without thought. The Ng had gone around behind the vat and squatted, their arms resting along its rim. He stared back at their one-face across it, tired past caring even to resist the power of their look. He shivered in the dawn wind that dried his shoulders and head, and felt his lightness and nakedness. "Spit of my tongue, hair of my upper lip, *what do I possess other than the thing you have given?"*

A movement made him pull his eyes from the Ng, and he saw the dirty Azur, squatting beyond them, grinning at him among the impassive scholars. The Azur Twel patted his own pate and his brother's and nodded sagely. How crazy they are! he thought. They are the only ones here who are as I am, we are well crazed, I and my father-friends! He felt no shame in front of the great throng, when the Ng motioned him to stand and face them. He feared only that his children would pity him. But when he glanced at them, he saw only sorrow. Ask met his eyes, and smiled, and took his brother's hand, and Saska smiled at him also, wanly. Ard looked too tearful to see him clearly, but Tared's face had a stern, closed look, as if she were willing him a share of her own childish pride.

He saw them dressed anew in garments none of them had ever seen, the three blue, but Saska's white with a blue slash over his heart, because he had begged this of the Ng when they took away his old dress. There were tucked pockets on the head-sleeves; and the blue was of such a sweetness that it took away the breath: the sky was not more clear. And then they were made to kneel at the vat and were painted with their father's dirty clay—wide, whitish streaks from brow to chin, over and over by the Ng's dark dipping finger.

As they traced, the Ng said *"This is better food, and more necessary water"*—it was in remembrance, because there had been bound food and water to Atwar when he went away.

Then the three clean blue dolls, and Saska's somewhat repaired one, were passed to the Azur to press into their pockets, which the old men did gleefully; Betwar watched them muttering and puffing over his children with their sweetish-sour mouths.

The Moon was near setting now, its barrens reddish as it drew down into the dust-haze past the city, its seeded plains purple and blurred. The night was far spent.

Then the players of reeds came pushing through the midst, and the Children of Atwar were carried for the last time around his Doll. Betwar, naked, was made to walk behind them among the scholars. This time, the people would not stay still but got up and rushed towards them to follow them, so that the Square became a swirling and circling mass. Many a lamp was trodden on and extinguished, and one flared as it caught a careless quarriers' dress: there was a whoosh of brightness but they made no sound—this was the only hurt in that night; their name was Tseth of Pevek and they died later of their burns.

The curtain was drawn down behind the blue strands, and the blue-clad Children of Atwar, stepping over its gathered mass, passed between the airy lines at dawn as through a waterfall. Betwar stayed behind, near the overturned vat among the scattered cloths and bowls. He put on his shirt and sat down beside the Azur who, oblivious of the noise and commotion, had curled up and gone to sleep there on the ground. But he was soon fetched by the Ng and some others into the buildings, so that he would not harm himself at this time, and he fell asleep among them. Many lights had been lit in the maze of rooms, and Ard and Tared were separated from their brothers.

Outside, the low sun streamed across the empty Square, picking out a kicked bowl, ashes, a rag and a dirty water-cloth, two little dolls torn and abandoned. It picked out all the puckerings and mendings on the right side of the great Doll, that was leaning strangely forward over its extended leg. The leg seemed to be shorter, bunched together. The Fu-en people, dispersing, looked at it askance—and strangers, following them down into the streets to find shade in which to sleep, glanced back over their shoulders. But some sat down at the edge of the Square and waited.

Nine

Inasmuch as this present world is our prison, the
ruining of prisons is surely a cause for joy.
Which is the road by which I came? I would
return, for it likes me not here.

1

Tared and Ard were carried farther in, to separate
rooms, by separate corridors of ever darkening, red-
dening house-cloth that brushed against their faces. At
first, Tared could see the shadows of Ard and the
people carrying her, over to her left, and then, as she
was brought past even darker hangings, she could not
see them any more.

In that last, inner room the cloth was the darkest
Tared had ever seen; even the earth floor was covered
with it, and the morning sunlight scarcely penetrated.
Her attendants laid her in a low, stiff sling that was so
deeply dyed it was nearly black, and went away from
her.

It was very still. Strain as she might with her ears
and eyes, she could make out no people near her. She
slept despite herself, and when she fought free of her
dreams and came suddenly and alertly awake, the sun
had moved; an oval pool of the bloodiest light lay on the

roof close over her head—it was almost in itself a darkness. The door was pushed up then, and Betwar entered.

His vague, shaven head and face moved forward, smaller, moonlike, almost unrecognizable. She could not read his expression in its new strangeness and in the gloom. He sat down carefully on the edge of the sling with his feet on the floor, and turned deliberately toward her.

"Tared, you know why I am here, and why they have brought you and Ard here into these secret places." He spoke very quietly.

"Yes—for Atwar."

As she spoke, Tared pressed her hands into the sling and sat up awkwardly. She began to undo the blue dress, which was half caught under her pallid, unbound legs. Immediately he grasped her by the arms.

"Do not, Tared."

"I must." She squirmed from him, dragging at the cloth, her head down and her face hidden in its sleeve. A strand of the fiercely tied hair had as usual come loose and hung unknotted on her shoulder, with his own hair meshed in it and unravelling. He caught at her arms more tightly and at last, in his grip, she stopped trying, and lifted a hand to her mouth in a gesture so innocent, so familiar that he almost gasped. She stared at him in the darkness. Her lips were parted, like an absence.

"I must, you must." He had relaxed his grasp and she slipped suddenly free of him, and pulled the head-sleeve down under her small, downy breasts, and pushed her face at him and tried to kiss his mouth. But he turned aside, and held her again, farther from him.

"Little Tared, do not. *Do not*—" for she had reached to touch him. The tears he had been unable to weep into the clay now burst from his eyes. His daughter was struggling towards him, whispering and whispering, her voice fast and rote and almost a whistle. "They told us you would perhaps be afraid, and not agree, and forget Atwar, that this you must give him. You must remember Atwar. You must remember him. *What do you possess other than the thing you have given?*" Again she reached out.

"Do not raise your voice." He covered her mouth with his hand. "They have told you much that I have not corrected; I have allowed them to teach you many foolish things. But this last—ah, you could not do other than listen to their words, I know. But now you must listen to mine." Her voice had stilled now, and she was motionless, but tensed as a bent stem and he did not trust her yet and held her. He went on:

"Tared, Atwar is not a god, that the seemly ways of men and women are upturned for his sake. He is a man like me, and if he could ask any thing of us, do you think it would be this?"

Carefully he drew his hand away from her mouth, watching her earnestly. "Tared, have you heard me?"

She had drawn back a little and her hands had fallen into her lap. "The Ng did not—however—insist about the red dresses," she said finally, in a little, childish voice.

He sighed and smiled. "No. Because I am your father, and it is my authority in the end. I have not forgotten Atwar—sometimes I think I am the only one who remembers him. Ah, the spirit of the world is turned inside out like the skin of a snake, nothing is right or has been right, since he went away."

"You tell us so often, nothing is right—when nothing is right then everything is right," she said, but doubtfully.

"Then, even right is unright. Do not touch me so

again, you are breaking my heart. There is more love between us than this."

He turned her away and drew her carefully in against him, holding her wrists crossed tight against her little chest, that trembled as fragile as Saska's asafir when the boy held them. They remained some moments in silence; as he waited, her breath steadied a little.

"Do you know, my Tared," he said gently at last, "that you are much like our-mother Tasman, now?— do you know that she was very young when she bore us, no more than twelve years old? And in those years at Siya in the clearing, when Atwar and I were unweaned, she and our-fathers played with us, milk-play—you were weaned early, all of you, because of what happened to your-mothers. Yet when the Linh lived, we played with you also, such touchings, and strokings— tongues, hands—how you glowed in all your forms, you and little Ard, how you arched and glowed! and threw yourselves joyously against your-mothers' breasts!"

"I do not remember."

"No, and that is why you cannot remember now, or understand, how to separate the touch of your father from the touch of other men."

She wept. "I do know it! It was the Ng—they said, they said—"

He rocked her. "I know what they said. It was not your fault, or any fault in you. The Ng invented these rooms, as they invented what they desired to happen, cunning images, violations—Do you remember our-fathers, the Sorud? I would have wished, that you remembered them," he went on, talking low and comfortingly.

"No—"

"Yet I set you and Ard before them as they were

dying, to bond into you the image of their faces—theirs were the first you looked into, and Ard squinted, and slept but you stared! It was just after you were born."

Tared stammered. "Their eyes—were they blind?"

"Why do you ask that? You know the Tale. Twar Sorud my Fadar was blind from before I was born. But he regained his sight in Fu-en; he was given the eye of his brother." Betwar sighed, and smiled a little. "They looked ever strange, from then on, seeing each with one eye—and the other eye, the inward one, shut and sunken. Well, if you cannot remember, ask Atwar when you see him, he will tell you they were good men."

"But, I do remember them," said Tared slowly in a new voice, that was soft and wondering. "For I have dreamed of them all my life, but I did not know it." She asked, doubtfully, "Were they always good and kind, as you are, Fadar?"

"More kind than me, or any who live now," he answered somewhat bitterly. "This is no good place any more, so how can any be good in it?

"And the Ng, twisting their one-face and their red darkness like a knife into my heart! To do thus, and thus for Atwar, they said—and believed it—how they believe it, I cannot understand! But I knew even then I would not obey them, yet would pretend to agree, so they would not otherwise interfere with you. They required that I should give over to you everything, everything I had, to give to Atwar—not just my hair and the earth under my feet, but my semen also, the children of my children.

"But you are my children, not Atwar's, you are my gift and this gift is enough—more than enough—He knows nothing of any more, and must not."

Tared sighed. "Fadar—we will never tell him! But I will speak to him of the Sorud, and tell him I remember them well, and am not afraid of them any more. But

Atwar—we are to be bonded to him."

"*God-bonded*—ah, that is what they have taught you,
but apart from the Ng they scarcely believe themselves
that he lives, who have conjured up this ugly snake-tale
for us to enter, this overturned imagining! This, they
have taught you, fair as you are!" He paused, and went
on more gently. "Their teaching cannot follow you so
far, Tared, it will fall away, as dirt from a thrown stone
falls back from its trajectory. Remember Saska's dream
of the new city where everything is wiped away? May
it be so for you there, and not just in walking!"

Then they smiled, and kissed each other quietly, and
spoke secretly of how they would deceive the scholars.
Betwar stayed a little longer with her and talked with
her of the caged asafir, and they planned and argued
lightly about how the Sanev could perhaps get them
into their pockets and this be kept from the Ng also, and
from everyone except the Azur, and they laughed
softly about the Azur—"who would be the best keepers
of the secret, telling it aloud and none believing them!"

"Nevi has a plan," said Tared, "Otherwise, you
would have heard Saska complaining, endlessly."

After that, Betwar embraced her tenderly and left
her, and went to Ard.

2

The water lay hard against the barrier, and at their feet
the tile was already wet, when the Children of Atwar
took leave of the triumphant, foolish Ng, whom they
had deceived, and of their friends and their father. The
Sanev were there close to them, and the Siri with babies
at their breasts, and the Azur with twinkling eyes—
these old twins had even cleaned themselves up for the
occasion, and braided their napehair, and allowed

themselves to accept a washed dress. Their tattered face-board was gone but they wore no new one, and their eyes were benign.

There was no ceremony, for that was not the way of Atwar, but the bay behind them was crowded with scholars, and as they were set down at the barrier a silence fell, so that the sound of dripping water could be heard from overhead.

They were numbed with excitement and apprehension, and gazed through the glass tremblingly, for the cars were not as they had imagined them, even though Betwar had said, "They are like trees." Saska kept turning back, and the Sanev came close behind him and whispered, "not yet, till the last"—for they had the living asafir hidden inside their sleeve, and their hands over them. But a fourth they had not found.

It was day, and daylight fell through the water and illuminated the cars, that seemed to reach up like stems budding. This glass barrier would be pierced for the children to reach the cars, then shattered by their trajectory. Yet, before that the water, flooding briefly through the pierced barrier, would all be drawn off and burned away. For the watchers there would be time to escape upward into Book and the city, but the bay and barrier and basin would not survive the thrust of the launching—the walls had been too hurriedly pushed into place—the Sorud would have taken greater care, but the scholars forsaw only the journey—nothing would remain of all this, after the cars were gone; it would be collapsed forever under the sea.

Already the water in the basin shuddered with a new, heavy hum; and the barrier trembled—the machines were awakening to the pulse of their strange hearts. So that the water had begun to warm up and diminish: the light of clear air was filling the upper part of the basin, and the intricate upper branches of the cars were emerging from their long water-burial, glistening and steaming.

Betwar moved a little back, and stood beside the Ng; they did not matter to him any more, or their machinations. He mattered no more to them either. He had already seen, in their look and in that of the others, that they believed he would choose death, and thus they would be rid of him and what they thought he had done.

Somehow, he did not know how, it had worked; his daughters had accomplished the deception. Who had then examined them? Had the Siri, and not told? Had the Ng themselves? so intricate and sexual in their minds, yet who had never bonded, whose body was caught in immaturity and a deathlike chastity so ignorant it caused them to be misled? Could their eyes and hands have lied to them for the wanting of it? He glanced at the Siri, who stood near him, but they would not look at him. Their eyes were withdrawn—it was not they, who had helped then in the deception, he was sure from their downlook they did not know of it—now with the Qam close by, leaning over their infants, they were retreating up the ramp. They too believed what did not correspond, and it was well. Somehow, this had been achieved.

Still the Sanev stayed, crouching with their arms around his children: he saw Ard turn and put her face into their throat, then lift it to Nevi's kiss. Adult Ard! Unlike Tared, she had required no argument; she had first looked up at him in passive terror and despair, and then heard his quickly whispered reassurance with a joyous burst of tears. Watching her now, Betwar decided that this daughter's body had not forgotten the ardent milk-play at her mothers' breasts.

When the water was low enough, scholars came

forward carrying lamps, and carefully unsealed the glass at the barrier with fire. It hissed out with the rush of water, and they waded hurriedly back to the ramp, but the Sanev stayed, standing now chest-deep and then deeper with his swimming children, talking with them hurriedly as the water flooded into the bay. Betwar saw them give Ask a little airy bag, that they had concealed in their sleeve, and Ask said something to them, smiling, and turned with it, pushing it before him as he swam through after the others. He saw their four dark heads—then the Sanev threw themselves back to him and he reached out to catch their hands. Already the water touched his neck; there was a slick of blackish oil on it and it smelled sharp and salt. He and the Sanev stumbled and waded up the ramp, backwards, clinging to each other, straining to see the children's heads past the gap where the glass had been burnt away. His leg scraped painfully against one of the instruments, and his own blood ran out into the water. But he saw also on the submerged surface one small, steady light—it was a promise.

Now they must go up quickly into the bay, back to the surface where the brief flood would not reach them, back to the Great Book and the city. Betwar walked with his arm over the Sanev shoulders. Ahead of them were the voices of the others. But for a little time they could still hear Saska's childish voice as well, calling out excitedly behind them, and then its echo, diminishing.

3

In childhood Betwar had witnessed Atwar's departing; and now again he was that witness, earthbound and helpless in all his longing. From the southern hill of the city he heard the prolonged explosions and saw, one after the other, three bursts of fire rise from the offshore Sheath and vanish into the bright day. Beneath them, in lurid and diminishing light, the promontory seemed to swallow itself, coughing and roaring, the whole farthest familiar outline sinking inward in a great gush of steam. One wave hurled outward, its edges fiery, and pounded the shore; there was a crackle of house-stems as the low buildings took its impact and were sucked outward, people pushed to climb higher though they were above the reach of it.

Three only, though they waited for the fourth long after there was any hope that it would follow. The scholars, counting and calculating, would determine whether it was the first that had failed, or the last. Tared or Saska? Ah—the screens would tell it soon enough, if they could not. He was not sure how he could bear to be told.

He saw the Sanev weeping near him, hard, adult sobs, but he did not go to them. People were still standing and staring at the Sheath as if unable to move. He passed up the street, and only the Azur called after him, and came shuffling forward, their arms outstretched in some kind of comfort or supplication, but he could not meet their eyes. There is nothing here any more, he thought. Could I have prevented, could I have learned of it, I could have kept at least Tared or Saska— Tared who would not or Saska who dreamed, who perhaps—*Grief raves into anger like a hurt snake, who turns on its own body and snaps at its wounds;*[45] he knew this—he would be clean in grief though it was worse—

rage did not correspond, it was deceptive and too easy. Ah, he would go into grief as into the darkest of houses! How much easier to welcome death now, how much easier that anger—death for the Ng as well, an odd embracement—ah, how much more difficult to walk forward into this house of utter grief.

He entered his door to emptiness, and slowly as if he were blind he touched the mats, and the walls and the inner door. His hands brushed across the known stems, the hollows where the children had picked out pebbles, the drooping roof-cloth with its dirty scatter of leaves. His eyes saw every familiar mark and shadow yet it was by touch he said them farewell—the new room hardly occupied with its strange curving wall, and the mats and dresses so carefully folded by Tared against their return (for the children, like Atwar, were allowed leave-taking). In the main room he stooped over the bowls in their tilted stack, the loose-folded drinking cloths in and beside them. His feet touched the well-known dips in the uneven earth floor; there was the trace—he knelt and pushed aside sleeping cloths and touched the whole length of the smooth metal, shiny with the play and polish of his children's growing hands. He stood up: there was the dirty wall-pocket; he touched it tenderly, then reached in and brought out the Linh arrows, and closed them into his left hand. Saska's proud-pit was empty, but under it at his feet lay a sufur feather: gently he lifted it, and straightened it with his tongue; it had a taste of salt and Saska. He took it as well.

He walked above the canal to the turning. The Ludh had just returned, and were stooping into their door.

"You are going from-us," their Twel said, simply and expressionlessly.

Betwar looked briefly into their faces. Then he

reached down to them, and put a Linh arrow into each of their hands.

"Do not listen to any Tale they will make," he said, gazing with love at their heavy, indifferent-seeming faces. Ah, how his heart clenched and eased as he saw their look clear in a rare softening of comprehension, and the Twel's, then the Twar's, change and crinkle from openness into satisfied complicity. So will they become as old women—wise after all, he thought.

"*If women are refused madder/ They will crush hibiscus*,"[46] quoted the Twel Ludh suddenly, her Twar joining in on the last words. The proverb made no sense to him, yet in their mouths it comforted him.

He mounted to the Square, where a few people, one pair light-haired, were milling about preparing to leave. Past them the curtain hung askew and the rooms behind it were half-dismantled; he saw some city twins carrying off an armful of cloth and children following them trailing one of the blue bands. Somewhere voices were raised in plaint, but there was no gathering of folk, the scholars would be in Book, and the people, if they cared, waiting in front of the Great Book to hear their words of appeasement or explanation. What he had felt before this, his life, seemed now like a jittering—then, he had thought he had grieved and known grief, and had in truth known nothing.

He looked his last on the Doll of Atwar. Ah—how he had despised and pitied it after all! yet it seemed drained of even that consequence now, in the plain light of day. "And if Atwar is ever gone from me, and is ever with me in the world," he thought, "no where and every where, then he is here-and-not-here also, no less and no more."

The Doll had slipped farther forward, and leaned

almost precariously over the nearest house; the great face with its pulled scowl squinted searchingly almost straight down. One eyelid had fallen shut. Atwar winked. He would lunge soon at the city and break their roofs, if the scholars did not come and right him. Stooping for a moment his living brother pressed his mouth against the nearest of the bulging, dusty toes. Then he jumped up, threw his sleeve over his head, and walked over towards the travellers.

Just as he crossed the Square, a rushing sound filled the air. He stared upward as it came closer, and a rushing shadow hid the sun. It was the asafir heading south.

The End

Tales and Songs

The Tale of Tasman[1]

The Tale of Tasman exists in several versions. This is "the Forty", the earliest and simplest, and was chanted in the *Månskead* (solar eclipse) ceremony. Other longer and more fantastical versions were sung in the streets.

Tal Tasman Ottahåndos —"The Forty"

1

Hiintid Utdod triv in Wo,
Fro fro thom frodik Mån.
Fromehim u tilvardehim gå
Efter Tretusindår for boorn
Nermeer Werd Werdas
Gathart stemt sprekendas.

The Outdead lived once on the World,
they seeded the Moon,
they travelled to and fro,
so that in three thousand years
closer to the Earth, two worlds,
in harmony, joined in conversation.

2

A thom Stamfolk snoglikos
Huvdalen småtroldikos
Wit in Skep u fel in Sind
Lerthom Alen Harm betwan.

They were a race like snakes
and had but one head, small as trolls they were
clever in craft but blind in mind
loneliness taught them to hate each other.

3

Katastrofas thom så
Werd smalt over Wo,
Hedh Hedh Werdlift ebrim
Hedh in Havor utbrand ehim.
Alen Liv in Hojwerdas
Ringt Werd Skeith in kerkerik Obsus.

Disaster followed disaster,
the world melted across their cities
great heat filled the World's air
the seas burned off in those days
only at the poles was it possible to live
the Earth girded by a sheath of terrible obsidian.

4

Than for fa os utan Wud
Fel Utdod start for hiin Bud
Gathart somlikos thom så
Janus u al thama små,
Had u såros thi vi liv
Hog u somlik, thom wud rev

Os from Liv evan na kan.
Inin Stamtal alen Twan
Dodbevor thom irst began
Kvinnos kvinnas Manas Man.

The Outdead fathered us against their will
they stared at that summons
they saw, conjoined as is seemly
Janus and all their children
they hated and hurt us because we lived
tall and seemly, they wanted to tear us
from life but they could not.
In one generation twins only.
They died as we first began
women (replaced by) twin women, twin men (replaced) men.

5

Evan sharmos? Na na harmos.
Foros Al skept, ekik u fageros
For Månfald hinder.
Thom os rinder.
In Dod skamwendt
Lifr for stemt
Vora Spar Esparar in Tro.
Tasman in frodik Tid ethoma Fro.

No, they did not hate us.
For us (they left) all they had shaped, useful and
beautiful,
against Moonfall.
They remembered us.
Dying, their hearts repented,
they ensured us salvation in trust.
Even Tasman was their seed, (to appear) in ripeness
of time.

6

Blandos Tasman Thiindag
Eboornt in Månfald utan Glay
Wend rund Sol Tretusindår
Utdodlik a felboornt evar.
Huvud een u hutht in Wald
Håndas fodas grim u bald
Hutht thi blandos thom wud glaylikos
Slak hiin Bodhi in Utid dod fromos.

Then among us Tasman in the present days
born during Moonfall without joy
after three thousand years
born like the Outdead, ah malformed she was.
One-headed, hidden in the wood
hands and feet sad and bald
there were those among us who would gladly
have (untimely) killed that body.

7

In Lofot Månfald Mar fulkomendas
Iningå Pyt for boorna Utansindas.
Felboornt thaytro nathay wud holdehir
Evan felstemt, Tasman Esparar.

In Lofot in Moonfall impeccable mothers
entered the pit pool to bear, the twinless,
a bad birth, they believed, and desired not to keep
her,
but they were wrong, (she was) Tasman Redeemer.

8

Tasman na twant u Klarglay utan
List from Folkesin eensprokt alen
Felboornt u thay utan Wit,
Thay så ehir u greet.
Thi Sindas list Gaev,
Thaytro wud brandehir
Askmak for standehir
Evan in Lofot thay ladehir liv.

Tasman untwinned, born without laughter,
last of her race, one-voiced,
malformed and they without understanding,
they saw her and wept.
The less brave would have burnt her
make her into ashes to stop her
but in Lofot they let her live.

9

Her blandos thom u thom rinderu
Månfald u wabhelik Werd dragendu
From Månvind. Talaras kam
Til Tasman thay wit ehir Nam.
From Stembok Fu-en thay Breevehir bring,
Thaytro for him hinder in fel Faldesin.

There are those among us who remember Moonfall,
how the earth was pushed like waves
by the Moon's wind; when messengers came
for Tasman, they knew her name.
From the True-Book in Fu-en they brought her letters
they believed (she could) prevent his (the Moon's)
fall.

10

Lang bevor Stormflodas
Fram mild Namaras
Sorud ehir from Lofot bar
Efter tulv Kåmos
Makt ehir Maderlist
Bekam for Tasman ehir Pasaras u Far.

Long before the floods
Sorud the mild Namers
carried her away from Lofot,
after twelve Darkenings
made her motherless
they became her fathers and guardians.

11

Se Say in ehir Voksanwo
Felrod gav for ladehir fro
Utfrandt In Skinwant camfelik
For Sorud thay wit ehir liklik
A wud
Ehir rid
Kortbondas fro forhindert Bud.

Look how the Say in Tasman's room
gave her false Root; so she would conceive
for they were not her friends,
to make mischief in jealousy, knowing Sorud loved
her,
ah then they (the Sorud) would want to abandon her,
for to make the short-bonded pregnant is forbidden.

12

Sorud twatid Moscvard gå
Wer wer thama Reksan in Dustgoldwo
Sogefter Ordar for standa Mån
Hutht in Skeith wohiin began.
Sandstorm makt Twar Sorud blind
Kåm hoydrag Obard sin vaker Sind.
Sid Gredil Hevitgredilstam.
Thay fand Dodos, hid thoma Nam.

Twice towards Mosc Sorud went,
very hard their journey in the dust-desert,
seeking directions to prevent Moonfall,
hidden in the Sheath where they were planned.
A sandstorm blinded Sorud Twar,
Darkness closed the threshold of his beautiful mind.
The ruin held only skeletons.
They found the dead there, these are their names.

13

(a list of the names of those who perished at Mosc)

14

A skindwan in Skeith lik Smådrokstamos
Tidwatardragt u drokt in Strandos.
Thom brandt ne Nojd thom brend
A utan Ard ne ardthom kan
Een alen Vind
for ebolr Plint
U thoma Ask
In Liftob edht.

Ah their shrivelled bodies like dry stems
dragged about by tides and dried up on the beaches.
They were burnt, no need to burn them,
without earth, no way to bury them,
only the wind to play their lament
and their ashes eaten by the air's mouth.

15

Månvind nu nerthom ekam
Hard Ard watarlik bekam
Stemskum slak flad Lofot inland
Flodas flodas overhim stand
Fjelos start for findthom Eyos
U dodfald Dalos.

The Moon's wind neared,
the solid earth became as water
a surf of stones broke on level Lofot,
powerful floods covered it.
Mountains were surprised to find themselves small
islands,
vales perished.

16

Tasman u Menesk in Valkendwo
From flad Lofot folgehir u gå
Lofot Hemhir behinehir feld
Ostvardin valk for Oldlov opfild.

She came with the people, in the Walking City,
they followed her from level Lofot,
it perished behind her, her home land,
eastward walking to fulfil the ancient promises.

17

Sorud mildas Manas Manas
Husbond Tasman esin Pasaras
Sansindas fa thay u tham fram
Likthama Mar Avskel thama Nam
Mundasnam Atwar u Betwar
Ran bevorthom inin Pechor.

The gentle Sorud were great men,
they were her house-bonded, and her protectors,
fathered her small sons and guided them,
like their mother, "Separated" was their name
we call them Atwar and Betwar,
Running before them into Pechor.

18

A rinder Liv boornt liftendas
Irst from Manga in Obard nekendas,
Got u glay, a wud tham huth.
Dod in Dirth.
A hiin grim Marsksump than
Lang u lang,
Utan Sang
Emakt tham smal u wan.

Alas remember the Liv born living
after many times refusing (life) at the threshold
well-born and bonny, ah, would they were hid.
They died in Dearth.
Alas the grim marshlake
gradually, with no (memorial) song
made them thin and sick.

19

Tham u al hiin Inbring Småa
A from sot sot Inbring dodos Al
Dodbrandt under Splintstamos
Sot sot Ask in vora Mundos.
Een Stam
Na bar Nam
Hid thom namt thoma kirtl Namos.

Them and all that harvest of newborns
alas all that sweet harvest
cremated under the stripped stems
in our mouths their sweet, sweet ash.
One generation did not (live to) carry their names,
Hear them named with their short-lived names.

20

(a list of the named infants, including the Liv, who
perished in Dearth)

21

Huvl Tasman u from Livask val
Lift-hevitstamas skoort u smal
Tham ebar ehin in Armrodas
Tham eber ehin betwan Werdas
Wohiin Tasman, erinderi
Wohiin Tasman, eberendi.

Tasman mourning took from the ashes
two ribs, scorched and narrow,
se she wore ever around her arms
she wears everywhere, wherever she is,
ring them, remembering.

22

Semer sogefter ehir, Frandas from Små
Saywo skiklikas iningå
Say skinhold Sorudgav in Camfel
Semer spar fromtham u thama Skamfel.

Semer sought after Tasman, friend from her childhood,
he entered the house of the Say courteously,
they had kept her gift from the Sorud,
taken in mischief, but Semer escaped them and their
shame.

23

(*Nakd Semersang*)—Naked Semer Song

Semer Oldpasaras slak
Thi wud standtham in Bok
Nakd skinskelvikas in Sand
Dagard skoort tham Fodas brand
Over Nakdhet ljusendos
Hår sonsomerblomlikos
Fan in Twelhånd
Stembok in Tweltandh
Dagard skoort tham Fodas brand.

Semer defeated the ancient keepers
in (Lenh) Book who wanted to stop them
and ran crazed over the sand
burning earth of daylight
daylight scorched them, burnt their feet
over their nakedness
hair (spread) like two sunflowers brightly

True-Book between Twel's teeth
a knife in Twel's hand.

24

Evan Stormflodas Semer spar
Semer mak Raft from Meneskhår
Lad Flog tham tilvard Ost e-ber
Svem indland
In Watarrand.
In Pechor thay Tasman ner
Gav Stembok Lins u Raft ehir.

Only the Semer escaped the (two) floods, swimming,
they made a raft of human hair,
rode the flood into the east,
swam inland in the water-courses.
At Pechor they joined Tasman,
gave her the raft, and True Book of the Disk.

25

Under Fjel Narod Fjel Fjel
Got u glay ran Avskel
Huth thay tham for folga Semer
For Twel Skam thay wud tham gathar.
Betwan Stamos over Gård
under Ardfald wer u hard
Inin Smalval wern from slak
Thar er Fara, Snog in Vak.

At Narod greatest mountain
the Avskel ran gleefully,
hid themselves, to follow the Semer,
for Twel's sake they wanted to join them.
Between trees and through farms,

under the earthfall dense and hard,
into the defile, wearied by (its) blows,
there was the hazard, snake ever wakeful.

26

Thar efand Snog tham, in Vak sindwitik
Ob Oy under Gruvsmat bejglik.
Eslak for opfildi Oldlav grim
Eval Atwar, 'slak kerkerik, ekrubehim.

There the Snake found them, waiting with intelligence
its eye opening baleful from its bed of gravel.
It struck to fulfil the harsh, ancient promise,
it chose Atwar, it struck terribly, it crippled him.

27

Thi lovt mut Semer Twar
Fand Lins in Yar
Fram hiin sin Broder Sind
Varsl Menesk, stikik varsind
A al Werdskelv listbevor
Flog from Oyas irstos Tår.

Mute Semer Twar as was promised
found the Disk in Yar, leading his brother,
warning the people, resolute.
Ah, just before every earthquake
out of his eyes flowed the first tears.

28

Began thom red Lins from Sand
Skoort Oyskindlik blind from Brand

Svart u sandbrandt
Forhuvd nu svart-tandth
Makt for Mån Wendglas klar u stemt
Thi in Lins esin Smil glimt

They began clearing the Disk from sand,
scratched like an eye blinded by fire
black and sand-burnt
a newly black-teethed face
making for the Moon a mirror clear and plain
so in its lens his (adult) smile could be seen.

29

In Fu-en red thom Tasman
For hiin nojdik Reksan
Werd eskelv in Ker u så
Ner hin estand in hiin Wo
A hoy estand Havor
For Fu-en dodfaldover.

In Fu-en they prepared Tasman
for the necessary journey,
the earth shook in fear when she stood in that city,
the sea stood up and fell on Fu-en to destroy it.

30

Helt in Fu-en Sorud Twar
Glim fager Ljus in Twelhuvd klar
Halvsikt u nemeer blind
For Broder Oyskind
Thiin Frandgav Frand betwan
Ogas in Mannas Man.

In Fu-en blind Twar Sorud was healed
beautiful light he saw in his brother's face
he was blind till his Twel gave him half his sight,
this is friendship, two eyes in two men (as) one.

31

Prudh Helaras wud ingå
For mak want Atwar gro
Hog lik al athar Man
In thoma Sind
Thom him utbind
A utwendt bevor thay kan
Helaras Blindhet,
Blind bevor Vakerhet.

Proud the healers,
they would have caused Atwar to grow
as tall as other men,
and in their minds
(already) unbound him,
ah he was gone before they could,
healers of blindness,
blind to his beauty.

32

Red nu Tasman
Tilvardin Mån Reksan
U Ordaras in Hånd
For maki ehim stil u Frand.
In Forhuvud tham mal
Vaker vaker Skel
Thay redehir
Al hevit hevit Leer.

Tasman was readied to journey into the Moon,
to take the directions, to calm and befriend him.
They painted her face with a beautiful parting,
with white clay they prepared her.

33

Than bring Betwar
Leer in Fingar
Glay for emali Broder Skel
From Kvinnas forhindert
Thay na wit
Wyp thay sin vaker Forhuvd sval.

Then Betwar took the clay on his finger
In play, to paint a parting on his brother,
Women prevented him, they were without understanding.
They washed the clay from his beautiful face.

34

Semer hevitas huvlendas
Utgå himlikas
Twel wud hugt sin felmut Twar
Thi alen for Grund Grund tham sår
Evan na kan.
Thiin Gav na triv.
Ne ne tha nekan giva
Liv for thama Frand.

White Semer mourning went out secretly
Twel desired mute Twar severed from their body
(to be) alone for a great purpose he would wound them,
but he was unable.

This gift cannot succeed.
It is never, it is never
You can give your life for your friend.

35

A nu Tasman redt bevor
Reksan a nekan iningå Car
A ehin meer hog meer somlik
From Utdod grimos kortfodlik.

Ah, now Tasman, ready to journey,
ah, she cannot enter the car,
alas she is too tall and seemly,
not like the Outdead, who were short-legged.

36

Alen Atwar ekrubt ekan
Smal from Snog neendmak han
In Armrod Fodrodas for bar
Hastik band thom Edh Watar
In esin kerlist Hånd
Smar thom Månfaldstand.
Blandos thom u thom him så
Klarglay klarglay iningå
In Brand Brand fromos revt
In Bristbrand fromos dragt.

Only crippled Atwar could enter,
thin from the snake with no farewell,
to carry on his arms and thighs
they quickly bound food and water,
inside his fearless hand
they wrote (how to) stop Moonfall.
Those (still) among us saw him

enter (the car)laughing aloud,
in a great fire he was torn from us
in explosion he was propelled away from us.

37

Na kan egå eran in Mån.
Evan for Ordlov endmak eran
Over Månard utan Start
Ordaros in Baldhånd smart
Efald een u eran.
In Mån ne Skamfel alen kan,
Fald een u ran.
Fald een u ran.

He could not walk, but he ran on the Moon.
Running, he fulfilled the promise,
over the Moon's sward without hesitation
the directions hurt his hairless palm
he fell once and ran.
In the Moon (being able to be) alone is no shame:
he fell once and ran.
He fell once and ran.

38

Thiin Tasman Sang
Sin Mar een een
Sparend Bodhi Esparar boorn.
Snog ekrubthim for thiin Grund
Thi ordart Utdod for Månfeld End.

This is the Tale of Tasman his mother
her saving body bore our savior.
The snake crippled him for this purpose,
as the Outdead directed, to prevent Moonfall.

39

Nu Mån mild, Fro frodikos
Gro in Sklerawaldos
Fager fager Watarrandos.
Hiin Atwar evalki,
Thiin Werd evaki
Atwar redi klarmak bevoros.

The Moon is clement, its seeds flourish
green in the distant forests.
Beautiful its water courses.
There Atwar walks, the world is watching,
He prepares to reveal himself to us.

40

Fulmakt Tal for Tasman Sind u Skam.
From Fu-en Semer ehir fram
Skeadlika tilvardin West.
Hemwendendu utan Hem
Månskead ehuthi thom
Werd helt in glay Glayfest.

The Tale is completed for Tasman's sake,
out of Fu-en the Semer have taken her
shadowlike towards the west.
Returning homeless home
Moon's shadow (eclipse) hides them.
The world is healed in joyous celebration.

Plint Betwar—Betwar's Lament

Neting stemtu. Hiintid ner va Småa u Atwar wend
fromwerd u Mån Wendt in esin Håndas gestskulik in
Sonljus
U sotmakt stilmakt Lift u hiintid
Ner Werd began heli al esin Sår,

"Nothing is right. When we were children, and
Atwar went away from the world and the Moon was
turned between his hands like a dish of yeast turned
in the sunlight, and the air was made sweet and quiet
and the Earth set about to heal all her bruises,

Hiintid ner va Småa u Folk glay from End Ker
U klarglay klarglay hogsprok gathart
U Kvinnos nekt edhu Rod
Thi meermak Glay thoma Wud,

"When we were children and the people were
made joyous by the end of fear, and laughed and
called to one another, and the women refused root,
because to increase happiness was their desire,

Hiintid ner va Småa u slak Håndrod in Siristam
U in Rand Ostfolk valk in hiin Slak
U klarglay hoyklarglay thi Werd hard underthom
U nameer skelv watarlik underthom
U Wo u Stofwo werdstemt hang
U nameer rev u spar in Månvind from Mån,

"When we were children, and wrists clapped
against wood and the eastern people stepped to that
beat in the streets, and laughed aloud because the
Earth was hard and no longer shook like water under
them, and their house-cloth hung straight down and

no longer tore and fled with the Moon's wind,

Hiintid ner hemewend Månvind in Mån
U va nameer Småa evan Sindi alen,
Hiintid ner Atwar ewend werdfrom u bekam
Eadsindi, Gotsindi,
In thoma Oyos Ebarar Sindi Esparar Sindi,
Hiintid ner kam Pilskeparos nordfrom u glaymak in Wo,
Hiintid ner va alen,
Hiintid ner Tasman Mamin skelvsindik
In Gret stand al Sprok u hindert erindermi
Hiintid ner Fa wend fromi iningå Sindaswo
Ob hogdrag eftertham...Hinntid ner haldover lang u lang
Wo,
Hevitlik stoflik from Vavaras Håndas
Lang u lang
Tidsind Hiintid flog flad u sank overos, Stilhet u Tidsind,
Utidsind, hevit Frok, Slaksprok utan Svar, Hiintid ner je
alen—

"When the Moon's wind returned to the Moon, when we were no more children but alone,

"When Atwar went away from the world and became a child-king, a god in their eyes,

"When the shapers of arrows came down from the north and rejoiced in the city,

"When we were alone,

"When my mother Tasman mad with grief ceased to speak, or to remember me,

"When Sorud my fathers turned away entering the house of their minds and pulling up the door, when over the city gradually, as a white cloth from the weavers' hands gradually, the temper of the times spread and sank down, a silence, a temper, a distemper, a white garment, an argument without answer, when I was alone—"

Spir Tared—Tared's Prayer

Atwar beremas, beremi.
Na stand in Stilhet
ner hidendas.
Na stand in Wald
ner vakendas.

Beremas beremi.
Rinderas rindermi.
Smalik estandi
Smakerikeri.
Atwar beremas beremi.

Atwar, help me.
Do not continue in silence
when we are listening.
Do not remain in the forest
when we are watching.

Help us, help me.
Remember us, remember me.
Standing here weakly
a little terrified.
Atwar help us, help me.

Smaspir Tared—Tared's Small Prayer

Atwar wyp from Febrwan
Sindvav bevormi
In Sval evakendi
Utwyp a na ladmi iningå
Meer hiin kerik Wo
Lad Vavsindstof hiin standi.

Ladmi from hiin Wo ewendi.
Ladmi espar in Reksan
Forhuvd dybt
Skotwatarwypt
Inin din Wo u Bond.

Atwar wipe my fever,
the dream before me
in the evening wakening.
Wipe it out, let me not enter
that fearful house again.
Let it remain in there.
Let me turn from there.
Let me escape in journeying
my face dipped,
in clean water wiped,
into your house and bond.

Fiirsmásang—Song of the Four Children

A gatharu wud
In Atwar Forhuvd.

Ne Smart evan Forvent,
Ne Smart evan Glay,
Atwarlik valkendu
In Helglay helendu

We will stand together before his face.

It is not pain, it is expectation
it is not pain it is joy.
We will walk as Atwar walks
In the joy of health healing.

Na endmaku skiklikos
Evan lik Atwar fromos
Neendmak mak u maki
Evan vaker vaki.

We will not take leave formally,
even as Atwar did not,
he made and makes no finishing
but watches in beauty.

Spiru svaros,
Al Werskepos
Sthi een har fel(?)
Se thom redt Alting al.
Al Fulkomendhet
Evan nekan wit
Vaker vaker Stemhet.

We are asking, answer us,
has any one instrument of the Outdead ever failed?
See what they have prepared for us!
it is all perfect, only we cannot understand it.

Thi from Utdod thiin Gav
Gavos for Hinderliv
Thi vi lik Små for sit
A nekan sind ath wit
Evan redt in hofik Håndos
Nekan sår ath såros
In Sår felwit Fel
Een een alen Hel.

Because the Outdead gave us these gifts
as to children, who cannot reason or understand,
and prepared them for us so that even with our rude
hands

we could not harm them, or with them
do ourselves any foolish harm, but only good.

In Alinrod Fodrodas for bar
Hastik band thom Edh Watar
for Reksan a Atwar in os
Edh meer nojdik Watar meer nojdikos.

A gatharu wud
In Atwar Forhuvd.

On his arms and thighs
they bound food and water
for the journey. Ah Atwar, with us
is more necessary food, more necessary water.

We will stand together before his face.

Circles and Ceremonial Songs

Wend Tasman—Tasman Circling

Tasman gathart Menesk in
From Lenh ran thom bevor ehin
Ottatusind Kvinnas Manas
Fodaros slakunder Gras.

Tasman gathered the people
from Lenh they ran before her
of pairs eight thousand
their feet beating down the grass.

For Tasman Skam wendu, rundwenduvi,
For hir Gras slaku, ne Stami splinti
From hard hard Ard efter thiin rirendi.

We circle, we beat down
the earth as grass, no blade of grass
breaks the hard ground after such a memory.

Tulvwend—The Twelve Turns

Tulvtid Avskel utan krimpendas
Wend under Snogbro overtham ewendi
Setham from sin rundik Bolr
Wit tham Snog, sin Oldsind rindrendi
Utdod, så tham u val Atwar.

Wend for Atwar Sind u Skam.

Twelve times the Avskel unflinching
circle under snake-arch circling over them
it watched, its round brain
knew them, its old brain remembering
the Outdead, it saw, it chose Atwar.

Circle for Atwar's sake.

Tulvtid for Atwar under Tulvbro
In Atwarglay for sindehim estandendi
Stilik under Narod wohiin han slakt
For Grund Grund Fodas sotas splintendas.

Wend for Atwar Sind u Skam.

We circle, at the twelfth arch standing
to honour the mind of Atwar, stalwart standing
under Narod, where he was struck down
for a purpose his sweet legs splintering.

Circle for Atwar's sake.

Wend Fodas-Huvudas—Heads over Heels Turn

Hin hutht in Wald,
Så Noss over Watar,
Wendover fodas-huvudas wend
Tek inin Wo for wendu Hem.

She was hidden in the forest
she saw Noss over the water
it turned on its heads, that was a sign,
they returned to the city.

For Inch Noss vi rundwendu
Vaku Oldwo wendoverendu
Fodas-huvudas Tek
In Alinas Ek.

Because of Noss we stand circling
we watch the Old City overturned
overturned was the sign,
in the crook of our elbows.

Noss over Watar
Huvudas-fodas,
Rund u rund wendendu
Wendu in wendendos.

Noss over the water,
heads over heels,
round and around
we turn in our circling.

Ead Werdas—God of the Worlds
(last Circling)

In Atwar ker
In Atwarglay
Rindu rundwendu in Nerdag Dag
Ead Werdas.

Lomu wer wer
In him ker
Se Son eskeli bejglik Havor
Ead Werdas.

A hemwend nu
In Sling slipu

Sindos in Slap for felglay Wan
Ead Werdas.

Vak vaku evan
Gaev in Tvan
For Atwar vaker hem ewendi
Ead Werdas.

In respect of Atwar
in honour of Atwar
we remember, we circle in dawning day.
God of the worlds.

Wearily we tread,
him we dread
see the sun harshly parts the sea.
God of the worlds.

Oh return now
in our slings
we slip into sleep, poor and weak.
God of the worlds.

But the Watch wakes
bravely two and two
for beautiful Atwar's coming.
God of the worlds.

Oldludhsang Suidfolk—Old Ludh Song of the Southern Folk

Over Skeith Al wendfromlik,
Twar Twel u Twel Twar,
Werd Mån u Svart Hevit,
Forhuvdos Suidfolk hevit Mån.

Whalsayrotos thoma Hår, hevitos Forhuvdos
Ne Kåm in Oyos, sonvard skotos,
Klargladu ner vi greetu, Gret thoma Klarglad klar.
Herboornt, tham Småatwan småa,
Spirtham thi rindera Fodas-huvdaswo,
Spirtham Sirisprok Al betwan Werdas.

Past the Sheath everything is backwards,
twar is twel and twel is twar,
the Earth is the Moon and black is white
the faces of the southern people are white as the
Moon.
Pink as Whalsay their hair, white their faces,
in their eyes no darkness, they squint at the sun
they laugh when we weep, weeping is their laughter.
If they are born here, ask them as babies,
whether they remember the place all upside-down,
ask them to tell us about it.

Tvasprok utanatwar sang - early secular song
(for 2 f. voices)

Semerhevit Hevit-tvan
Reda in Suid
Lagmat Lagbodh.
Framos Sindstof skler tilvardin
U lik Vavaras wern u wan
Thama Oyos wendt from Lom
In Sklerglay Sklerfjel glima.

White twins, Semerwhite,
in the south you are preparing
your bed, your body
you send us your distant thoughts

our eyes like weavers worn and weary
look up from the loom
have pleasure in far (blue) mountains.

A vil laya a layreda
Svart u Hevit in hiin Dag
Vaker Småatwan boorna
Gotgathart va tham lerna
In fager Atwarglay.

Ah we will lie and play
black and white in that day
beautiful twins we will bear
together we will teach them
to honour Atwar in beauty.

Oldlov—Prophecies

Thama Sindos vil bro Goldwo
Wohiin thama Bodhi nekan wend,
Betwan Werdas werdstemt Werd.

Your thoughts will cross the barren place
your body cannot pass
between worlds, and we will be one world.

Tistedi Sprok betwantham in Hiin Dag
Wenda Huvudas in Frandglay.

There will be conversation between them in those
days;
they will turn their faces to each other in kindness.

from *A Gentle Rain in a Distant Autumn*[48]

A gentle rain in a distant autumn
And the birds are blue, are blue,
And the earth is a feast.

Sang for Feltrohinder—Song against heresy

Feltro in Obardos stand
Fel Feltrodragaras hemwendu
From vava Sindstof fel.
Feltrodragt lik witlist Små
Framt from Atwar Felfolk gåu
Thom wud wendu Huvud al.

Heresy stands (stays) in our threshold
false heretics return
from weaving false imaginings.
Swept by heresy like witless children
foolish folk are persuaded from Atwar
the heretics want to turn every head.

Felbokfolk Atwar spir
Wud Asafir mak Meer
U Suidfolk hevit
Thomtro meer Wit
Fu-enwit felskamu
Skam Suidwit for framu.

False scholars doubt Atwar
desiring to increase the Asafir (power)
and believe South-folk white
are more bright,
Fu-en wisdom they put to shame
in order to persuade (us) of South-folk wisdom.

Feltrodragarsang—Heretic Song

Sufur estand blandos estand
Over Skeith from skler Suidland
From Suidfolk Frand
Na ker him Brand.

The Sufur stopped and stayed
from the distant South over the Sheath
from our South-folk friends.
Burning did not scare him.

Ne skoort from Skler
Sklera han eber
Wern Reksan wer
Glay efram him her.

Unscorched by distance
carrying distance (blue)
worn (from) difficult journey
guided here by joy.

Sufur eframt in Atwarsind
In Sklerglay hemewend
Mån neros estand
In Atwar Hånd
Sufur inatwar Smart emak End.

Sufur guided by Atwar's mind
In the pleasure of blue he has returned.
The Moon stopped close by
In Atwar's hand
Sufur in (the mind of) Atwar ended pain.

Tvasprokt Gret Atwar—Atwar's Grief (for 2 voices)

Hiin Brand makas forhuthikas
Thiin va spreka nakdmaka Forhuvdas in Felskam
Vara Tår begin blandu in Drosas
Thi va nama hiin Brand u Atwar Gret.

The fire made us forgetful
we will say this, baring our faces in shame,
our tears will mingle at our throats,
when we speak of the fire and Atwar's Grief.

Een een sma Smatid alen
Wend va, a wendfrom ehim,
Fel Brand var Fel Brand
Ne-evan Vakaras felutan.

Only a small time
we turned away, yes we turned from him.
Fire's fault it was, fire's fault
but we are not faultless watchers.

Atwar! ereni over Sward,
Så under, sprok u va na svar.
Ne ne nekan glim vara Forhuvdas.
Evan hul Wo, u Brand over Hoy.

Atwar! running on the sward,
you looked down and spoke, and we did not answer.
No you could not see our faces.
Only the empty places, and fire on the hill.

Atwar Atwar for hiin faralik Brand,
Atwar Atwar for hiin din Gret.

Ne ne nameer vilva forlada'u.
Lad Wo underbrend u vara Små, thi va forladu meer.

Atwar, it was that dangerous fire,
Atwar, it is your grief.
Never again will we forsake you.
Let the city burn and our children, if we forsake you.

Atwar evalki—Atwar Walks

Atwar 'valki, u vi vakendos,
Atwar valki vaker somlik
Atwar valki in Månwald Hjert.
Nemeer etugti Smart
From Slak Snog, thi ehan helt,
Månvind Lift in Mån
Eberihim, evalki, eberihim.

Atwar walks, we are watching,
Atwar walks well and seemly
Atwar walks deep in the forests of the Moon.
No more does he suffer pain
from the snake's blow, he is healed,
the moon's wind is a light breath on the moon
bearing him: he walks, it bears him.

Atwar valki, u vi vakendos,
Atwar valki vaker somlik
Ner Watarrandos Merk from Fodas,
Ekan svimi over Wataros.
From Nat opstandi
Vil Ljusbrand tindi
A vaku for glim Ljus Atwar tilos
Over Havor betwan Werdas.

Atwar walks, we are watching,
Atwar walks well and seemly
along the watercourses are his footsteps,
he is able to swim across the Moon's water.
In the night he rises up
he will make a bright fire
we will discern the light of Atwar
across the sea (space) between the World and the
Moon.

Atwar valki, u vi vakendos,
Atwar valki vaker somlik
In Månmorn obardi Sward
Klarglay spreki ostilvard.
Ne ne nameer standu from Atwar Vak
Thihan forgavos Al sin Gret,
In sin Fagertid u tilos
Vilspreki Witsind u vil helos.
Werdas nu bekoma Frandas,
Thi Lov, ne mutas evan sprekendas.

Atwar walks, we are watching,
in the Moon's morning he will enter the sward,
he will laugh down towards us.
Never will we cease to watch for him,
he has forgiven us his grief,
in his good time
he will speak in wisdom and heal us.
The two worlds (Earth and Moon) will be friends, as
it is foretold,
not silent, but conversing.

Edhet Atwar—The Small Eating

Begint Edh Atwar, Skead Werd
Begini kåmmak edhtmak Mån.
Evan di edht svi sindslipu Atwar(?)
Ne ne na slipu, evan edht fromos.
Skeadvora, Skeadvora du Atwar edha.
In Obard Skeadvora, in Obard Skead Obos.
Over Obard inos Wo, Atwar edhmakios.
Hemwendi from Irstmån kåm
Glimu Ljushet lang u lang.

Now begins the eating of Atwar.
The shadow of the World begins to make invisible
the Moon.
Will we forget you, Atwar, if you are eaten?
No we will not forget you, although you are eaten.
It is our shadow, our shadow eats you.
You enter our shadow, you enter our mouths of
shadow.
Into us, into us, Atwar is nourishing us.
He will return with the new Moon, we will see his
brightness.

Linhtal—Tale of the Linh

Valt Linh from al Menesk
Formist thama Glay.
Thay boornt from Brand
Nekt framgiv Brand
Slip in liftik Lift skoorbrandt from Felskam.

The Linh were chosen of all the people
and forfeited their joy.

Born of the fire
they refused to relinquish the fire
and left the vivid air scorched with their infamy.

Dod eran bevorthama Hånd
Graslik treawlik in Vind
Thay kortljusmakt Fanas.
In Wo Atwarsmåa
Wostof ran in Bandos, Bandos ran in Brand.

Death ran before their hands
like grass, like trees in wind
they flashed their blades.
At the house of the Children of Atwar
the cloth ran in ribbons, the ribbons ran in fire.

Opstand in Dag, Piilas bristljusendas,
Thay ob Lifr Atwar
Himalik in Wo, hald esin Rot,
Thay brandehim in Blud.
Over Fu-en brist Forhuvd, smalt Fodas.

They rose in day, their arrows flashed,
they opened the liver of Atwar
secretly in the City, his red spilled,
they fired him in blood.
Over the City his face burst, his limbs melted.

Nakan vi nerehim.
Nakan endbrandehim.
Thiin Linh, sind u rindertham.
Ask ask ask ask ask.

We could not come near him,
we could not extinguish him.
This was the Linh, remember them.
Ash, ash, ash, ash, ash.

Irst Sufursang—First Sufur Song

A Sindos Sindos
From Sklera Sklera in Obardos standu
Fjel skleros standendos
In Nerfiil Håndos
In Sklerglay Oyos bevorthom liftwanu.

Ah they are great thoughts
From a great distance they arrive on our thresholds.
The distant mountains are standing
in touch of our hands.
In the pleasure of blue our eyes are drowning before
them.

In Obard Atwar huthvi
In Sklerglay din, Sklersindi.
Skler er ner
In Oyas her
Wend tilos hemwendendi
Werd in Helglay helendi.

In your sleeve, Atwar, we have hidden
this blue (distant) thought for your pleasure.
Distance is close by
in every eye
turn to us, returning
the world heals for your pleasure.

Utanatwarsang—A secular Song (after sapphire)

From Overskeith skler
A vaker Folk vaker Twan vakendas
Glim va Sindos betwan Håndas sprekendos Skler
A va in Sklerglay, a va in Safirglay

Tilvardas kom liftendas, tilvardas kom valkendas,
Tilvardas in Skler, tilvardas in Safir,
Skindhevit u rotbehårtas
Skler in thama Frokstof, Skler Skler in thama Frokstof,
Safir in thama Frokstof.

Far beyond the Sheath
ah beautiful people, beautiful twins awaiting
we have seen your thoughts, between our hands they
speak of distance
our pleasure is in distance, our pleasure is in sapphire
come towards us living, come towards us walking,
come towards us in distance, come towards us in
sapphire,
white of skin and red of hair
blue in your garment, distance in your garment,
sapphire in your garment.

Sindskelvsprok Azur—Azur gibberish

Inin Rotfat u semertos Al.
Blind e-var u blind e-erdi Hiindag.

Into the dye-cauldron, and boiled clean, all of them.
Blind he was then, and blind you are now.

Atwar mild in Suid, hiin estandi huvd-fodas in Mån.
Estandi Mån huvd-fodas e-obi Mund esin. Fat Fat, inin
hedh Rotfat! Semersemer hiin Huvd u sithim in esin
Liftwo. Semert meer fager Rot, semert Safir in Asafir
Blud.

"Atwar is benevolent in the south, there he stands
on his head in the Moon. The Moon stands on his
head and opens his mouth. It is a cauldron - into the
dye-vat! boil that head clean and put it at his breast.
We have boiled a better colour, we have boiled
sapphire in the blood of birds.

A bejglik Huvdskel Forhuvd! Thom vil faldu in hiin
Forhuvd asafirlik, thom vil svimu inin Skler, thom vil
svimu inin Safir. Thom vil faldu inin Suidfat, sidehan
Skul al felmånik from felboornt Håndas felmånikas
Leerskeparas, Skept lik Felmån.

"Ah, malevolent face-board face! they will fall into
that face like birds, they will swim into distance, they
will swim into sapphire. They will fall into the
cauldron of the south, it has a bowl all humped from
the humpbacked potters' crooked hands, the shape of
the gibbous Moon.

Wan, wan, makthom meer u meer små, thoma
Hevitgredilfod smalskept Småstam. S'vo Raftos betwan
Werdas? Kliklik Stamos, kliklik kliklik gathartos. S'thom
rou in Damp, s'gistu Stam in Matarwatar, s'vaku thi Lift
u nemeer Lift thom giva Hold? Sva slak in Dod Asafir in
Hjertslak thama Håndas? Sva Liftwana Sufur witskepik
in Thradh thama Håndas Hår?

"Sicken, sicken, they make them smaller and
smaller, their leg bones are little stripped sticks.
Where are the rafts of the heavens? Click, sticks, click
together. Will they row clouds, will their staffs stick
in rainwater, will air and absence of air give them
purchase? Who has killed the small birds in the pulse
of the hands? Who has strangled the small bird with
a string of hand-hair artfully?

*Dook Blindsid ewendi eredi slakfald over Wo. Al Folk in
Rand, ren from u til for esin Sind u Skam. Een Suid alen
emak Atwar mild. Wend esin Eenhuvd over Dros smal.
Asafir asafir, pluk een u een Tradhi Tradhi, wend ehim in
Suid in Tid esin Hemwend!*

"The Doll turns his back and prepares to lunge
across the city. All in his path, run to and fro for his
sake! Only the south makes him kind. Turn his one-
head on its narrow neck. Birds! take each one a
strand of his hair, and turn him to the south at the
time of his coming!

Di vil bidi Dod, ner Thiin endmakt emaki.

"You will choose death, when you have done it."

Framsprok Ng—Ng Persuasion

*Di bar for Atwar hel, sid esin Utwend u tistedi in Werd
Tradh, ingatharend Sind u Sind u evan vora Sindos. Ne
ne di kan sindslipehim, ne ne di ehim sindslipi. A ne
Nojed di Betwar gathart in Skik for Broderglay, thi
Bodhidin him sindi vakend ath wern, Liv edin ehim
emindi.*

*A va list list u soma na holda edir in Tal, evan vi holda
u evan vi sindadir u wita edi him meer ner; een alen edin
Sind ewitihim. Na kom di Dookbevor, di na nojdi Dookos
Likskik. In Hjert Hjertatwar, in Lifr Lifr edin Broder. In
Liftwo Tasman dragt Thiintwan witskepik in Skel, thi
thaytro da kan liva avskelt til Hinderdag Skel in Stemthet.
Thiin Tal for edi Betwar, Betwar Atwarbroder, u ininthiin
Inlik, lik Månskead Mån efolgefter Mån, lik Kåm
hemewendi efter Ljus u Svalhet efter hedh Daghedh. Utan
Betwar na tilstedi Atwar, evan thi Betwar elivi, eglimi*

*Werd Skead Atwar bland Folk, blandthom evalki Betwar
in Skead Atwar lik in Stand Treaw, uthom sinduhim utan
Sprok, thom witu ehim Sind u Skam. Thom inhim glay.*

"You have served your brother well, since his
going away your being in this world is the conjoining
braid, the ingathering of his mind with your mind
and so with our-minds. Never can you forget him,
never can he forget you. You Betwar have no need to
partake in the ceremony to honour your brother,
when your body honours him awake or asleep. Your
whole life honours Atwar.

"Ah, we are less than you and we seem not to
account you, yet we do account you and know you
are closer to him; you are the only mind who truly
knows him. Do you not come to the Doll, who have
no need of dolls and replicas. In your heart is the
heart of your brother, in your liver is the liver of
your brother. In Tasman's womb were these drawn
deftly apart, that you might live separately until you
must separate in purpose, to rejoin in purpose at last.
There is a Tale of you, Betwar brother of Atwar, in
which you are his equal, as the shadow of the Moon
follows the Moon, as the darkness returns after the
light and coolness after great heat. Without Betwar
could there be no Atwar, while Betwar lives does
Atwar live also, the world beholds Atwar's shadow
among the people, among the people Betwar walks
in the shadow of Atwar as in a stand of trees and
they acknowledge him without speech; they know
and acknowledge him. They honour him.

*Thi va felsindikas rundwenda Dook, thi va Tal Talu
Gret Atwar skikspreka, rindera Betwar over Strand,
himalik ewendi Forhuvd tårblerti in Mån. Thi vi
utanstandikos vaku in Skerm, rinderu Betwar evaki Mån*

*for hoyestandi over Werdmerk. Oyas esin red glima
Irstljus. Betwan Betwar u Atwar ne Nojed Sprok u
Skikvakt. A redi for Reksan, a redi esin Små for hiin sklera
Reksan. Tradh sidhuvdlik, Tradh Tviintradh holdu, brotu
betwan Werdas for utwendu Små, wendufrom Fa for
hemwendu in Fa, thom beru in thoma Bodhsmå
Atwarbroder inin Twan.*

"When we who are ignorant circle the Doll, when
we tell our Tales and recite Atwar's Grief, we remember Betwar on the strand, who lifts his tear-
blurred face directly towards the Moon. When we
watch unceasingly at the screens, we remember
Betwar waiting for the Moon to rise over the horizon,
his eyes ready to catch the first light. Between Betwar
and Atwar there is no need for words or watching.
Ah, he is preparing for the journey, ah, he is preparing his children for that journey of distance. The
braid will tighten, the braid will hold; across space,
between worlds his children will go to him, they will
leave their father to return to their father, they will
bring in their small bodies the brother of Atwar into
his conjoining."

Rumi fragment

What do I possess other than the thing you have
given? What are you searching for in my pocket and
sleeve?[49]

Snogsay —Snake proverb

Gret thvari inin Thvar
Lik Snog sårt ewendi
In Thvar tindi tindi
U revi esin Sår.

Grief raves into anger like a hurt snake, who turns on
its own body and snaps at its wounds.

Say Ludh—Ludh proverb

Nekt Rotrod Kvinnas
Gruvsa Hibis
In Want Hibis
Rotl thay rotendas.

Ardrotel in Håndas
Maku meer vakeras
From Rotrod ath Hibis
Vavt betwan Werdas.

If women are refused madder
they will crush hibiscus,
if hibiscus is wanting
they will pretty themselves with reddle.

Earthy reddle in the hand
makes them more beautiful
than madder or hibis
woven in space (imagined).

Notes

[1] *The Tale of Tasman*, p. 179

[2] *Betwar's Lament*, p. 198

[3] *Circles and Ceremonial Songs*, p. 204

[4] *Atwar Walks* p. 213

[5] *Atwar Walks 3*, p. 214

[6] *Song of the Four Children 1*, p. 221

[7] *The Small Eating*, p. 215

[8] *Atwar's Grief*, p. 212

[9] *Song of the Four Children 1*, p. 201

[10] *Circles and Cermonial Songs*, p. 204

[11] *Atwar Walks 1*, p. 213

[12] *The Tale of Tasman 37*, p. 186

[13] *Song of the Four Children*, p. 202

[14] *Song of the Four Children 3-4*, p. 203

[15] *The Tale of Tasman 14*, p. 186

[16] *The Tale of Tasman 26*, p. 191

[17] *The Tale of Tasman 36*, p. 195

[18] *Tared's Small Prayer*, p. 201

[19] *Song of the Four Children 5*, p. 203

[20] *Old Ludh Song of the Southern Folk*, p. 208

[21] *early secular song*, p. 208

[22] *from A Gentle Rain in a Distant Autumn*, p. 210

[23] *Prophecies 2*, p. 209-210 (*ref. Tale of Tasman 1*, p. 179)

[24] *Song against heresy*, p. 210

[25] *Heretic Song*, p. 211

[26] *The Tale of Tasman 40*, p. 197

[27] *Moonfall*

[28] *Tale of Tasman 4*, p. 181

[29]*The Tale of Tasman 5*, p. 181
[30]*The Tale of Tasman 24*, p. 190
[31]*The Tale of Tasman 11*, p. 184
[32]*The Tale of Tasman 26*, p. 191
[33]*Atwar's Grief 2-3*, p. 212
[34]*First Sufur Song 1*, p. 217
[35]*First Sufur Song 2*, p. 217
[36]*a secular song (after sapphire)*, p. 218
[37]*Tale of the Linh*, p. 216
[38]*The Tale of Tasman 34*, p. 195
[39]*Azur gibberish*, p. 218
[40]*Ng Persuasion*, p. 220
[41]*Tared's Prayer*, p. 200
[42]*lit.*, Will we remain?
[43]*Song of the Four Children 2*, p. 202
[44]*Rumi fragment*, p. 222
[45]*Snake proverb*, p. 223
[46]*Ludh proverb*, p. 223
[47]*Mythic background to the present text, not to be depended on factually. A translation follows each stanza.*
[48]*Mahmoud Darwish*
[49]*Jalal al-Din Rumi*, p. 211: 186.8

Dictionary

Riksprok in Translation

The task of the translator is to tell the story plainly, and to avoid encumbering it with explanatory text whenever a concept is unfamiliar or a word not directly translatable. Notes or an aftertext can go far to replace such interruptions. Yet a society is most wonderfully elucidated through its language, which quietly and naturally provides for all its idiosyncracies. Fortunately for us, insight into the distant world of Fu-en is transluminated by an extra layer of (ablbeit coloured) light, making it at once more strange and more clear. This is the intervening, nonobjective "objectivity" of Riksprok, which, for itself and by itself, attempted to explain what was observed and then lived— it is Fu-en through the eyes of Betwar and the diaspora people.

Riksprok, Function and Change

The dictionary is an introduction to diaspora Riksprok, and thus reflects both the western society of its origins and the eastern society in which it came to be spoken.[1]

Riksprok in Fu-en had the double function of ceremonial (formal) language (*Skiksprok*) and minority or "house" language (*Wosprok*). As a minority language, it took a new look at Fu-en, and had to attend to aesthetic and moral concepts it did not know. Thus it had either to incorporate them ironically, or extend itself in forms which were highly colourful and biased, with an (originally) skeptical or critical overlay.

One could take for example the word for facial beauty (*Vakerhet*) as applied by Fu-en folk quite naturally to their

---

[1] For a shorter account of the explainable vagaries of Riksprok see *Moonfall*, Appendix, pp. 235-239.

own shaped heads. Diaspora Riksprok continued to use the word, but with the courteous connotation: "pleasing to Fu-en" (*Fu-englay*); *vaker* became *utvaker*: unattractive and outlandish. In Fu-en Riksprok, the status of the common word *fager* (fair) was elevated to mean beautiful.

Definitions of such terms are foll. by *(Fu-en)*; of words particular to Lofot society by *(Lofot)*.

Linguistic irony, in the case of Betwar's children, was not always apparent; Riksprok was appropriated by the scholars of Fu-en as Atwarsprok, "Atwar's language", and learned by all Book children. Formal Riksprok was, despite its internal ironies, a serious, courteous language spoken in Book and during the ceremonies, and the metaphor of Fu-en entered it to some extent as well, as witnessed to in many new compounds. The children's relation to the father-tongue identified their ambivalent relationship to their father and was complex and uncertain. At any rate, Fu-en Riksprok did not survive as a living language: it was imbedded in the ritual and otherwise lost. Betwar's was the last generation speaking a colloquial Riksprok in the eastern lands.

Riksprok is a simple, muscular language. It uses pudding-stone words when it runs into anything complex, and makes do with plain repetition for emphasis and the superlative. The dictionary includes a few of the most common compound words, as well as new "snows" or images compounded to meet new circumstances. The reader of English will recognize many Germanic origins that are the tough roots of English as well; as will the reader of any Germanic or Scandinavian language: most common words have remained unchanged, or nearly so, down the centuries.

Most interesting for the browser, however, is the way words and compounds illuminate Fu-en social structure and ceremony—from the upbringing of children to the sexual, aesthetic, moral and spiritual complexity of this extraordinary society.

The action of the book records a period of relative stability and increasing rigidity after violent change; yet even within this period (less than one year) more change had to be accomodated. All this—change, stability and more change—the language, with its chunky basic tools, shapes clear, reflects, incorporates and even at times anticipates.

Grammar

I have used a somewhat erratic alphabetic. *å* (originally *aa*) appears before *a* but is a separate letter, pronounced *oa* -(*ō*) (*o* is lighter *o*). Choice is sometimes arbitrary between initial plosives *b & p*, initial clusters *tv & tw*, clusters *dh & th*, borderline fricatives *f, v, w,* & final dipthongs *-g, -j, -y.*

Colloq. words & speech patterns are marked as such. *sl.* indicates a new meaning. *Duals,* usually referring to human physical place and action, are marked. Such duals have no singular. For our monocephalic users, the way around this was to plunge straight ahead using *we* for *I,* etc. or, in formal speech, to use the *archaic singular prefix e-* (used anyway in personification of Moon, Earth, snake, bird, etc., and in the very occasional, formally permitted, use of the body by one twin. In reality, each twin had control over the appropriate hand, but to refer to its use in the *s. poss.* was considered discourteous.

It will be noted that many *ns.* (*f. ex.* the words for water, cloud, blood) which are singular in English are *pl.* in Riksprok. These have been translated in *s..* Again for stylistic reasons, I have for the most part dispensed with translating the inalienable dual as *pl.* when used by, to or about the monocephalic characters.

Another perhaps more difficult anomaly is anatomical nomenclature—as the body is not conceived of as being divided into the same named parts. The dictionary attempts to give a definition of Riksprok divisions but the text sticks to "ordinary" ones: the most glaring example is the term *Huvud* (*tr.* "head") which in Riksprok includes the neck as well—in fact, it means that part of the body unshared by the other twin. "Hand" includes wrist and probably lower arm, and the arm consists of upper arm plus "armroot" (*Alinrod*)—shoulder. A final example— *Mund* ("mouth") refers to the inside of the mouth only, and "mouth-muscle" (*Mundsen*) is not the lips, but includes the entire muscle.

Perhaps not unexpected in a society that lives and observes by night, colours are ill-defined in Fu-en Riksprok. The reader will have noted there was no word for blue - it is the same word as "distance" (*Skler*). Green and "grow" are synonyms. Red, the only colour the Fu-en dyers used, means "colour" in general, as well as serving as *a.* "pretty" or "pleasing". The term *Hu* is better translated as "tone" than as "colour".

There is no article. The objective pronoun forms the reflexive, usually (like other *obj. prons.*) as *suff.* to the verb. *Adjectives & adverbs* tend to function as nouns in the predicate or as ultimates of strings (and are then marked for number); *pl. number* (except in formal speech) is omitted; the dual is marked always, as are participles - but not passives; however, passives that have taken up a life of their own as adjectives may be. For the sake of simplicity I have not listed *advs.* forming regularly from adjectives; nor have I noted that duals with no *s.* are obviously ordinary plurals as well. Present verbs inflect but the *f.* gender ending -*a* did not survive into Fu-en. *Auxs.* are usually followed by the uninflected present. Word-order does not change in the *interr.*, but a *pref. s* occurs in formal speech; the facial sign of the (completed) interrogative is the "fixed" open mouth. The *imperative* is an initial (uninflected) *pres.* Word order is otherwise fairly free-for-all and seems to depend on emphasis, the most important word in the sentence or phrase taking precedent. *Numerals* are so close to Scandinavian that it would be tedious to list them; the only ones included are those which appear in the text.

It is to be noted that, while the dictionary does not record every form and compound, in terms of the text it is complete. The diaspora Riksprok of the original book is therefore available to the reader.

Thematic Root Clusters of Interest

The interested browser is directed to unusually large clusters of words pertaining to religious and homely ceremonies (*Skik*), weaving and dyeing (*Rot*), the Moon (*Mån*), childbirth and upbringing (*boorn*, *Bònd*, *Små*, *Voksan*), language, education, medicine, space travel & government (*Bok*, *Sprok*), the twinned individual in a shared body (*Twan*, *Sind*), the face as aesthetic and moral focus (*Huvud*, *Sen*), harmony as the highest moral goal (*stem*), and sexual mores and practice (found, as in all dictionaries worth their salt, dispersed throughout).

Dictionary Riksprok-English

A

~a *n. a. & adv. f. suf.*, *arch.*

a *int.* ah, alas, oh

År *n.* year

Al *n. & a.* everything, all, every, ever

alen *a. & adv. arch.*, *prohibited (Lofot)*, *avoided (Fu-en)* alone; *arch.* een een ~, only

Alenhet *n. arch.* loneliness

Alinbu *n.* elbow

Alinrod *n. Anat.* area incl. upper arm & shoulder

Aln, Alin *n. Anat.* lower arm, *usu. incl.* hand

altid *adv.* ever, always

Amadu *n. dual* m. twins, messengers (from Sakhalin)

An *n.* **1.** darkness (*f. Chin.*); **2.** *n. dual* f. twins, doctors (Fu-en)

Ard *ns. & v. dual* **1.** *ns.* earth, floor; **2.** daughter of Betwar; **3.** *n. dual* "the Ard", daughters of Betwar, b. 5460; **4.** *v.t.* bury, imbed (*f. Arab.*)

ardbu *v. dual* kneel, squat down

Ardfald *ns.* "earthfall", eroding fall of earth & gravel (Narod)

Ardhu *n. & a.* **1.** brown *or* yellow colour, ochre; **2.** *a.* earth-coloured, dirty; ~glay (*dual colloq.*), good and dirty, earthy, acceptable

Ardrot *n. & a.* brownish, madder-red colour

ardutan *a.* transparent, clean, pure, pristine

Ardwo *n.* area near house, yard

~as *suf. forming dual n., a. & part.*

as *see* **va**

Asafir, **'Asahfeer** *see* **Sufur**

Ask *n.* **1.** son of Betwar, b. 5463; **2.** *ns.* ashes

ath *prep. & conj.* or, rather

athar *pron., a. & adv.* another, other, different, otherwise

Atwar *n.* son of Tasman, named (with Betwar) Avskel; brother of Betwar, b. 5441

Atwar-glay *n.* "ardent for Atwar", reverent; **in ~**, honouring *or* in honour of Atwar

Atwarker *n.* respectful; **in ~**, in respect *or* fear of Atwar

Atwarsindi *n. dim.* "little-one" (child) of Atwar, formal title for one of Betwar's children

Atwarskik *n.* "the way of Atwar", Atwar's manner, as Atwar did

Atwarsmåa *ns.* "Children of Atwar", formal title for Betwar's children

Avskel *n. dual* ("separated ones", *lit.* separation), name of Atwar & Betwar, sons of Tasman, b. 5441

Azur, Azr *n.* **1.** *arch.* enclosing with helpfulness (*f. Arab.*); **2.** *n. dual* twins, "great scholars" & governors, Fu-en, b. 5401

B

bald *a.* bald, hairless

Baldbro *see* **Bro**

Band *n. & v.t.* **1.** knot; **Hår~**, knot of hair; **2.** binding-cloth, bandage **3.** *v.* (*part.* **bindend**; *pres.* **bind**) knot, tie up, bandage; **rund~**, wind up; **skep~**, shape (infant heads) by bandaging (eastern continent); **ut~**, unwind, untie

Bandsmåa *n. dual* infant twins (up to 1 year) with bandaged heads; **~tid**, infancy (Fu-en)

bar *v.* (*part.* **berend**; *pres.* **ber**) hold, carry, wear, put on; **end~**, carry through, manage; **~ for**, serve; **~ Nam**, live, *as*, stay alive, live beyond infancy

barbar *a.* heavy; *colloq.* pregnant

Bardel *n.* inner "shoulder" (of twins)

Barendaras *see* **Bokaras barendas**

Barting *n.* parcel, burden

bartlad *v. dual* ride

began *v.*(*part.* **beginend**; *pres.* **begin**) plan, begin

behårt *a.* haired, hairy, hirsute

behin *adv. & prep.* behind

bejg *n. & v.* **1.** risk, threat; **2.** *v.* threaten, risk, impose on

bejglik, beyglik *a.* baleful, ominous

bekam *v.* (*part.* **bekomend**; *pres.* **bekom**) become

Besm *n. & v. dual* **1.** bound twigs, for sweeping, broom;

2. *v.* sweep

Betwan *n., adv. & prep.* **1.** stripe, row; pause, interval; **Sma~**, moment; **Tulv~**, hour; **2.** *adv. & prep.* between, through

Betwar *n.* son of Tasman, named (with Atwar) Avskel; brother of Atwar; b. 5441

bevor *adv. & prep.* before, in front of

Bevorhang *n.* curtain

Big *n., a. & v.* **1.** centre, middle, midst, gist, theme; **2.** *a.* main, important, central, principal; **3.** *v.* matter, concentrate on, attend to

bim *v.* "beam", look on benificently, approve

Bimbrand *see* **Brand**

Bimlag *see* **Lag**

bimt *a.* benign, condescending

Bjost *n.* breast

Bjostwort *n.* nipple

bland *prep. & v.t.* **1.** among; **2.** *v.* blend, mingle

Bler *n., v. & a.* **1.** blur, slur; **2.** *a.* blurred, slurred, bleary

Blind *n., a. & v.* blind

Blindsid *n.* back (of torso)

Blom *n.* rose

Blomedh, Somerblomedh *ns. prob.* dried pulverized rosehip

Blomsind *n.* bud, idea

Blomsvart *n. & v. dual* **1.** black resin, *unkn.*; **2.** *v.* stain black

Bludel, Blud *ns. & v. dual* **1.** blood, *colloq.* violence; **2.** bleed

Bludelrot *a.* "orange as blood", orange-red colour

Bludelsip *n.* menstruation

bludlik *a.* violent, brutal, fierce

Bodh, Bodhi *n.* body

bodhik *a.* physical, causing (physical) sensation

Bodhlift *see* **Lift**

Bodhwer *see* **Wer**

Bodhwo *n.* in **~**, having room, space

Bogdan, Bogdan-a *n.* **1.** gift of god (*f. O Slav.*); **2.** *n. dual*, f. twins, midwives from Joensuu, b. c. 5370, d. 5448

Bok *n.* **1.** school, library; **2.** learning; **ler ~**, study

Bok Bok *n.* "Great Book", library, centre of learning

Bokaras *n. dual* twin scholars; **~ Bokaras**, "great scholars", learned governors; **~ barendas**, "carrying scholars", twin governors who bear (*lit. & fig.*) the people's burdens; **Ler~**, apprentice scholars, nepophytes (Fu-en)

bokså *v.* (*part.* **boksåend**, *pres.* **bokse**) read

Boksmå *ns. pl.* "Book-children", school-children

Bokstam *n.* letter (alphabetic symbol)

Bokvav *n. & v. colloq.* "scholarly weavings", complex discourse, inapplicable argument, nonsense

Bolr *n. & v.* **1.** ball, bundle, group, flock, crowd; cheek, *colloq.* brain; **~tal**, duet, two-voiced song using other twin's mouth as vibrator (Plains);

Rod~, reed basket; **2.** *v.* puff, blow

Bolraras, Stambolraras *n. dual* "blowers of reeds", twin flute-players, musicians (Fu-en)

Bolredh *ns.* fruit, edible seeds

Bolt *n.* roll of cloth, sieve

Bond *n. & v.t. dual* **1.** agreement *usu.* sanctioned sexual relationship (**kort~**, **Hus~** *etc.*); **2.** *v.t.* enter sanctioned sexual relationship, marry

boorn *v.t. dual* give birth to, bear; *v. i.* evolve, come into being, come to pass

Boornbondas *n. dual* those (*usu.* the old or dying) formally presented to newborn twins to be remembered; whoever first is seen by newborn twins

Bord *n.* wall; **Stik~**, sluice, floodgate

Brand *n. & v.* **1.** fire, congflagration; **Bim~**, *colloq.* (children's) contained, approved fire; **~ Brand**, "great fire", the Great Fire of Fu-en, 5464; **2.** *v.* (*part.* **brendend**; *pres.* **brend**) burn; **end~**, extinguish; **ut~**, burn up, burn away

Brandbrist *n. & v.* **1.** explosion **2.** *v.* explode, burst into flames

Brandglay *n.* (of children) pleasure in seeing & playing with fire

Brandleer *see* **Leer**

Brandsår *n & v. dual* burn; **~skar**, burn scar

Bred *n. & a.* **1.** expanse, space; **2.** *a.* broad, wide; **ut~**, long

Bredbro *see* **Bro**

bredgrin *see* **grin**

Breev *n.* "letter", memorized oral message

Breevtalaras *n. dual* "letter tellers", twin messengers

Brim *n. & v.* **1.** brim, edge, verge, extent, limit; **2.** *v.* fill up, *metaph.* be filled (with emotion)

Bring *n. & v.* **1.** collection, harvest; **2.** *v.* get, fetch; **in~**, harvest, collect, gather in

Brist *n. & v.* burst, snap, rupture, break; **in~**, implode, implosion

Bro *n. & v. dual* **1.** arch, bridge; **Bald~**, hairless face of eastern peoples; **Bred~**, "broadbrow", *colloq.* western folk outside Lofot, unshaped face, separated eyebrows; **~hår**, conjoined eyebrows, growth of hair on forhead (Lofot); **2.** *v.* cross, pass over

Broder *n.* brother; *usu.* twin brother; (*also dual*) male twins, (*dual & pl.*) brothers, siblings

Bu *n.& v.* **1.** bow, curve, crescent; **2.** *v.* bow, bend, curve

bud *v.t.* (*part.* **bidend**; *pres.* **bid**) "invite", (courteous) *usu.* summon, require, cause to appear (*as*, set in motion, interfere during, childbirth); **~ Dod**, (as, "choose, invite death"), welcome death, embrace death willingly, commit suicide

but *a. & adv. usu. dual* bent, bowed, ducked down, bent over

Butstam *n.* bamboo

C

Camfel *n. & a. colloq.* 1. mischief; 2. *a.* interfering, mischievous; ~**skept**, (of machines) infernal

Camp David *n.* ancient Outdead centre of power; *metaph.* (as in Tales) bad place, *as*, hell

camrid *see* **rid**

Car *n.* "car", Outdead vehicle; **stand~**, controllable, maneuverable vehicle; **hima~**, self-functioning, inactive or not understood vehicle (Outdead remnant)

Chern *n.* ancient, extinct city: ancient catastrophe

Chmedes *n.* Archimedes, lunar crater

Crisium *n.* lunar *mare*

D

da (tha) *pron. subj. & obj.* (*poss.* **dara, thara**) *dual pron. of 2nd pers.*

Dag *n.* day

Daghedh *n.* "dayheat", daytime, discomfort; **in ~**, uncomfortable

Dal *n.* valley

Damp, Damphevit *ns.* cloud, haze, steam, vapour; **Mån~**, clouding on Moon

dara *see* **da**

Datteras *n. dual* twin daughters

Del *n. & v.t.* 1. part, piece, chunk, cell, share, fragment, division; 2. *v.* share, divide; **gredl~**, divide, compartmentalize

di *pron.* (*subj. & obj.* **di**; *poss.* **din**) *sing. pron. of 2nd pers.*

din *see* **di**

dir *a.* valuable, precious

Dirth *n.* "Dearth", plague winter which no infants (of Walking City) survived, 5450-5451

Dod *n., a. & v. dual* 1. death; 2. *a.* dead; 3. *v.* die; **slak ~**, kill

Dodas, Dodos: *ns. dual & pl.* (the) dead

Dodask *n.* of mourning, edible ash

Dodbodh *n.* corpse, carcass

dodbrand *v. dual* cremate

dodfald *see* **fald**

dodhuvl *see* **huvl**

Dodsump *n.* "Lake of Death" Lacus Mortis, lunar lake

Dook *n.* "doll", replica, statue; ~ **Dook**, "the great Doll", large statue of Atwar (Fu-en)

Dookhoj *see* **Hoj**

Dookhuvd *n. & v.* 1. mask; 2. *v.* manipulate or disguise facial expression

dookhuvdik *a.* impassive, expressionless

Dookmakaras *n. dual* twin "doll-makers", makers of cloth replicas of Atwar (Fu-en)

drag *v. usu. dual* push, pull, press ahead, write; **fel~**, scorn; **hog~**, pull up, close; **lag~**, tease; **skik~**, repeat, drill; practice; **ut~** stretch, extend, prolong; **~ in Skead**, withdraw; **~ utanslip**, besiege, torment

dragt *a.* bedraggled, messy

drok *a.* dry, ironic

drokbrist *a.* caked, flaked, dried out

Drokdod *n.* **1.** dead wood; **2.** carcass

Drokgras *ns.* straw

Drokhuvd *n.* cactus; **Valkend ~** rootless cactus

drokmundik *a.* ironic

drokwan *v. dual* thirst

Drokwant *n. & a.* **1.** thirst; **2.** *a.* thirsty

Dros *n.* throat (of twins, throat-join)

Drospyt *n.* pit of the throat-join

du *pron. subj.* (*obj.* **er**, *poss.* **era**) *pl. pron. of 2nd pers.*

Dun *n.* soft, short hair

dunlik *a.* downy, furry, soft

Dust *ns.* dust

Dyp *n., a. & v.* **1.** well, trench, dent, depression, ditch; **~Dyp**, sea floor or bottom; **2.** *a.* deep; **3.** *v.* dip, bob (*v. dual*) nod (in assent), dive (in water); **lift~**, *sl.* swoop (of birds)

E

e~ *pref., arch. sing. marker (for dual verbs of place & motion)*

e-sinsind *pron. arch.; subj. sing. pron. of 2nd. pers. emphat.*

Ea *n., adv. & v.* **1.** obedience, agreement, confirmation; **2.** *adv. of affirmation* yes; **ea~**, *emphat.* yes indeed, certainly; **3.** *v.* obey, acknowledge, acquiesce, agree, be resigned to

Ead *n.* authority; **~Werdas**, godlike, total authority (ascribed to Atwar)

ealik *a.* resigned, obedient

Eb *n.* ebb tide; **in ~**, *colloq.* aging, celibate

ebik, ebt *a.* low, shallow

Edh *n. & v.* **1.** food, act of eating; **2.~Atwar**, "Eating of Atwar", New Moon ceremony; **Sma~**, "The Small Eating", waning Moon ceremony (Fu-en); **3.** *v.* eat

edhmak *v. dual* feed, nourish

Edhwo *n.* kitchen market

Edhwud *n.* appetite; **in ~**, willing to eat

een *num. & adv.* one, once; **~ een,** *a. & adv.* simple, single, singly; **~ ~ alen**, only; **~ u ~**, each one

Effa, Eva *n. dual* name of twin foremothers (*myth.*) evoked at childbirth

efter *prep. & conj.* for, after, when

ehim, *pron. arch. m. obj., sing. pron. of 2nd pers.*

ehir, *pron. arch. f. obj., sing. pron. of 2nd pers.*

Ek *n. & v.* **1.** angle, corner *colloq.* elbow, knee; **2.** *v. dual* use well, frugally

ekik *a.* useful, frugal, careful

ekvalk *see* **valk**

End *n., a. & v.i.* **1.** end, resolution; **2.** *a.* last, final; **3.** *v.* end, come to an end

endbar *see* **bar**

Endmak *n. & v. dual* **1.** "finishing", ceremony of completion; **2.** *v.* finish with, resolve

Endmak-neendmak *n., int. & v., as, au revoir,* farewell till we meet again; *colloq. int.* **neendmak;** *euphem.* **got neendmak,** "take good leave", say final farewell

endstemt *a.* inevitable

er, era *see* **du**

ersind *see* **varsind**

Esparar *see* **Spararas**

evan *conj.* but, though, yet, however *colloq. a.* only

Ey *n.* small island

F

Fa *n. dual* fathers

Fadar *n.* right-sided father

Fadel *n.* left-sided father

Fafa *n. dual* paternal grandfathers

Fafrandas *n. dual & voc.* "father-friends", twin friends of fathers

fager *a.* fair, beautiful

Fagerlay *n.* lovemaking, act of intercourse

Fagerljus *see* **Ljus**

Fald *n. & v. dual* **1.** fall, descent **2.** *v.* fall, fell, fall down; **dod~,** fall dead, perish; **over~,** attack

Famar *n. dual* maternal grandfathers

Fan, *n.* knife, blade, vane

fand *v.t.* (*part.* **findend;** *pres.* **find**) find, discover

Fanskeparas *n. dual* "shapers of knives", twin forgers (Novaya Zemlya)

far *v.t. dual* beget

Fara *n.* danger, threat; **ner~,** imminent danger

Fast *n. & v.* fast; **in ~,** hungry; **in Wer~,** ravenous

Fat *n.* vat, basin, dyeing tub; **Brand~,** cauldron

Fatpis *see* **Pis**

Febrwant *ns.* fever

Fed *n.* skein

Fel *n., a., adv. & v.* **1.** fault, failure; **2.** *a.* false, faulty, not; **3.** *adv.* badly, strongly **4.** *v.* fail, go wrong

Felard *ns.* filth, debris

felboornt *a.* "birth-faulted", malformed

feldrag *see* **drag**

felfast *v. dual* forget or decline to eat

felfram *v. dual arch.* deceive, mislead, betray

Felframhet *n. arch.* betrayal, deceit; **Lov~,** sexual deceit

Felfrand *n. arch.* bad influence,

bad company; **~lov**, complicity

Felglay *n.* fool, folly; **in ~**, foolish, freakish, thoughtless, poor (*as*, ignorant, subservient, pitiful)

felgrin *see* **grin**

Felmån *n.* gibbous Moon

felmånik *a.* hunched, warped

felmist *see* **mist**

Felnat *n.* darkness during solar eclipse

felrid *see* **rid**

Felrod *see* **Rod**

Felskam *n.* & *v.* **1.** shame, infamy; **2.** *v.* shame, exclude, ostracize

felskept *a.* makeshift, marred, spoilt

felsmar *v. colloq.* write

Felstam *n.* sprout, sapling; *n. dual colloq.* naughty children

Feltal *n.* discrepancy

Feltroskik *n.* heresy, heretical practice; **~dragar**, heretic (Fu-en)

felutan *a.* innocent, faultless

Felwo, Felglaywo *n.* shack, hovel

fend *v. dual* protect, avert, defend, justify, attend, care for

Fendaras *n. dual* twin attendants *usu.* scholars (Fu-en)

Feng, Ng *n.* **1.** wind, hill (*f. Chin.*); **2.** *n. dual* (called **Ng**), twins, "great scholars" & governors, b. 5433

Fest *n.* celebration

Fiil *n.* & *v.t.* (*part.* **filend**; *pres.* **fil**) feel, touch; **Sma~**, brush against, graze; **in Ner~**, against, in contact with

Fiir *num.* four

Fiirathotta *a.* & *adv. colloq.* "four-or-eight", several, much, many

Fingar *n.* & *v.* **1.** finger; **~tind**, fingernail; **2.** *v.* point, show, demonstrate, refer to

Fist *n.* & *v.* **1.** palm, footsole; **~ Fist**, (clenched) fist; **2.** *v.* clench, clutch, lock together

Fisthår *ns.* hair growing out of palms & footsoles (see **Håndhår, Fodhår**)

fistik *a.* cramped, constrained

Fjel *n.* mountain

Fjelob *n.* pass

Flad *n.* & *a.* **1.** surface; **Skept~**, panel, metal surface or part (Outdead); **2.** *a.* low, level, flat; **sem~**, polished, sleek, smooth, shiny

fladflog *v.* spread, cover

fladskep *v. dual* smooth out, flatten

Fladwo *n.* continental plains

flit *v. dual* move, move house, go away

flitik *a.* active, fluttery, jittery

Flitmerk *n.* & *v.* gesture, motion, flash or slash of hand (with its after-image)

Flod *n.* incoming tide

Flog *n.* & *v.* **1.** current, river; **2.** *v.* flow, pour, suspend, float; **skum~**, gush, rush

Fod *n. Anat.* foot, *usu.* foot & lower leg, member, limb; **~fingar**, toe; **~fingartind**, toenail

Fodalinbu *n.* ankle, knee

fodas-huvudas *adv.* heads-over-heels, tumbling

Fodhår *n.* "foot-hair", hair growing out of footsoles

Fodlofas *n. dual* "foot-gloves", shoes

Fodpudh *n.* stringed pouch, bound on thigh or upper arm

Fodrod *n. Anat.* "leg-root", area incl. thigh and sources in hip

Fodslak *n. & v. dual* kick; **Skik~**, knock

folg, folgefter *v. dual* follow

Folk *n. & v.* **1.** people, race; **2.** *v.* populate, live at *or* in

folkskiklik *a.* social, sociable

Folkstru *see* **Stru**

for *prep.* for, at, in favour of, in order to, because of

forbud *v.* (*part.* **forbidend**; *pres.* **forbid**) frown on, caution, advise against; *arch.* ban, forbid

forgav *v.* (*part.* **forgivend**; *pres.* **forgiv**) forgive

forhinder *v.* prohibit

forhindert *a.* prohibited, taboo

Forhindertid, Hindertid *n.* the future (Lofot)

forhuth *v.* forget

Forhuvd *n.* face, visage, *esp.* hairless part of face, features

forlad *v. dual* forsake, abandon

formist *see* **mist**

forskam *prep. & adv.* despite, even so

Forskik *n.* precedence, preface

forthiin *conj.* so, therefore

Forvak *n. & v.* **1.** intention, anticipation, hope; **2.** *v.* intend, await alertly; **glay~**, anticipate, hope for

forvakt *a.* alert, keen, expectant

Fosfor *n.* phosphorus, irridescence

fram *adv. & v. dual* **1.** forth, forward; **~ u til**, to and fro **2.** *v.* send, proceed, continue; lead, guide, persuade, coax; argue for, insist on, propagate; **~bring**, present, bring to light; **~ utanwud**, *colloq.* transport, exile

Framaras, Framaros *ns. dual & pl.* twin guides, propagators

framklar *v.* show forth, reveal

framsit *v.* postpone

Frand *n. & v.t.* **1.** friend; **2.** *v.* befriend

Frandgav *see* **Gav**

Frandglay *n.* kindness; **in ~**, kindly

Fro *n. & v.* **1.** seed; **2.** *v.* spring up; **3.** *v. dual* sow, seed, breed, impregnate, conceive

frodik *a.* frothy, lush, pregnant; **frod~**, **hog~**, ripe, in last weeks of pregnancy

Frodikhavor *n.* "Sea of Fertility", Mare Fecunditatis, lunar *mare*

Frok *n.* gown, dress, garment

from *prep. & compar.* from, of, out of, belonging to, pertaining to; (*introducing 2nd member of compar.*) than

Fu-en *n.* eastern province and city (*uncert.* Ayan)

Fu-englay *a. colloq.* **in ~**, "pleasing to Fu-en" (Lofot)

fuld *v.t. (part.* **fildend;** *pres.* **fild)** fill, inform, engage; **ob~,** fulfil

ful, fulkomend *a.* complete, perfect, impeccable

Fus *n. & v. imit.* whish, whoosh, flare up

G

gå *v. dual (part.* **gående;** *pres.* **ge)** go, move; **in~,** intervene; **inin~, inunder~,** enter; **~over** *(usu.* **over~),** cross, exaggerate

Gård, Gårdos *ns.* "farms", cultivated area outside city

Gaev *n. & a.* **1.** courage; **2.** *a.* brave, daring

Gap *n. & v.* "stare"; **1.** fixed facial expression, indicating strong emotion; **2.** *v.* gape, stare fixedly

gapt *a.* interested; **~ u rapt,** fascinated, *colloq.* in love

Gapsen *see* **Sen**

Gapsind *n.* amazement, surprise

Gapstart *see* **Start**

Garwa *n. uncert. Medic. herb prob. fam.* yarrow

Gasmin *n.* pleasing scent, jasmine (Lofot)

Gasminglay *n.* **in ~,** enjoying heavy scent (Lofot)

gathar *v.* join, include, assemble, share as one

gathart *a. & adv.* composite, united, together; **got~,** *usu.* joined and sharing as twins

Gav *n. & v.* **1.** "gift", *rare, usu.* of confidence or sacrifice; **Trost~;** gift in trust, offering; **2.** *v. (part.* **givend;** *pres.* **giv)** offer, provide

gavhold *v.* receive; be exposed to; learn effortlessly *(f. ex.* by children, language); freely have, freely partake of

Genog, Nog *n., a. & adv.* sufficient, enough

Get *n. & v. dual* **1.** achievment, household, family, happy or successful life; **2.** *v.* win, achieve, succeed

Getglay *n.* triumph, self-satisfaction

Gist *n. & v.* **1.** yeast; **2.** *v.* stick, fasten

Gistpyt *n.* yeast-well

Givting *n.* concession, accommodation, small present, favour

Gjan *n. & v.* **1.** bay, slit, recess, alcove, insertion; **2.** *v.* insert (Fu-en)

Gjeld *n. & v. dual* **1.** orgasm; **2.** *v.* yield, reach orgasm; **ut~,** climax

Glas *n. & v.* **1.** glass; **2.** *v.* glare, reflect, fit, match, copy

Glasbrandaras *n. dual* twin glass-makers (Severnaya)

Glay, Glee *n., a. & v.* **1.** joy, pleasure; **2.** *a.* content, happy, satisfied; **3.** *v.* please, rejoice, gladden

Glayfest *n.* celebration

Glaylag *n. & v. dual* **1.** antics, nonsense; **2.** *v.* dance, prance about

Glaysen *see* **Sen**

Glaysip *n. colloq.* menstruation (term used to & by girl twin children)

Glaysval *n.* coolness, delight

Glaywud *n.* goodwill; **in ~,** eagerly, willingly

glaywidik *a.* eager

Glim *n. & v.* glance, glimpse, discern, descry

glimsprok *see* **Sprok**

gog *v. dual* preen, look or strut lustily

gold *a.* barren

Goldwo *n.* desert

got *a. & adv.* good, well; **~ u glay**, bonny, healthy, good-natured

gotboornt *a. dual* well-born, healthy

gotmak *see* **mak**

Gotsindi *n. & voc.* "child-god, god", Atwar; **in Bond ~,** "god-bonded", bonded to Atwar (Fu-en)

Gras *ns.* grass, small plants; **hel~,** medicinal herbs

Grasbring *n. & v. dual* **1.** sheaf, turf; cut, bound herbs or fibre; **2.** *v.* harvest fibre

Graswo *n.* meadow

Gredil *n.* pattern, grid, frame, set, system of joined supports (on Moon, structure containing & maintaining atmosphere); **Smar~,** (cloth) map; **Hevitstam~,** skeleton; **Wo~,** ruin

greet *v.* weep, cry; **sma~,** sniff, whimper

Gret *n.* grief, sorrow; **~ Atwar,** "Atwar's Grief", ceremony commemorating the Great Fire of Fu-en (5464)

grim *a.* stern, austere, ugly, harsh, forbidding

Grin *n. & v.* smile; **Fel~,** grimace; **Bred~,** "wide smile", twin smile (Fu-en); **Sma~,** giggle

Gro *n., a. & v.* **1.** green, growth; **2.** *v.* become green, grow, increase

Grund *n. & v.* **1.** purpose, reason; **~ Grund**, great purpose, quest; **2.** *v.* explain

Gruvs *ns. & v.* **1.** gravel, shale; **Små~,** powder; **2.** *v.* crumble, erode, pound, grind, cough

gruvsdrosik *a.* hoarse, rough-voiced; changing-voiced (of adolescent males)

H

Hånd *n.* hand

Håndhår *ns.* "hand-hair", hair growing out of palms

Håndrod *n.* wrist

Hår *ns.* hair, beard

Hadley *n.* lunar mountain

Halv *a. & adv.* half; **~mån** *n.* half-moon

Halt *n. & v. dual* limp

han *pron. subj. (obj.* **him,** *poss.* **sin)** *m. sing. pron. of 3rd pers.*

Hang *n. & v.* **1.** draped cloth; **in ~,** suspended, in abeyance; **~stof**, cloth hung to bleach or dry in process of dyeing; **2.** *v.*

suspend, hang down; hang up; droop, drape

Hap *n. & v.* **1.** chance, event, circumstance, accident; **2.** *v.* happen, befall

hapik *a.* accidental; **hap~**, haphazard

hard *a. & adv.* strong, firm, extreme, hard

hardhold *see* **Hold**

Harm *n. & v.t.* hate

Harmsår *n.* wound

Harmwant *see* **Want**

Hast *n. & v. dual* **1.** haste; **2.** *v.* hasten, hurry

hastik *a.* sudden, quick, urgent

Havor *n.* sea, ocean

Hedh *n. & a.* **1.** heat; **2.** *a.* hot

Hel *n., a. & v.* **1.** care, healing, help; **~hold**, comfort; **2.** *a.* good, whole, entire, healthy, hale, vigorous, strong; **3.** *v.* help, heal, cure

Helaras *n. dual* twin healers, doctors

Helbok *n.* "Medical Book", hospital

Helglay *n.* pleasure in recovery

Helgras *see* **Gras**

Helmån *see* **Mån**

Helskar *n.* scar, healed wound

helt *a.* healed, complete

Hem *n. & adv.* home; **~land**, homeland; **~want**, homesickness, longing; **in ~glay**, welcome

hemwend *v.* return

her, herhiin *adv.* here, in this place

Hersiros *see* **Siros**

~het *suf. formimg ns. of condition, etc.*

hevit *a.* white, blond, fair

Hevitnat *n.* "Whitenight", summer solstice festival (Fu-en)

hevitrot *a.* colourless, pale, pallid, pink

Hevitstam *n.* bone; **Lift~**, rib

hevit-tandht *a.* "white-teethed", childlike, childish

Hibis *n.* rose-mallow

Hibisrot *n. & a.* **1.** uneven dark-pink dye **2.** *a.* pale red

Hid *n. & v.* **1.** ear, hearing: **2.** *v.* hear, heed, listen to

Hidaras, Hidaros *ns.* audience, hearers

Hidgav *n.* vivid & accurate aural memory, recall (*usu.* of children, messengers)

Hidhud *see* **Hud**

hidik *a.* audible; **hid~**, noisy, loud

hidlist *a.* careless, heedless

hidmut *a.* deaf

Hidpudhas *n. dual* protective earmuffs, for babies

Hidsyparas *n. dual colloq.* infant twins

hidsypik *a.* babyish

Hidwo *n.* audible range; **in ~**, in hearing

hiin *a., dem. pron., conj. & adv. emphat.* what, that, which, that there, those there

Hiindag *n. & adv.* **1.** the past; **2.** *adv.* in the past, long ago

Hiintid *n., adv. & conj.* at that time, then, when

him *see* **han**

Hima *n.* secret, covert
Himacar *see* **Car**
himalik *adv.* secretly
Himalapas *n. dual colloq.* lips of vagina
Himamerk *n. colloq.* vagina
Himapudh *see* **Pudh**
hin *pron. subj. (obj.* **hir**, *poss.* **sin**) *f. sing.* pronoun of *3rd pers.*
hinder *v. dual* stop, thwart, prevent
Hindergav *n. uncert.* patent, pact
Hinderliv *n.* future life
Hindertid *see* **Forhindertid**
hir *see* **hin**
Hisis *n. & v. imit.* hiss, whistle
Hjert *n.* heart, centre
Hjertsid *n.* "heartside" left side (of the body); *Twar*, supposedly emotional twin
Hjertwo *n.* breast, chest, upper torso
hof *v. dual* lunge, heave, leap
hofik *a.* cumbersome, clumsy
hofutan *a.* delicate, graceful
hog, hoj *a.* tall, high; (of sounds) loud
hogdrag *see* **drag**
hoghidik *a.* (of sounds) piercing, strident
hoglift *v. dual* ascend
hogstand *see* **Stand**
hogtidik *a. & adv.* timely, imminent
Hoj, Hoy *n.* hill; city in coastal Scandinavia (Hoy); **Dook~**, "Hill of the Doll", open square on Fu-en; *also* **Skik~**, "ceremonial hill"

Hojsprok *see* **Sprok**
Hojwerd *n. Geog.* pole
Hold *n. & v. dual* **1.** embrace, purchase, hold; **2.** *v.* keep, hold, retain, last, endure, cling to, embrace; **hel~**, comfort; **hard~, skin~**, hoard, keep jealously
Hrof *n.* ceiling, roof; **~stof**, heavy cloth, *colloq.* serious matters
Hu *n.* hue, tone
Hud *n. & v.* sound, noise; **Hid~**, clamour, commotion
hug *v. dual* cut, sever; **huvd~**, behead
hul *a.* hollow, cleared, empty, deserted, vacated
Husbondas, Husbondt *n. dual* "house-bonded", husbands, wives
Huth *n. & v.* **1.** lap, embrace, sanctuary; **2.** hide
huthik *a.* shy, embarrassed
Huthob *see* **Ob**
Huthpudh, Huthpyt *see* **Prudpudh**
Huthwo *n.* isolated or regulated glass box for small infants (Lofot); *sl.* "little house", trap, birdcage (Fu-en)
Huvd, Huvud *n.* head; *n. dual* **Huvdas**; **~-eenforhuvd**, "composite face, one-face", illusory single face, twin faces perceived as one (*see* **Huvdskel**)
Huvdhoj *n.* nose
huvdhug *see* **hug**
huvdlik *adv.* singly, in unison, as one (head)

Huvdskel *n.* "face-board", stiffened cloth board worn between heads, projecting between faces (Fu-en); *phr.* **bar ~**, have authority; *a.* **~ealik**, obedient; **~rapt**, influenced, *prob.* hypnotized, by twins wearing face-board; **~skelvik**, confused, disoriented; **~sogendas**, "looking for the face-board", those (twin scholars) aspiring to be great scholars or leaders

Huvdstam *n.* "head-stem", neck (incl. insertions in head, jaw)

huvl *v.* howl, cry loudly; **dodas~**, mourn

I

in~ *pref.* inner

in *prep.* in, at, inside, within; in the mode *or* temper of; ever

Inbolr *n.* bag, bladder

inbring *see* **bring**

Inch *n.* island

ingå *see* **gå**

inin *prep.* into

iningå, inundergå *see* **gå**

Inland *n., a. & adv.* inland

Inlik *n. & v..* **1.** example, comparison; **2.** compare, liken

Insår *n. & v.* **1.** interfere; **2.** interference, contamination, invasion

inskoor *see* **skoor**

Invalkaras, Invalkaros *n. dual & pl.* emigrants, foreign settlers, members of the Walking City (Fu-en)

Inwit *n.* intelligence, ingenuity

inwitik *a.* canny, clever

inwo *a.* private, intimate

irst *a. & adv.* first

Irstsprok *see* **Sprok**

Irstwo *n.* womb

J

Janus *n. dual* twin forefathers (*myth.*) *c.* 2650

je *pron. (obj.* **mi**; *poss.* **min**) *sing. pron. of 1st pers.*

jetro-netro *see* **tro**

Joensuu *n.* western city (Joensuu)

Jomi, Jomu *n.* m. or f. virgin body

Jomwo *n.* virgin vagina

Jomwud *n.* chastity, celibacy

K

Kåm *n. & a.* **1.** darkness; **2.** *a.* dark; **3.** **~sprokt**, "dark-voiced", deep-voiced (*usu.* of women)

Kåmend *n.* "Darkening", eighth month following summer solstice

Kåmos *n.* shortest days, winter solstice (*f. Finn.*)

Kåmsår *n. & v. dual* bruise

Kaj, Kay *ns.* tea; **Kaytreaw** tea-bush

Kald *n.* calling, vocation

Kalk *n.* calcium, edible chalk;

Stofsilt~, dyer's soda for mordant

Kalkhoj *n.* bluff, cliff

kam *v.i.* (*part.* **komend**; *pres.* **kom**) come

Kamchat *n.* eastern range

kan *v. aux.* can, be able to

kanik *a.* possible, able

Kap *n.* point, promontory

Katastrof *n.* catastrophe, disaster

Ker *n. & v.* **1.** fear; **~**, terror; **2.** *v.* fear

kerik *a.* wary, chary, anxious, afraid; **sma~**, nervous, doubtful

kerlist *a.* fearless, carefree

kid *v.* chide, scold

kilik-kilik *int. & n. imit.* noise of looms (Fu-en)

kilt *a.* direct, straight, steady, even, earnest, serious; **ut~**, frivolous, tangled, crooked, askew

Kirtl *n.* shirt, tunic; untenable or briefly held idea or (*usu.*) desire

kirtlik *a.* quick, thoughtless, unconsidered, childish, temporary

klar *a. & adv.* bright, visible, adept, eager, ready; **Bok~** (of children), ready for school

Klarglay *n.* laughter; **in ~**, funny, comic, humorous

klarmak *see* **mak**

kort *a.* short, brief

Kortbond *n.* "short-bond", sanctioned temporary relationship, *usu.* between adolescents & older adults

Kortljus *n. & v.* spark, flicker, flash

kreprot *n. & a.* madder, alizarin

Kreprotrod *n.* madder root

krimp *v. dual* cringe, cower

krub *v. dual* creep, cripple

Krubstam *n.* "generation of cripples", *derog.* term for the four children (ancient, *f.* Rabin, 20c., *ref.* lost)

kudh *a.* sensitive, fine, fragile

Kupl *n.* outcropping, overhang

Kvin *n.* twin of f. twins; **Kvinnas** *n. dual* f. twins

Kvinnasbond *n. & v.* **1.** sexual relationship *or* act of intercourse with f. twins; **2.** *v.t. dual usu. of ms.* bond to *or* have intercourse with f. twins

Kvinnos *ns.* women

Kys *n. & v.* kiss

kyt *v. dual* (of cloth) snip, cut; *colloq.* circumcise

L

Lab *n. & v.* **1.** lip, lid; **2.** *v.* lick

lad *v.* allow, let; *freq.* as **ladmi** ("allow me"), courtesy *phr.* by twin wishing to control body; *euphem.* fail to prevent, assist in (*as,* **~ Dod,** "allow" death)

Lag, Lay *n. & v. dual* play; **Bim~**, "beamed-on" play, approved play; **Brand~**, "play with fire", private play by children; *colloq.* brash, inconsidered act

Lagting *n.* toy

lang *a. & adv.* long (of time); ~
u ~, slowly, gradually

Leer *ns.* clay; ~pyt claypit, dig;
Brand~, tiles, pottery

Lenh *n.* ruined city (Leningrad)

Lenhbok *n.* library at Lenh

ler *v.* 1. *usu.* ~ Bok, learn; 2.
teach, impart

lerik *a.* learned, *colloq.* prating,
didactic

let *a.* slight, light, easy, lenient,
tolerant; (of sounds) high in
tone

Lifr *n.* liver; (*metaph.*) seat of
feelings, *as*, heart

lifrwant *a.* distressed, melan-
choly

Lifrwo *n.* belly, gut, lower torso

Lift *ns. & v. dual* 1. air, breath,
lungs, breathing; 2. *v. refl.*
breathe; 3. *v. dual refl.* live;
svem~, *sl.* "swim", fly; 4. *v.*
throw, cast

liftedh *v.* corrode, rust

Lifthavor *see* Havor

Lifthevitstam *see* Hevitstam

liftik *a.* alive; lift~, lively

Liftrand *n.* perceptual connection, envisaged *or* perceived
line *or* boundary, trajectory,
perimetre

liftwan *v. dual* suffocate, choke,
drown; *metaph.* sink, sub-
merge, founder

~lik, ~ik *suf.* forming *as. & advs.*
f. ns.

lika *v.t.* like, enjoy, pertain to;
~lika *colloq.* love

likwidik *a.* loving, affectionate

lin *v.* ring, reverberate

Linh *n.* 1. ping, tiny ringing
sound; 2. *n. dual* twins, wives
of Betwar, b. 5439 d. 5464

Linné, Linay *n.* brilliant lunar
crater

Lins *n.* disc, lens; *usu.* the great
Disk near Yar

list *a., compar. adv. & conj.* 1.
just, less, somewhat; ~list-
bevor, just before; ~utan,
hardly, scarcely: ~list, least,
last; 2. *conj.* unless

listik *a.* weak, frail, powerless

Liv *n.* 1. living creature, life; 2. *n.*
dual infant daughters of
Tasman, b. 5451 d. 5451

Ljus, Lyus *n., a. & v.* 1. light,
lamp; Pyt~, lamp set into
ground; Stem~, Fager~,
"True light", Outdead light,
coloured light (Lofot); 3. *v.*
light, make visible

Ljusend *n.* "Lightening", eight-
month following winter
solstice

ljusik *a.* bright, light; lift~, radiant, shining; ljus~, brilliant;
son~, sunny, dangerously
bright

Lof *n.* leaf, glove, slipper; Små~,
ns. "small-leaf", moss, lichen,
edible algae

Lofot *n.* coastal Scandinavia
(Lofoten)

lofwant *see* Want

Lom *ns. & v. dual* 1. loom; 2.
trudge, tread

Lond *n.* ancient western city,

destroyed *c.* 2700 (London)

Lov *n. & v.* pact, promise, love

Lovbond *n.* "love-bond", sexual relationship

lovwidik *a. dual* ardent, fervent, passionate

lud *a.* solid, dense, compact

Ludh *n. & a.* **1.** *n. dual* twins, wives of Nev, b. 5442; **2.** compression, density; **3.** alum

---

M

Mån *n.* Moon; **Hel~, Thik~,** full Moon

Månalin, *n.* "Arm of the Moon", telescope, projector

Måndamp *see* **Damp**

Månedht *n.* new Moon

Månfald, *n.* "Moonfall", period of Moon's erratic orbit, threat of Moon's collision with Earth, culminating 5452; **~stand,** prevention of Moonfall

Månotta *n.* "eight-month", half-year; **Hedh~** summer; **Sval~,** winter

Månskead *n.* solar eclipse; **~fest,** celebration of solar eclipse (Fu-en)

Månsump *n.* "Lake of the Moon", depressed arena in Fu-en Great Book, used as projection screen

Månvind *ns.* "the Moon's wind", tidal wind; winds observed on Moon

Ma, Mar, *n. dual* mothers; *arch.* **Madar**

madarlist *a. dual* motherless

mak *v.* do, cause to happen; **~end** (*usu.* **endmak**), finish; **~klar** (*usu.* **klarmak**) exonerate, explain; **~ nakd,** (*usu.* **nakdmak**), bare; **~fuld** (*usu.* **fuldmak**), complete; **got~,** do good, make good, mend, rectify; **meer~,** increase; **sår~,** cause harm, do harm; **~ for &** *inf.,* begin to, be about to

Mamar *n.* of twins, "twarside" or right-handed mother

Mamel *n.* of twins, "twelside" or left-handed mother

Man 1. *n.* twin of m. twins **2.** *ns.* men

Manas *n. dual* m. twins

Manasbond *n. & v.* **1.** sexual relationship *or* act of intercourse with m. twins; **2.** *v. dual usu. of f.* bond to *or* have intercourse with m. twins

Manga *ns. & a.* many, myriad, multitude

Manj'u *n.* northeastern continental plain (*uncert.* Manchuria)

Mar *see* **Ma**

Marfa *n. dual* maternal grandfathers

Marmar *n. dual* maternal grandmothers

Marsk *n.* marsh; **~sump,** marsh-lake

Mat *n. & a.* **1.** rug; **2.** *a.* soft, opaque, vague

Matar *ns.* rain; **~watar,** rainwater (*f. Arab.*)

Matarhavor *n.* "Sea of Rains",

Mare Ibrium, lunar *mare*

Meer *n., a. & compar. adv.* more, also, too; ~ **from**, more than

Meermån *n.* waxing Moon

meermak *see* **mak**

Melk *ns.* breast-milk

Melkfiil *n.* "milk-touching", *usu.* parents' sensual play with children, proscribed after weaning

Menesk *ns.* people

Meneskhår *ns.* human hair

Merk *n.* **1.** footprint, snakespoor; **2.** "trace", Outdead track

mi *see* **je**

mild *a.* mild, clement, placid

mildsindik *a.* tender, gentle, lenient, kind

min *see* **je**

mist *v.t.* lose; **fel~**, forfeit, relinquish

Morn *n.* morning

Mosc, Mosc-ininskeith *n.* city ruin within Sheath (Moscow)

Mu, Mø *n. & voc.* "Marie", maiden, (*usu.* first spoken word, nickname used by infant f. twins in referring to each other)

Mund *n.* (inside of) mouth

Mundas *n. dual colloq.* "two mouths", argument; **in ~,** "in each other's mouths", privately

Mundasnam *n.* **in ~,** called, named

Mundsen *see* **Sen**

mut *a.* mute

N

na~, na *pref. & adv. negativing vs. & advs.*

nakd *a. dual* naked

nakdmak *see* **mak**

Nam *n. & v.* name

Namaras *n. dual* "Namers", twin name-givers

nameer *adv.* no more, no further

Nap *n. & v. dual* **1.** nape; trap, trick; **2.** *v.* seize, snatch, catch, grab, trap, trick

Narod *n.* Mountain in Urals (Narodhaya)

Nat *n.* night

Natwo *n.* "night-place", working place, school

ne~ *pref. negativing ns. & as.*

ne *a. prep. & conj.* no, not, without; ~ ~, *a., prep. & conj. emphat.* no, not, without; ~ ~ **na,** *adv. emphat.* never

neendmak *see* **End**

nekan *v. aux. pres. irreg.* cannot

nekt *v.* refuse, refute, deny

nelik *a.* unlike

ner *a., adv., prep., conj. & v. dual* **1.** almost, close, soon, near, nearly; **2.** *conj. & interr. adv.* when; **3.** *v.* approach, overtake

Nerdag *n.* dawn

Nerfara *see* **Fara**

nerfaralik *a.* precarious

Nerfiil *see* **fiil**

Nermån *n.* perigee

nermeer *a. & adv.* closer

Nernat *n.* twilight

net *a.* neat, brisk, exact, "just so"

Neting *num., a. & adv.* nothing

netwitik *a.* particular, fastidious

Nev *ns.* 1. *arch. unkn.* "snow", congealed air; matchless verbal image (Lofot); 2. *n. dual* twins from Pechor, husbands of Ludh, b. 5438

Nevi, Nevar *see* **Sanev**

Ng *see* **Feng**

Nip *n. & v.* neap, extreme tides; 2. *v.* of tides, to ebb, flow maximally

Nog *see* **Genog**

Nojed *n.* need; ~ **Nojed**, necessity

nojedik, nojdik *a.* ordained, unavoidable, necessary

Nord *n. & a.* north

Noss *n.* island off Lofot

Novaya Zemlya *n.* northern highlands

nu *a. & conj.* new, now, presently

Nua, Nuatid *n. & a. dual* youth, young

O

Ob *n., a., prep. & v. dual* 1. sleeve, door, cloth door (Fuen); *colloq.* mouth; **Huvd~**, "head-sleeve", (of shirt or dress) loose neck-opening; **Huth~**, hood; **~ ~**, great opening, vault; **~inard**, cave, cavern; 2. *adv. & prep.* up, upward; 3. *v.* open

Obard *n. & v. dual* 1. threshold; **over ~**, visiting; **under ~**, in-

active, not involved or responsible, (of unborn infants, subjected to labour); **in ~**, prepared to act, ready, being born; **over ~**, involved, committed; ejected, born; 2. *v. dual* sit in threshold; 3. *v. metaph.* observe passively, consider

oben *a. & adv.* up, open, obvious

obfuld *see* **fuld**

Obsus *n. Geol. uncert.* obsidian *or* agate

Obwo *n.* adult (penetrated) vagina

Og, Oy *n.* eye

Ogpudh *n.* eye-socket

Ogskind *n.* cornea

Ogsen *see* **Sen**

old *v. dual & a.* 1. age, grow old; 2. *a.* old, ancient

Old~ *n. suf.* **~bok**, history; **~bokar**, historian; **~lov**, ancient prediction or prophesy; **~sind**, ancient knowledge; **~sprok**, "Old Speech" (*New Norw., Sw.*); **~wo**, ruined city; **~tid**, ancient times

Oldas *n. dual* old twins

Oldas-skik *n.* custom, customary act

oldas-lik *adv.* "as the old", deliberately, cautiously

Or *see* **Ur**

Ordar *n. & v.* 1. "directions", instructions, plan; 2. *v.* command, direct

~os *suf. forming pl. ns., a. & part. (ommitted in speech)*

os *see* **vl**

Ost *n., a. & adv.* east

Dictionary

Otta *num.* eight

Ottahåndas *num. colloq.* forty; "the forty", 40-stanza *Tale of Tasman*

over~ *pref.* upper

over *prep.* over, on, across

overfald *see* **fald**

Overfod *n.* thigh

overflog *v.* overwhelm, overcome

Overland *n., a. & adv.* by, on, across the land

overtak *see* **tak**

overwend *see* **wend**

P

pas *v. dual* catch, keep, store

Pasaras *n. dual* twin protectors, custodians

Paswo *n.* ward, store

Pechor *n.* city west of Narod (Pechora)

Penek *n.* northern highland; *colloq.* quarry, rocky ground

Penis *n.* penis

Piil *n.* arrow

Pilhuvd *n.* arrowhead

Pilskeparas *n. dual* twin "shapers of arrows" (northern Manj'u)

Pis *n. & v. dual* piss; **Fat~**, "vat-piss", two-day-old urine used in dyeing

plin *v.* whine, complain

Plint *n.* complaint; **Skik~**, formal lament, elegy

Pliny *n.* lunar crater

pluk *v. dual* pick up, pluck, collect, scratch

Plukfingaras *n. dual* apposed fingers (thumb and forefinger)

Polder *n.* diked land

Polderbrim, Pold *n.* dike

Prop *n. & v. dual* buttress, support, stopper, plug; **2.** *v.* support, hold upright; lift, raise, fill in (of dikes, Lofot)

prudh *a.* prim, proud, sagelike

Prudhpudh, Prudhpyt *n. colloq.* "proud-pit", small pocket or depression for possessions (*also*) **Huthpudh, Huthpyt**

prudhsid *prep. & v. dual* **1.** in the possession of, owned by; **2.** *v.* own, hoard

Prudhsprok *see* **Sprok**

Prudhsten *see* **Stamsten**

Pudh *n. & v.* **1.** mound, patch, pouch, pout, pocket; *colloq.* testicles; **hima~**, "pout of sex", mons Veneris; **2.** *v.* pout, sulk

Pudhfingar *n. colloq.* penis

Pudh-mø *n.* "Pillowmarie", prostethic head (Lofot)

Pyt *n.* pit, hole (in earth), pool, puddle; **~-Pyt**, "pit-pool" *or* "pit", small pit dug by pregnant women for childbirth, (water-filled: Lofot)

Pytljus *see* **Ljus**

Q

Qam *n. dual* m. twins, scholars, husbands of Siri, b. 5456 (Fuen)

Qamar *n. arch.* Moon (*f. Arab.*)

R

Raft *n.* litter, sledge; **Stand~**, platform

ran *v. dual* (*part.* **rinend**; *pres.* **rin**) run

Rand *n.* street, passage, path

rapt *a.* preoccupied, obsessed; **lov~**, in love

rebl *v.* ripple, ravel, ruffle, shake

reblik *a.* coarse, wiry, curly

red *v. dual & aux.* prepare, groom (*usu. as pass.* **redt**, ready); *colloq.* lie down; *aux.* prepare to

Redmat *see* **Stofmat**

redsindslip *v. dual* lie down (to sleep)

reks *v. dual* travel

Reksan *n.* journey

Reksaras *n. dual* "Travellers", twin porters *or* walkers between cities

rev *v.* (*part.* **rivend**; *pres.* **riv**) tear (cloth)

revsindik *a.* distraught, frantic

Revsprok *see* **Sprok**

Revstof *n.* rag

rid *v. dual* discard, drop; **cam~**, punish; **lift~**, throw away; **fel~**, lose

Riks *n.* realm, civilized or inhabited world

Riksprok *see* **Sprok**

rinder *v.* remember

ring *v.* gird, surround

Rip *n.* rip-tide, stretch of broken water

ro *v. dual colloq.* "row", crawl, propel forward

Rod *n.* root, reed, rod; *colloq.* contraceptive herb (*also*, ~ **Rod**, "strong root"); **fel~**, inactive or innocuous preparation said to have been fed Tasman by the Say at her initiation

rodgoldas *a. dual* of initiated f. twins, (temporarily) infertile

Rodgoldtid *n.* effective period (about 4 years) of contraceptive herb

Rot *n, a. & v. dual* **1.** dye, red; **~brandpyt**, firepit for dying; **~fat**, dyers' vat; **~pyt**, dye pit; **~skulpfat**, rinsing vat; **~skotsplintas**, dyers' mangle; **~stam-gredil**, system of stakes for hanging cloth to bleach, drip *or* dry; **~wo**, dyeing shed; **2.** *a.* red, ruddy, pretty; **3.** *v.* colour, stain, redden

rotbehårt *a.* fair, red-headed

rotblomik *a.* rosy, roseate

Rotglay *n.*; **in ~**, "in the pleasure of colour", experience of seeing bright (red) colour

Rotl *ns.* reddle, red ochre, red earth dye; *colloq.* stained skin (of dyers)

Rotpyt *see* **Rot**

rotmak *v.t.* "dye red", dye, beautify (Fu-en)

Rotmakaras *n. dual* twin dyers (Fu-en)

Rotwo *see* **Rot**

rund, rundik *a. & prep.* round, around

rundwend *see* **Wend**

S

s~ *suf. marking interr. sent. usu. omitted in speech*

så *v.* (*part.* **sånd;** *pres. & imp.* **se;**) see, look at; **stil~,** gaze

Sår *n. & v. dual* **1.** wound, ulcer; sorrow, sadness; **2.** *v.* wound, hurt, disappoint

sårmak *see* **mak**

Sårsen *see* **Sen**

Sårud *see* **Sorud**

Safir *n. & a.* **1.** sapphire; **~gruvs,** ground sapphire; **2.** *a.* brilliant cerulian blue; unearthly; **efter ~,** after 5474

Safirglay *n.* **in ~,** "in the pleasure of sapphire", experience of seeing bright blue

San, Sansindi *n. & voc.* son, one of twin sons

Sand *ns.* sand

Sandbrand *n.* "burnt sand", ancient glass

Sandstorm *n.* sandstorm

Sanev *n. dual* "Sons of Nev", m. twins, Nevi & Nevar, b. 5459

Sang *n. & v.* **1.** "Song", song, chanted story; **2.** *v.* sing, chant

sank *v.* sink, gulp, swallow

Sap *n. colloq. & v.* **1.** spittle, dark tea (Lofot); **2.** *v.* spit, soak; **rot~,** soak in dye

sapik *a. colloq.* sour, unpalatable (Lofot)

Sapstof *n. colloq.* old (or stained) drinking cloth

Saska *n.* son of Betwar, b. 5463 d. 5474

Say *n.* **1.** saying, proverb; **2.** *n.*

dual f. twins, b. 3390 d. 5451 (Uppsal)

Semer *n. & v. dual* **1.** refinement, clarity, purity; **2.** *n. dual* twins from Lofot, b. 5402; **3.** *v.* cook, simmer, shimmer, cleanse by boiling, clarify

Semer Rand *n.* "Semer's Way", path from Fu-en to Yar

semik *a.* metal-coloured, silvery; pristine, pure

Sen *n. Anat. & v.* **1.** muscle, sinew *usu.* facial muscle of expression; **Glay~,** *Zygomaticus minor* (smiling muscle); **Klarglay~,** *Z. major* (laughing muscle); **Gap~, Mund~,** *Orbicularis oris* ("gaping" *or* mouth muscle); **Og~,** *O. oculi* (eye muscle); **Sår~,** *Depressor labii inferioris* (muscle of sadness); **Skuvl~,** *D. anguli oris* (scowling muscle); **Sner~,** *Levator anguli oris* (sneering muscle); **Start~,** *Frontalis* (staring muscle), *etc.;* **2.** *v.* express; **3.** *v. dual* reach, strain, stretch, exert

sendod *a.* numb, *metaph.* stunned

Sensmar *n.* facial expression

Severnaya Zemlya *n.* northern highland

Shelik *n.* bay N. of Fu-en

Shui *n.* **1.** waters (*f. Chin.*); **2.** *n. dual* f. twins, short-bonded by Sanev 5775 (Fu-en)

Sid *n., a., prep. & conj.* **1.** side; **~huvud** (of head) temple; (of loom) device to keep cloth stretched; **2.** *a.* parallel; **3.** *prep.* near, beside, against, in the possession of (*as v.* have); **4.** *conj.* since

Sidflog *n.* tributary

sidhuvdik *a.* taut, tight, stretched

Sikt *n. & v.* **1.** sight, gaze, direction, general view, outlook, visual field; **Små~**, exceptionally clear sight (as childrens'); **2.** *v.* poise, aim, direct

Siktgav *n.* vivid, accurate visual memory (*usu. of* children); vivid or prophetic dream

siktlik *a.* visible, perceptible, materialized

siktutanwud *a.* oblivious

Siktwit *n. & v.* **1.** attention, awareness, recognition; **2.** *v.* attend to, recognize

Silt *ns.* salt

siltbring *v. dual* harvest salt

Siltgras *ns.* "salt-grass", sourgrass

Siltwatar *ns.* saltwater

Siltwo *n.* salt flats, saltings

Sim *n.* seam, fold

sin *see* **han**

Sind *n. & v.* **1.** self, mind; **2.** "twin", individual, one of two individuals constituting bicephalic human being; **for ~ u Skam**, in honour of, for the sake of; **3.** *v.* think seriously, bring to mind, keep in mind, honour

Sindbludel, Sindblud *ns.* "mind-blood", violent thoughts or images

Sindhu *n.* "colour of mind", *metaph.* disposition, nature

Sindi *n. & voc. dim.* "little-mind", individual of twin children; *colloq.* one of Betwar's children

Sindsikt *n.* attention

skindskar *v. arch.* harm mentally, craze

sindskart *a.* inattentive, deranged (by previous experience)

sindskelvik *a.* crazy, "rattled", unexplainably deranged

Sindslip *see* **Slip**

Sindstof *n.* thought; *also*, **Slip~**, (verbal) image, dream, imagining; **vav ~**, pretend, imagine

sindtas *a. dual* twinned, two-minded

sindutan *a.* careless, impetuous

sindwitik *see* **witik**

Sindwo *n. colloq.* "the house of the mind", mind

Sip *n. & v.* **1.** damp ground, seep, possibility; **2.** *v.* seep, dimly appear (*as*, first light)

sir, siir *a. & v.* **1.** strange, odd; **2.** *v.* speak strangely, mumble; **sir~**, stammer

Siras, Siros *n. dual & pl.* strangers, foreigners; **Her~**, diaspora Scandinavians (Fu-en)

Siri *n. & v.* **1.** *n. dual* Fu-en twins, wives of Qam, b. 5555; **2.** infant plaintive crying, gurgling, piping sound; **3.** *v.* squeak, pipe, babble, prattle; **~siri**, *sl.* warble, chirp (as birds)

Sirisplint *n.* flute, reed (Fu-en)

sirsang *v.* lull, croon, hum

Sirsind *n.* confusion of mind

sirsindik *a.* confused, irritable

sirsprokik *a.* talkative, verbose

sit *v.* put, place; *v. dual refl.* sit; over~, superimpose, overlay; ~ **Stam in Bro**, "place a stem across", refute, win or redirect argument with new evidence (Lofot)

Siya *n.* old city site in northwest (*uncert.* Tsilma); *colloq.* new field, clearing

Skael *n.* scale, feather

skal *v. aux. forming imper.* must

Skam *n.* sake

Skamfel *n. & v.* 1. shame, regret; 2. *v.* put to shame, blame, condemn

skamfelt *a.* regretful, remorseful, ashamed

skamwend *v.* repent

Skar *n. & v.* 1. scar; Sind~, compulsive recurrent thought, idea, or memory ; 2. *v.* carve, score, incise; *arch.* write

Skarsprok *see* **Sprok**

Skead *n.* shade, shadow; in ~, shy, withdrawn

Skeith *n.* barrier; "Sheath", barrier, uninhabitable zone of continent, extending S *f. c.* 60 N; ~bord, Sheath wall, rising boundary of Sheath; ~brim, abrupt northern edge of Sheath surface

Skel *n.& v.* 1. part (in hair); 2. *n. dual* ~sindas, (between twins)

difference of opinion, lasting quarrel; 3. *v.* part, separate, try, test, prove, distinguish

skelrapt, skelskelvik *see* **Huvudskel**

skelv *v. dual* tremble, shake, jitter; ut~, shake off

skelvstart *v. dual* startle, jump in surprise

Skep *n. & v. dual* 1. shape, device, instrument; 2. *v.* shape, devise, make; vaker~, beautify by shaping head, *thus*, flatten (Fu-en)

skepik *a.* excelling, proficient, deft

Skepsplintaras *n. dual* "shapers of wood", twin woodworkers

Skeptflad *see* **Flad**

Skerm *n.* "screen", Outdead computing device

Skik *n.* ritual, custom, manner, way; courtesy

skikdrag *see* **drag**

Skikflit *n. & v.* gesture, flourish

skikfromwend *see* **Wend**

Skikglay *n.* pleasure in ceremony

Skikhoj *see* **Hoj**

skiklik *a. & adv.* courteous

Skikplint *see* **Plint**

Skikslaksprok *n.* ritual quarrel, debate

Skiksprok *see* **Sprok**

Skikwend *n.* "Circle", circling dance, ceremony, pageant, turn, (Fu-en)

Skind, Skindos *ns. lit.*, "skincells", skin; Snog~, snakeskin

skindgathart *a.* wrinkled, shrivelled, puckered, tucked

skindhevit *a.* albino, redheaded (rare); of, related to people supposed to inhabit Southern Hemisphere

skinhold *see* **hold**

skinwant *a.* jealous

skler *a.* blue, bluish-gray; distant; ~**werd**, distant scene blued by aerial perspective; ~**wald**, distant woods, woods seen on Moon

Sklera, Skler *n.* distance; sclera: white of eye, (blue in Lofot people)

sklerarot *a.* cold reddish colour, purple

Sklerfolk, Skleroyos-folk *n.* "The people of distant eyes", Lofot people (Plains)

skoor *v. dual* scour, scrape, scratch, shave; **brand**~, scorch; **in**~, pierce

skot *v.* squeeze, wring, squint, frown

Skotwatar *n.* clean water, drinking water

Skul *n.* bowl, vessel; pate, scalp, bald or shaved head (of the old)

skulp *v. dual* rinse, stir; *colloq.* stir about or mess with (food)

Skulpfat *see* **Rot**~

Skum *n.* surf, splash, breaking wave

Skutel *n.* shuttle, shaft

Skuvl *n. & v.* scowl

skuvlik *a.* sullen

Skuvlsen *see* **Sen**

Slak *n. & v. dual* strike, beat, clap

Slaksprok *n.* quarrel

Slam *n.* grease; ~**rod**, milfoil

Slamstam *n.* torch, taper

Slap *n., a. & v. dual* **1.** sleep, nap; **Slap** ~, long, heavy sleep; **Wern**~, exhausted sleep; **2.** *a.* asleep, relaxed, sloppy

Slent *n., a. & v.* **1.** cliff, slope, sly glance; **2.** *a.* steep, oblique, slanted, (of faces) "steep", gaunt, sly; **Skik**~, dissembling, dishonest; **små**~, (of half-grown twins) shy, secretive, devious; **3.** *v.* tilt, slant, divert, look askance; **4.** *v. dual* saunter, walk off (without formal leave-taking)

Sling *n. & v. dual* **1.** hammock; **2.** *v.* swing, lull to sleep (Fu-en)

Slip, *n & v. dual.* **1.** mud; **Smar**~, ceremonial slip, wet clay, wet reddle (Fu-en); **2.** *v.* escape from, drop, abandon, relent, relinquish, let fall, let go; *colloq.* forget; **sind**~, forget

slipik *a.* runny, slippery, clever

Små *ns. & a. pl.* **1.** children: **2.** *a.* small

Småa *n. & a. dual* **1.** twin children; **2.** *a.* small

Småatwan *n. dual* baby twins

Smålof *see* **Lof**

Småsikt *see* **Sikt**

sma *a. sing.* little

Smabetwan *see* **Betwan**

Smabok *n.* "little Book", Betwar's children's school in Fu-en

Sma-edh *see* **Edh Atwar**

smagreet *see* **greet**

smagrim *a.* shrunken, stunted

Smal *a. & v.* **1.** narrow, meagre, sad; skinny (of twins); **2.** *v.* shrink, diminish

smalt *v.* (*part.* **smeltend**; *pres.* **smelt**) melt, mesh, merge, mould, run together

Smalval *n.* gulch, mountain defile

smar *v.* paint, smear

Smarslip *see* **Slip**

Smart *n.* pain

Smasten *n.* pebble

Sner *n. & v.* sneer, taunt

Snersen *see* **Sen**

Snog *n.* "snake", large limbless reptile (rare) believed to be intelligent; dragon

snogik, snogwitik *a.* devious, guileful, secretive, shrewd

Snogmelk *n. colloq.* semen

Snogslam *n.* lamp oil

Snogsogaras *n. dual* twin snake hunters

sog, sogefter *v. dual* search for, forage, hunt

som *v.* seem

somlik *a.* seemly, goodly

Son *n.* sun

Sonhår *ns.* solar corona

sonhevit *v. dual* bleach, whiten

Sonnevi *n.* **1.** **Göran ~**, Outdead poet, author *ca.* 1980 of Lins fragment (*see* **Moonfall**); **2.** "little sun-snow", childrens' inadvertant imagery (*see* **Nev**)

Sonsomerblom *n.* flower, *uncert. prob.* sunflower *or* rose

Sorud *n.* **1.** (*f. arch.* **Sårud**)

deliverance; **2.** *n. dual* twins, husbands of Tasman, b. 5402 d. 5460

Soster, Søster *n.* sister *usu.* twin sister

sot *a.* sweet

Sothavor *n.* "Sea of Sweetness", Mare Nectaris, lunar *mare*

spar *v. dual* save, deliver, rescue; *refl.* avoid

Spararas *n. dual* twin rescuers; **Esparar** *arch. sing.* savior

sparsog *v. dual* seek refuge

spartas, spart *a. dual & pl.* safe, rescued, free; "spared", alive (of infants)

Spartwo *n.* refuge, deliverance; **in ~**, home safe, secure, *euphem.* dead

Spil *n. & v. dual* **1.** waste, overflow; **Brim~**, abundance, plenty; **2.** *v.* waste, spend incontinently (of dye, semen, water)

Spir *n. & v.* doubt, question, wonder

Splint *n. & v. dual* **1.** worked wood, stripped or split branch **2.** *v.* work (wood), *also* **skep~**; break apart, splinter

Sprok *n. & v.* **1.** voice, speech, language, word; **Atwar~**, "the speech of Atwar", corrupted diaspora Scandinavian (Fuen); **Irst~**, "First Speech", original language of Manj'u (Fu-en); **Rik~**, modern Scandinavian language; **Skik~**, formal speech, interview; **Stem~**, "True

Speech" (Riksprok); Wo~, "house-speech", colloq. speech; 2. *n. & v.* Hoj~, call, shout; Prudh~, boast; Rev~, shriek, scream; Stil~, murmur; 3. *v. (part.* sprekend; *pres.* sprek) speak, converse; for~, commit, convince; fram~, provoke, tease; glim~, decipher, "read" (facial expression); stand~, protest, condemn, contradict

Sprokas *n. & int.* "two voices", *int.* (childbirth); in~Klarglay, joy at hearing two infant voices

Sprokdel *n.* phrase

stakr *v. dual* stagger, hobble, falter, stumble

Stam *n.* stem, reed, trunk, spar, staff, torso; Sma~, twig, *colloq.* alphabetic letter

stambludik *a.* related by blood, consanguine

Stambolraras *see* Bolraras

stamfram *v. dual* perpetuate

Stamsten *n.* inherited stone *uncert.* gemstone; *also* Prudh~

Stamtal *n. & ns.* generation; "the generations", orally transmitted family history or Tale

Stand *n. & v. dual* 1. stand, grove (of trees), fallow part of farm, preserve, leaving; 2. *v.* stop, stay, abide, remain, interrupt; hog~, get up, rise; slap~, stall, loiter, linger; ~ evan, "Remain as you were", courtesy phrase (Lofot)

Standcar *see* Car

standik *a.* resolute; stand~, stubborn

standlist *a.* restless, shiftless

Standwabh *n.* "standing wave", stationary wave

Start *n. & v. dual* 1. start, surprise, stare; 2. *v.* startle, hesitate; Gap~, stare

stem *v.* correspond, fit, befit, be right, true

Stembok *n.* "True-Book", ancient printed paper

Stemhet *n.* correspondence, likeness, harmony

Stemljus *see* Ljus

Stemsprok *see* Sprok

stemt *a.* corresponding, right, in harmony

Stemtind *n.* accuracy

Stemtro *n. & a.* 1. true belief, certainty; 2. *a.* sure, convinced

Stemtvan *n. dual* "true twins", *uncert.* telepathic or *(prob.)* having commisure conjoined ventrically at stem

Sten *n.* stone; ~brist, quarry

Stenbristaras *n. dual* twin quarriers

sthi *see* thi

Stik *n. & v. dual* 1. ladder; *(also,* ~stam); 2. *v.* climb, clamber

Stikbord *see* Bord

Stikwatar *see* Watar

stil *a. & v.* still, quiet

Stilhavor *n.* "Sea of Quiet", Mare Serinitatis, lunar *mare*

stilså *see* så

Stilsind *n.* serene consciousness, awareness; Mut~, non-verbal consciousness & intelligence (*usu.* non-human *but also*, of infants, the deaf); **Treaw~**, consciousness (& intelligence) of plants

Stilstand *n. & v. dual* **1. in ~**, motionless, calm, laid aside, neglected; **2.** *v.* stand still, be motionless

Stink *n. & v. dual* stink, *usu.* smell of human excrement, decay or death

stinkstemt *a. dual colloq.* "having the right, or privilege, to stink", of the old *or*, newborn

stir *v. dual refl.* move, stir, bestir (*usu.* after "fixed" staring)

Stof *n.* cloth, *colloq.* thought

Stofgras *ns.* "cloth-grass", large, cultivated herb with copious inflated fibre-pods *prob. fam.* milkweed

Stofhu *n.* untreated cloth fibre

Stofmat, Redmat *n.* sleeping mat (Lofot)

Stofrand *n.* narrow hall or covered street (Fu-en)

Stofsilt, Stofsiltkalk *see* **Silt**

stoft *a.* fuzzy, vague, diffused

Stofwo *n.* tent (plains), cloth house (Fu-en)

stop *v. dual* rest; **~ for**, await

Storm *n. & v.* storm

Stormflod *n.* flood; **~as** *n. dual*, "the Two Floods" of Lofot, 5451

Strand *n.* beach, shore; **in ~**, ashore

Stru *n. & v.* **1.** scattering; **Folk~**, "diaspora", displaced Scandinavian people; **Fel~**, *colloq.* visible semen; **2.** *v.* scatter, disperse

Strum *n. & v. dual* stroke, rub, caress

Sufur, 'Sufur *n. sing.* (*dual* **'Sufureen,** *pl.* **'Asahfeer** *corrupt.* **Asafir**) bird (*f. Arab.*)

Sufurhuvd *n. & voc. vulg.* "head-of-a-sufur", one-headed (of Betwar, Fu-en)

Suid *n., a. & adv.* south

Suidfolk *n.* hypothetical race in Southern Hemisphere

Sump *n.* lake

sva *interr. adv.* (*colloq.* **'va**) what, who

sval *a.* cool, pleasant, comfortable

Svalhet *n.* coolness, comfort; **Nat~**, coolness of night

Svalmånotta *see* **Månotta**

svalwyp *v. dual* cool by wiping

Svar *n. & v.* answer

Svart *n. & a.* **1.** black colour; **2.** *a.* "swart", swarthy, black

Svart-rod *n. unkn.* indelible root, preparation applied at initiation to protect and beautify teeth

Svartsten *n.* slate

svart-tandht *a.* "black-teethed", adult, initiated

svem *v. dual* (*part.* **svimend;** *pres.* **svim**) swim

svo, swo *interr. adv.* (*colloq.* **'vo**) where

Sward *n.* sward, plane of grass

syp *v.* drink, suck

Sypstof *n.* drinking-cloth, cloth soaked with tea or clean water

T

~t *suf. forming p.p., pass. & adjs.*

Tår *n. & v. dual* 1. tear; 2. *v.* (of eyes) tear

T'ai *n.* 1. whiteness (*f. Chin.*); 2. *n. dual* m. twins, scholars, brothers of T'ien, deported 5452 (Fu-en)

tak *v.* take; **over~** *v. dual* inherit

Tal *n. & v.* 1. "Tale", orally transmitted story, *usu.* rhymed or repetitive, story, message, number; **in ~**, accounted for, respected; 2. *v.* tell, count, measure

Talaras *n. dual* twin "tellers", singers, story-tellers, letter-tellers

Talglay *n.* (children's) pleasure in counting

taltalik *a.* fabulous, fantastic, hypothetical, unbelievable

Tandh *n.* tooth

Tared *n.* daughter of Betwar, sister of Ard, b. 5460

Tasman *n.* monocephalic woman from Lofot, mother of the Avskel, b. 5428

Taygon, Tagon *n.* coastal range N. of Fu-en

Tchern *see* **Chern**

Tek *n. & v.* 1. sign, indication, significance; 2. *v.* mark, signify

tekik *a.* important, significant

tham *see* **thay**

thama *see* **thay**

than *adv.* then, at that time

thar *adv.* there

thara *see* **da**

thay *pron. subj. (obj.* **tham**, *poss.* **thama**) *dual pron. of 3rd pers.*

thi *adv. & conj.* if, because, thus, so; **s~**, if, whether

thiin *a., dem. pron. & adv. emphat.* this here, these here, such a

Thiindag *n.* today, the present, modern times

thik *a. & v.* 1. stubby, swollen, engorged, waxed full, lusty; 2. *v.* swell, distend, fatten (*as*, breasts, infant belly after nursing, penis, plant, Moon)

thikbuet *a.* rigidly adhered to, impervious to argument

Thiksind *n. colloq.* lust, desire

Thiksindas *n. dual colloq.* lusty twins

thom *pron. subj. & obj.* (*poss.* **thoma**) *pl. pron. of 3rd pers.*

thoma *see* **thom**

Thvar *n. & v.* rage, anger, pain

thvart *a.* angry, sore; **~ thvartik**, furious, painful

Thvarwant *see* **Want**

Tid *n.* time, occasion

tidik *a.* timely, eventual, sequential

Tidsind *n.* nature, disposition, temper; **Tvan~** (*dual*), shared (*usu.* physical) nature

Tidsikt *n.* attitude

tidwant *a. & adv.* late, belated

Tidwatar *ns.* tide, tidal wash

Tidwatarvind *ns. colloq.* tidal wind

T'ien *n.* 1. sky (*f. Chin.*); 2. *n. dual* f. twins, scholars, sisters of T'ai, deported 5452 (Fu-en)

til, ti~, til~ *prep. & pref.* to, at to, at, until, up to

tilvard, tilvardin *prep.* toward

Tind *n. & v.* **1.** tip, flare, *colloq.* nail; **2.** *v.* prick, light, catch (of fire); bite

Tindi, Tindsmar *n.* flake, speck; *colloq.* freckle

tindik *a.* abrupt, sharp, bitter

Tindwo *n.* "The Pointed Desert", area west of Fu-en, site of great Disk

Ting *n.* thing

tistad *v.i. dual arch.* (*part.* **tistedend;** *pres.* **tisted**): *v.* be placed, present (Lofot)

Torn *n.* **1.** thorn, thorny plants

Torntind *n. & v.* **1.** prick, reminder, painful memory; **2.** *v.* prick, stick

Tradh *ns.* rope, braid, string

Tradhi *n. sing. & v. dual* **1.** thread, wisp, tag, fibre, filament, single human hair; **2.** *v.* stitch, mend, embroider, elaborate; think consecutively

Tranqhavor *n.* "Sea of Tranquility", Mare Tranquilitatis, lunar *mare*

Tre *num.* three

Treaw *n.* tree; **Sma~** bush, shrub

Treawik *a.* "vegetable", concerning plants, plant-covered

Treawstilsind *see* **Stilsind**

triv *v. dual* thrive, prosper

Tro *n., v. & aux.* **1.** belief, conviction; **2.** *v.* guess, speculate, conjecture, believe; **3.** (*w.pron. pref.*) *v. aux. forming cond.,*

subj. may, might; **~-netro,** doubt

Trold *n.* troll, small, deformed creature referred to in Tales (*prob. ref.* Outdead)

Trost *n. & v.* trust

Trostgav *see* **Gav**

Tseth *n. dual* m. twin quarriers (from Penek), d. 5474

Tugt *n. & v.* **1.** tongue, taste, scent, quality; **2.** *v.* smell, taste, chew; sense, savour, linger over (also of sight, sound, touch); **in ~glay,** enjoying sensation, finding delicious

Tulv *num.* twelve

Turuk *n.* plains city (*uncert.*)

Tusind *num.* thousand

Tva *num.* two (rare, used only to count or measure)

Twan, Tvan *n. dual & v.* **1.** "twain", "twins", bicephalic human being; **2.** *v.* conjoin, combine; **~håndas,** *colloq.* "join hands", (of uninitiated twins) masturbate

Twanglay *n.* **in ~,** in harmony (between twins)

Twanfolk *n. pl.* bicephalic people, bicephalic race

Twar *n.* right-hand twin

Twarhånd *n.* right hand

Twarsid *n. & a.* right side, right

twarvé, twarvay *adv.* right, to the right

twastemt *a.* equal, symmetrical

Tvatal *n. & v.* **1.** name for the emphat. & superl. form (*usu. as* twice or thrice repeated *wd.*): *emphat. as* much, very, positively, strongly, extremely, indeed; *superl. as* greatest, most; **in ~**, in emphat. mode; **2.** rhyming verse, rhymed song, strain, refrain, echo; **3.** *v.* emphasize, repeat, mimic, rhyme, speak in rhyme

twatid *adv.* twice; **in ~**, at second hand

tvatidik *a.* simultaneous

Twelhånd *n.* left hand

Twelsid *n. & a.* left side, left

twelvé, twelvay *adv.* to the left

Twiin *n. & v.* dual. **1.** complex double braid of (twins') hair (Scandinavia); **2.** *v.* twist, braid

Twiinharm *n. arch.* cruelty

U

u *conj., prep. & adv.* and, with, again

u al *in v. phr. forming emphat. as v.,* ~, *participial n.; ex.* (han) vak u al Vakend, (he) watched with all his might

under~, under *pref., a. adv. & prep.* under, lower, down; ~**ard**, below ground level

undergå *see* **gå**

Undersikt *n.* "downlook", averted gaze signifying withdrawal

Uppsal, Uppsal-a *n.* western city (Uppsala)

Ur, Or *n.* **1.** origin, source; **2.** *n. dual* sons of Betwar, called Ask & Saska, b. 5463

urlik *a.* original, primordial

ut~ *adv. pref.*; un-, out-, utterly

ut *prep.* out of, from, away from; *usu.* ~**from**

utan, utan~, ~utan *prep., suf. & pref.* without

utanatwar *a.* secular

utanfilt *a.* "untouched", punished by withholding caresses (of children)

utanlert *a.* ignorant

utansindik *a.* unaware

utanslipik *a.* relentless, continuous

utanstandik *a.* irresistible

Utantugt *n.* "unsmell", lack of scent or taste

utanwendik *a.* unswerving

utanwo *a.* public, general

utanwud *adv.* "unwillingly", by force

Utbludel, Utblud *n. metaph.* shame

utbrand *see* **Brand**

Utbred *see* **Bred**

utbrimt *a.* extravagant, elaborate

utdamp *v.* condense

Utdod *n.* "Outdead", monocephalic race, extinct ca. 2700 A.D.

Utdodskep *n. colloq.* maze, puzzle

utdodskept *a.* complicated, intricate

Utdodwerskep *see* **Werskep**

utdrag *see* **drag**

utdyp *a.* very deep, fathomless

Utfrand *n. & v.* **1.** "unfriend", *arch.* enemy; **2.** *v.* quarrel with

utgå *see* **gå**

utglim *v.* dwindle, diminish, taper, fade

utglimt *a.* dim, faded

Utgret *a.* utter grief, despair

utidik, in Utid *a. & adv. phr.* early, untimely, premature

utkilt *see* **kilt**

utkudh *a.* coarse, rude, uncouth

Utland *n.* foreign country, primitive area or society

Utlandaras, Utlandaros *n. dual derog.* foreigners, curious-looking unfamiliar people, strangers

utlandik, utlandskiklik *a. derog.* foreign, outlandish, bizarre

Utliv *ns. & v. dual* **1.** survivors, the surviving race; **2.** *v.* survive

utrid *v. dual* destroy

utskelv *see* **skelv**

Utskep *n. & voc.* "unshape", reverted image or form, *voc. vulg.* one's twin

Utskik *n.* public spectacle, predicament

Utsprok *n. colloq.* "unspeech", unlearned (thus, incomprehensible) language; "unwords", wordless chatter, *as of* birds, babies

utstand *v. dual* withstand, resist, challenge

utstemt *a.* "not corresponding", false, wrong

Utstrand *n., a. & adv.* offshore

utvaker *see* **vaker**

utwendt *a. & adv.* lost, absent, gone

utwot *a.* "unhoused", mentally disturbed, inattentive

utwypt *a.* "wiped out", obliterated, erased, vanished

V

va *pron. subj. (obj.* **as,** *poss. m.* **vara,** *f.* **var)** *dual pron. of 1st pers.*

Vak *n. & v.* **1.** "the Watch", lunar watch, ceremony of watch, vigil; watchpeople, guard (Fu-en); **2.** *v.* wake, await, awaken, look out for, watch for, keep watch over, guard

Vakaras *n. dual* twin guards, members of Watch

vaker *a.* beautiful (Fu-en); **ut~, Fu-englay~,** "considered beautiful in Fu-en", bizarre, unattractive (Lofot)

Vakerhet *n.* beauty (of face) harmony of expressive musculature

vakerskep *see* **Skep**

vakerskept *a.* well-shaped (of heads, Fu-en)

vakt *a. & adv.* slow, late

vakwidik *a.* patient

Vakwud *n.* patience

val *v.t.* decide, choose

valik *a.* deliberate

valk *v. dual* walk; **ek~,** pace, walk carefully; **visk~,** shuffle

Valkendskel *n.* lunar terminator

Valkendwo *n.* "The Walking

City", those with or joining Tasman in journey E.; that journey, 5450-5451

Valkfest *n.*, celebration of twins' learning to walk, *usu. c.* four years old

var *see* va

vara *see* va

varsind *v.* (*part.* **ersindend**; *pres.* **ersind**) be alert, present

Varsl *n. & v.* **1.** threat, warning; **2.** *v.* warn

vat *a.* wet; **hel~**, drenched, soaking

Vav *n. & v.* **1.** *colloq.* dream; **2.** *v.* weave, think comprehensively; ~ **Sindstof**, pretend, dream, imagine (Fu-en)

Vavaras *n. dual* twin weavers

vavt *a.* woven; *colloq.* imaginary

Vept *n.* weft, transverse thread woven into warp; **in ~ u Verp**, *prep. phr.* "weaving together into one cloth", resolving, coming to completion (Fu-en)

Verp *n.* warp, lengthwise thread woven into weft (Fu-en)

vi *pron. subj.* (*obj.* **os**, *poss. f.* **vora**, *m.* **vor**) *pl. pron. of 1st pers.*

vil *v. aux.* forming fut.

Vind *ns.* wind

vink *v.* wink, wince

Visk *n. & v.* whisper; ~ **visk**, tattle, rumour

viskvalk *see* valk

Voksan, Vokson *ns. dual & pl.* adults

Voksanfast *n.* adult initiation

Voksanfest *n.* celebration after initiation

Voksankyt *n.* m. circumcision

Voksanwo *n.* "adult room", initiation & (until or unless bonded) private room for initiated twins

vor *see* vi

vora *see* vi

W

Wabh *n. & v.* **1.** wave, flap, flourish; ~ **Wabh**, great wave, tidal wave; **2.** *v.* waver, flourish, shake out, billow out (cloth)

wad *v. dual* wade

Wadhavor *n.* "wading sea", shallows

Wal *n.* wall; cloth wall (Fu-en)

Wald *n.* forest

wan *v. dual* sicken, contaminate

Wan, Wanbokaras *n. dual* twins, f. scholars, mothers of Ng, d. 5453

Wanmån *n.* waning Moon

Want *n. & a.* **1.** sickness; **in ~**, lacking; **Harm~**, *arch.* (of Outdead) sickening, consuming hatred; **Thwar~**, "(body's) anger", sickness; **2.** *a.* sick; **lof~**, sickly, greenish

Watar *ns.* water; **Stik~**, rising tide

watardous *v. dual* divine, dowse

Watardousaras *n. dual* twin dowsers, water-finders

Watarfald *ns.* waterfall

Watarrand *n.* canal, water-course

wen *v. dual* wean, be weaned

Wend *n.* & *v. dual* change, turn, circle; **2.** *v.* **from~**, leave, remove; **huvd~**, distract, entice, seduce; **3. lay~**, squirm, roll about (in play); **over~**, turn over; **rund~**, circle, rotate, turn around; **skelv~**, range, walk agitately; **skikfrom~**, take (formal) leave of

wendfromlik *adv.* backwards

Wendglas *n.* mirror, match, reflexion, (pictorial) image

wendlet *a.* changeable, volatile

Wendwatar *ns.* whirlpool

went *a.* weaned

wentgrim *a. dual* unattractive, of weaned children

Wentfest *n.* weaning

Wentsmå *ns.* weaned children

Wer *n.* & *v. dual* **1.** effort, difficulty; **~ Wer**, extreme difficulty; **Bodh~**, physical effort or difficulty; **Sind~**, mental effort or difficulty; **2.** *v.* fret, worry, attempt, try, endeavour, **~boorn,** give birth with difficulty; **~wend**, strive, wrestle

Werd *n.* world, the Earth, everything

Werdas *n. dual* "the two worlds", Earth & Moon; **betwan ~**, "between the worlds", anywhere, everywhere

Werdi *n.* star

werdik *a.* natural

Werdiwo *n.* space, the heavens

Werdmar, Werdmadar *n. dual* "earth-mothers", twin midwives

Werdskead *n.* shadow of Earth on Moon, lunar eclipse

Werdskel *n.* horizon

Werdskelv *n.* earthquake

Werdsmå *ns.* "World-children", children choosing not to go to school

werdstemt *a.* right, harmonious; (of people) steady, righteous, in harmony with the world

werik, *a. dual* busy; **wer~**, bustling, fussy, tiresome

werfram *v. dual* prise, force open

wern *a.* weathered, dull, worn, spent; *(dual)* bored, weary

Werskep, Utdodwerskep *n.* scheme, machination, contraption, machine fashioned by Outdead

Werskep-nersind *n.* "machine near-mind", functioning machine (Outdead)

werwend *see* **Wer**

West *n., a.* & *adv.* west, *usu.* Scandinavia

Whalsay *n.* western highland; **~hevitas**, *a.* dual *colloq.* of Whalsay, red-headed

widik, glaywidik *int.* please

wild *a.* naughty, uncooperative

Wit *n.* & *v.* **1.** knowledge; **2.** *v.* reason, know, understand

witik, sindwitik *a.* thoughtful, reasonable

Witsind *n.* wisdom, understanding

Witskep *n.* art, craft, design, tactic

witskepik *a.* canny, clever, artful

witwidik *a.* curious, inquisitive; ~**widik**, pestering, importunate

Wo *n. & v. dual* **1.** place, house, dwelling, room, city; **2.** *v.* dwell

Wogredil *see* **Gredil**

wohiin *adv., conj. & pron.* where, wherever

Wort *n.* mole, bump

woskep *v. dual* order, furnish dwelling

Woskik *n. & v. dual refl.* custom, habit; **2.** *v.* accustom

woskikik *a.* usual, familiar, practical, customary, ordinary, matter-of-fact

woskikt *a.* used, accustomed

Wosprok *see* **Sprok**

Wostof *n.* "house-cloth", wall or roof

Wud *n. & v.* **1.** wish, will, preference, desire; **Vak~**, patience; **2.** *v.* (*part.* **widend**; *pres.* **wid**) prefer, want, desire; **wid~**, plead, press for

Wudhinderhet *n.* disappointment, frustration

wyp *v.t.* wipe, cleanse, sweep across, flourish

Wypsind *n.* "wiped mind", state of grace, forgiveness

Wypstof *n.* wiping-cloth, soaked cloth

Y

Yar *n.* city in desert (*uncert.* Yakusk)

Acknowledgements

The italicized verses of the chapter headings are by the 13th-century Persian poet Jalal Al-din Rumi. Other fragments are from the poem *"A Gentle Rain in a Distant Autumn"* by Mahmoud Darwish, and from *Moonfall*. The *Tale of the Linh* steals, obviously, from Stephen Spender. Otherwise "I have no wish to sleuth down my own plagiarisms."

Copenhagen, 1992.

Rumi: *Mystical Poems of Rumi*, tr. A. J. Arberry, The University of Chicago Press, Chicago, 1968.

Darwish: *A Gentle Rain in a Distant Autumn*, from: *Victims of a Map*, Al-Saqi Books, London, 1984, p. 46. I have translated *hariifun* as "Darkening" rather than "autumn", *ardun* as "celebration", rather than "feast" - a term inappropriate in a society where eating is a necessity rather than a pleasure.

About the Author

Heather Spears is a poet, author and artist. She won the 1989 *Governor-General's Award* for poetry and is a two-time winner of the *Pat Lowther Poetry Prize*.

The second in the trilogy, *The Children of Atwar* is the sequel to *Moonfall*.

She lives in Copenhagen, Denmark and travels extensively throughout Europe and the Middle East.